Hints
of His
Mortality

The

Iowa

Short

Fiction

Award

University of

Iowa Press

Iowa City

*David
Borofka*

*Hints
of His
Mortality*

The publication of this book is supported by a grant from the National Endowment for the Arts in Washington, D.C., a federal agency.

University of Iowa Press, Iowa City 52242

Library of Congress Cataloging-in-Publication Data

Borofka, David, 1954–

Hints of his mortality / David Borofka.

p.   cm. — (Iowa short fiction award)

ISBN 0-87745-557-0

1. Men — Social life and customs — Fiction.   2. Boys — Social life and customs — Fiction.   I. Title.   II. Series.

PS3552.O75443H56   1996

813'.54 — dc20   96-26017

                                                              CIP

01   00   99   98   97   96   C   5   4   3   2   1

For Debbie

Our birth is but a sleep and a forgetting:

The Soul that rises with us, our life's Star,

Hath had elsewhere its setting,

And cometh from afar:

Not in entire forgetfulness,

And not in utter nakedness,

But trailing clouds of glory do we come

From God, who is our home:

Heaven lies about us in our infancy!

Shades of the prison-house begin to close

Upon the growing Boy,

But He Beholds the light, and whence it flows,

He sees it in his joy;

The Youth, who daily farther from the east

Must travel, still is Nature's Priest,

And by the vision splendid

Is on his way attended;

At length the Man perceives it die away,

And fade into the light of common day.

—WILLIAM WORDSWORTH, "Ode, Intimations of

Immortality from Recollection of Early Childhood"

Contents

ACKNOWLEDGMENTS

Stories in this collection appeared, in somewhat different form, in the following journals: "In the Shadows at Gaylord's," *Mosaic* (Spring 1994); "The Blue Cloak," *Manoa* (volume 7, number 1, 1995); "Tabloid News," *Southern Review* (volume 28, number 2, 1992); "A Blessing," *Northcote Anthology of Short Stories* (volume 1, 1992); "Reflected Music," *Carolina Quarterly* (volume 45, number 2, 1993), winner of the Wood Award for the best story published in *CQ* during 1992–1993; "The Children's Crusade," *Black Warrior Review* (volume 21, number 1, 1994); "The Summers of My Sex," Part I, "In My Father's Pool," *West Branch* (number 31/ 32, 1993); "The Summers of My Sex," Part II, "Bluebeard, Blackbeard, Light, and Little Women," *Modern Short Stories* (November 1989) under the title "Vacations"; "The Summers of My Sex," Part III, "O. Henry and the Harem," *South Dakota Review* (volume 31, number 2, 1993); "The Girl on the Highway," *South Dakota Review* (volume 30, number 1, 1992); "Strays," *Missouri Review* (volume 17, number 3, 1995); "Mid-Clair," *Santa Monica Review* (volume 8, number 2, 1996); "The Whole Lump," *Crosscurrents* (volume 9, number 1, 1990); "The Sisters," *Greensboro Review* (number 56, Summer 1994); "Hints of His Mortality," Part I, "Steam," *Crosscurrents* (volume 9, number 4, 1991) under the title "Steam"; "Hints of His Mortality," *Beloit Fiction Journal* (volume 8, number 1, 1993); and "Epilogue," *Missouri Review* (volume 16, number 1, 1993), winner of *Missouri Review*'s Editors' Prize Contest for 1992; reprinted in *Walking on Water* (University of Alabama Press, 1996).

Hints
of His
Mortality

─────────
▬▬▬▬▬▬

Prologue:
In the Shadows
at Gaylord's

Though only a coffee shop, Gaylord's does have a small patio that overlooks a canal and a ragged stand of pungent eucalyptus trees; when the sun goes down on late spring days, the evening breezes ruffle the umbrellas as if they were the awnings of a rich man's house, and my wife and I go there to sit, have our drinks, count the stars, and pretend.

On one such spring evening, we were to celebrate our eighth anniversary. I had saved the table nearest the canal. A box of roses was at my feet. A bottle of champagne, purchased an hour before, was chilling in a plastic bucket, and Sabrina, the owner's daughter, had—from somewhere—found the appropriate glasses. The sun had passed beyond the mountains in the west, and in the

cough-drop air the twilight seemed to hint at mystery and possibility, fate and chance. On another such fragrant night nine years
before, we had come to Gaylord's the first time—our first date.
Ann and I had been introduced by mutual friends, and in the center of a chaotic and rather terrible party, we had made plans to
meet; but then, uncertain as to whether or not she should keep
the date, she had arrived forty-five minutes late. I was already
five beers to the bad, and yet somehow the aquamarine of twilight and the seven-thirty breeze had worked a kind of magic—as
if the world and all that is within it had been designed from a
blueprint by Maxfield Parrish.

So now, eight years later, we were to meet here again, Ann's
choice, her hopes transparently obvious: that somehow a spring
breeze and its nostalgic rhythms might return us to our better,
more naive selves, that we might find it in us to untangle the
knots we'd made of our lives.

A year ago, I had been the cause of no small amount of trouble.
You can guess, I'm sure, how that was; the explanation is always
as tiresome as it is predictable: another woman from another
town not far from here, a claims adjuster for the same company
that I work for. Our pretexts for meeting did not require signifi-
cant manufacture, and every three or four days we'd run into
each other. Literally. I do not need to recite every unfaithful husband's lament: how much I dreaded coming home—those nights
when I was late, unwashed, and sullied—to Ann, who would be
finishing the dinner dishes or reading *The Cat in the Hat* to Leah
and Jacob, how much I dreaded facing the tilted cheeks of my children and my wife, who trusted the kisses I gave as articles of good
faith. There were times, I confess, when I enjoyed—I craved—the
sensation that everyone wanted me. However, most of the time I
was in shreds: guilty, yet, even so, calculating my next indiscretion; sensitized to the possibilities announced in each new glance
or gesture, yet numbed by my utter loss of principle and panicked
by the fear of being found out. I lost sleep and hair, and I longed
to put an end to everything.

Then, when Yvonne began to call the house, making demands
she had no right to make and yet every right to make, when Ann
had finally pieced the story together, her eyes shimmering with
reproach, when I confessed and ended things with Yvonne in a

horrible hour of further recrimination, from that day forward our lives became cautious, a pantomime of consideration and concern, each of us tiptoeing from room to room, careful not to disturb a house inhabited by the cracked and poorly repaired.

So on this night, my offering was champagne and roses and a willingness to return to our past. Then I waited. This time for an hour. I began to think that this was Ann's idea of revenge—she had decided nine years later that showing up was a bad idea after all. Twenty minutes into the hour, Sabrina offered to pour the champagne. I refused. I did not, however, refuse the bottles of beer that appeared on the table, and so I was feeling mildly quarrelsome when Ann appeared, rushed and apologetic. Her dark hair flew wild around her face, her face was flushed as though she'd been running, and her eyes were as green as I'd ever seen them.

"I've just heard the most amazing thing," she said.

I looked at my watch. "So tell me," I said.

"Yes, yes, I know I'm late. It's not such a crime. I had to take the kids to your mother's. Oh," she said, her eyes brightening further, "champagne! Flowers, too? I'd thank you, but I'm not sure that my appreciation for men is up to snuff just now."

"What? Why aren't the kids at Janie's?"

"Relax, that's what I have to tell you."

She stood and waved through the windows to Sabrina, who was inside.

"Janie's in no condition," she said. "She's had quite a shock, so I've been comforting and consoling."

Sabrina came with a towel, and Ann hugged her. "Did you see what he brought me?"

Sabrina nodded. "I've been waiting over an hour to pop it, but your sweetie, the little son of a bitch, wouldn't let me."

"Well go ahead," Ann said, "let's celebrate."

Sabrina twisted the bottle once and the cork flew out of her other hand, up through the patio lights, and into the darkness. When it left, it made a sound like an air rifle, and a moment later we heard the suggestion of a splash. In her hands it had looked like an obscene gesture.

"Bull's-eye," Sabrina said. "I love that." She poured, and the wine frothed over the sides of the narrow glasses. "Happy anniversary, dudes," she said. "Let's get to the next one, okay?"

Ann looked at me, holding her glass in front of my face. "Yes. Let's do that."

We touched glasses. "By all means," I said.

"Now," I said when Sabrina was gone, busy haunting other tables, "what's this about Janie?"

"I could hear noises inside the house when I knocked on the door," Ann said. "Janie crying and then yelling. And Peter. I know I heard Peter, but it wasn't quite Peter either. Just when I was going to ring the doorbell, some high-school-age kid came out the door. He was wearing the uniform of one of those pizza places, a delivery boy, you know. There was a Volkswagen at the curb with a sign on the top of it. And I remember that I thought, Good, at least the kids will eat something. You never know how wrong you can be. The delivery boy said, 'Excuse me,' or some such thing, hopped in, and buzzed off. Kind of a smirky little punk. You know the type, the kind that think adults have one foot in the grave and the other in senility.

"The door was standing open, so I pushed the kids inside. All the drapes were pulled and the blinds were turned so the place was like a cave. I called to Janie, but there was no answer, just the same crying I heard before, this horrible sobbing. It sent shivers up and down my spine. I thought somebody might have died or something."

Janie had watched the kids for us for two years. Ann met her through work, a head-injured adult who had come to Ann's office with state rehabilitation money in hand. She'd been hit by a Cal-Trans truck, and she needed to relearn things you'd teach your twelve-year-old. She was a sweet woman, maybe a little simple even before the accident, the sort of person that kids don't take advantage of because she's even more innocent than they are. She had not had much luck with men, however, a cause for worry where our kids were concerned. Every now and again, Ann or I would come home swearing that she was just too risky; Leah and Jacob, however, worshiped Janie and were her staunchest defenders. Since we'd known her, she'd lived with two different men who dumped her and stole either her stereo or her checkbook.

One of them took her car, an old Pinto. For Janie's sake, Ann and I took turns hoping for a rear-end collision. Three months ago, out of the blue, Janie introduced us to Peter as her husband. She said it was a sudden thing, but she knew it was right. He was . . . well, goofy-looking. He was wearing a suit that had obviously never been cleaned. His shirt collar seemed at least three sizes too large. He looked like LBJ's beagle—these big hanging ears and bad teeth. There was also some sort of skin condition—eczema or psoriasis, maybe—that traced his hairline, or what would have been his hairline, since he was nearly bald. But he was very soft-spoken, not the sort of person to cause trouble, we thought. We could not even begin to guess where they'd found each other. And the thought of them at home together made each of us cringe. But Janie was clearly happy, and Janie's life is Janie's life, though it is tempting to try and protect her.

"The kids were hanging on to my legs," Ann said, "and I felt as though I was wading through shallow water. We went down the hallway towards the bedrooms, and after the bright sun outside, it was pitch-black. 'Janie,' I said, 'where are you?' There was no answer, just the crying, but then there was somebody in front of us. 'Ann?' this voice said, and I knew it was Peter, but again something was not quite right. 'Janie's a little upset right now,' he said. 'Maybe we could talk for a little bit out here.'

"You know, I've seen a lot of strangeness, but I wasn't prepared for Peter. The kids and I waded back out to the living room, and I opened the blinds in the front window, just to let a little light in. Everything was a bit more chaotic than normal. Dirty dishes on the coffee table, dirty clothes on the floor, dust mice rolling along the baseboards. Unlike Janie. Usually everything is clean but in the wrong place. I cleared a spot on the couch for the kids and myself and sat down to wait. Peter had ducked back into one of the bedrooms, I guess, because he didn't follow us into the living room. All this time Janie's still crying this horrible cry, and I was just getting up again from the couch when Peter stepped into the light from the window. He was dressed in a woman's suit and wearing a wig, nice pumps, and I can't be sure, but I think false eyelashes and nails. I must have gulped half a dozen times. You read about these things—you don't ever see them in real life. 'Hello, Peter,' I said. I choked out that much at least. 'My name's Patricia,' he said in this awful falsetto voice, 'my life has been hell, and I can't keep going any other way.'

"The funny thing is that he looked so much better as a woman, such a definite improvement, that I really can't hold it against him. Except for what it's done to Janie. He said he's been fighting this thing ever since he can remember. He'd tried psychologists, faith healers, and gay bars. None of it helped. Until he and Janie got married, he'd been going to work as a man and living at home as a woman. Janie was sort of the last resort, I guess, and now that's up in smoke. Peter thought today was Janie's day for therapy, and she caught him undressing the pizza boy."

"Poor Janie," I said. "Tough enough to be a few bricks shy. Now this."

"Tell me about it," Ann said. "Men. You guys can't get anything right, can you?"

Before I graduated from college, there was a time when I thought I'd enter the ministry. I surrendered to the lovely and noble notion of letting go of myself as a way of saving the world. The problem was that I couldn't always maintain that floating feeling of emptiness and grace. If, as Paul maintained, Jesus gladly emptied himself for the sake of others, I was a bit more reluctant and erratic: there were simply times when I would have much preferred watching television. And too many times when I thought other people should just go to hell and stay there.

Then I left school. By that time, I thought I was maybe a writer of fiction. Not such a big change really—both jobs revolve around ego and its displacement, as well as a love for other people that is, above all, generous and empathetic. A vow of poverty is also involved, not to mention a kind of elevation of feeling and purpose. I believe now that, as with my ministerial days, my days as a writer were doomed, at least in part, by my love of the idea more than the actuality. And the same qualities that I would have lacked as a minister would have been equally damaging in the life of a novelist or a writer of stories.

When I met Ann, she told me that she knew who I was, that she had enough friends who knew me, that she knew I was pompous and dogmatic (the minister), cynical and pretentious (the writer), but that she could see better things. And yet, the night of our first date, the reason for Ann's tardy arrival had been her suspicions about me, about whether those better things had been merely the fruition of her own imagination.

But in those early days, I was never more faithful or single-minded! It was only some years later—when Ann was pregnant with Leah, when unspoken expectations about money and stability mounted and sent me to the insurance business and a rack full of short-sleeved dress shirts, when I had begun to feel as though I had traded myself away for a person I did not know, a person about whom I had not been consulted—only then did I become the prodigal. I knew I would have been a disaster in the ministry, and I had begun to guess that as a writer, I simply did not have any gift at all. I gave myself the excuse that if I couldn't save other people's lives or reinvent them, then I could at least help make them secure. But it was the hollowest sort of rationalization. I craved importance, but I sold insurance; I was unhappy, so I went to have my claims adjusted.

I watched Ann as she told me Peter/Patricia's story, watched the way the patio lights played shadow games with her face, the molding of her cheeks and mouth and hair, and the thought that I'd caused her as much pain with another type of duplicity was more than I could bear.

"Poor Janie," I said again.

"Yes," Ann said, "poor Janie."

"So, you lovebirds," Sabrina said, "you're not drinking fast enough." She poured the last of the bottle into our glasses, then held another in front of us. "Compliments of Dad, the last great restaurateur."

The cork flew like a rocket rising. And again with that barest hint of a splash at the end.

"Speaking of love, do you know that before they put the grates in near the dam, Dad used to see at least a couple of bodies every spring and summer? Love jumpers, he called them, though they probably just lost their footing. Strangest thing, I guess, to be eating your pot pie one minute, then watching a corpse go sailing by the next."

"Sabrina!" Ann said, "there was never any such thing."

The girl shrugged before she left the table, swinging the empty bottle in her hand: "Eleven, twelve years ago, you weren't around. It could have."

"I won't do that to you ever again," I said when she was gone. "I won't hurt you again." I gave her my promises, knowing the hollowness of my own resolve and, in the attendance of my own discontent, knowing that we had not yet come to the end of this.

"Men," she was laughing and weeping into a cocktail napkin, "goddamn you to hell, anyhow!"

*A Sleep
and a
Forgetting*

The Blue Cloak

It was one of the many ironies of their married life that Grimshaw's wife was never more amorous than when the house was filled with overnight guests. This was also true on the occasions of visits to friends and family, when they slept in beds not their own, when their love cries were well within earshot of others.

One might have suspected that at the root of her desires lay a compulsion to mock the social convention that would restrict romantic coupling to darkness and silence and the privacy of that group of two. Yet who could have predicted this of her? For Grimshaw's wife was the daughter of midwestern burghers, members of a conservative clan, whose topics of conversation were restricted by certain covenants: omitting the specific dollar amounts of financial transactions, discussing politics only in the abstract, and remarking the relationships of men and women as long as this was confined to the driest possible record of marriage and divorce, illness and recovery, birth and death.

In appearance she was the possessor of a face as perfectly molded as marble and yet as bland and unremarkable as a white sauce, hair the color of new corn, eyes that mirrored nothing but the blue sky overhead. She was tall, and her figure was full and ripe, her skin was flawless, a perfection having less to do with superiority than it did with negation, an absence of defect. As an attractive woman, she evoked her share of scrutiny at social gatherings, but early in life it seemed that she had learned one proverb and learned it well—*a fool uttereth all his mind: but a wise man keepeth it in till afterwards*—and her observers quickly understood that there was little beyond the decoration of her appearance except a second taciturn veneer. Even those kind souls who insisted on the presence of still waters finally resigned themselves to their own failure; unwilling to admit her fundamental superficiality, they claimed her reservoir of calm to be too deep. Upon their first meeting, Grimshaw could not have said whether she were fool or wise either—was it possible that in withholding herself she was giving vent to all that she knew?

She resisted all entreaties for conversation that she could, and those responses she could not avoid making, she limited to one breath or less. Under pressure from her family, she had once entered the Miss Hamilton County Pageant. During the interview, in response to the question of what she hoped for the future of humanity, she had stared bravely into the eye of the camera and said, "I would like to see fast food eliminated. I don't believe that so much speed in a person's eating habits can be good for anyone." The audience and judges were stunned. At that point she had been leading on the strength of her performance in the first two portions of the contest: swim suit (red, such lovely contours) and talent (uneven parallel bars to the tune of "The First Time Ever I Saw Your Face").

He was dealing with an extraordinary intelligence, he knew that much already; when he asked her to marry him, her response was typically oblique.

"Well," she said. Her top teeth touched her full bottom lip for one brief moment; she seemed puzzled and not a little bit irritated. "Well," she said again, "if you promise never to cut your toenails in the living room and then leave them on the carpet. My father does that, and it makes my mother hysterical."

He swore an oath of cleanliness, and that was that. If Grimshaw had harbored any secret desire for his proposal to prompt some sort of breakthrough—either communicative or analytical—he would have been sadly disappointed. The truth, however, was just the opposite. To those who asked directly, Grimshaw would freely admit that he had married her for her vacuity as well as her compromised beauty, that he had joined himself to her precisely for her lack of complexity, recognizing that his own ego, shaky enough even when accorded center stage and top billing, would not tolerate the competition of sharing.

He had married her, in short, to lie still. So, to discover this one quirk—that his vegetable wife could be transformed by strange beds or the presence of visitors into his agile mistress, his nubile Salome—was a shock, to put it mildly. During those days and weeks when company came to visit, the dark hours of night turned her oblivious passivity into erotic will and their bedroom into a bordello, a red room of wonders, leaving him bewildered as well as exhausted. She was beautiful, she was dim, and periodically she turned into a temptress whose skills rivaled his own adolescent fantasies. Year after year, it was a shock that did not lose its value.

He noted more than once that his wife's periodic passions could also contain a hint of sly aggressiveness. Within the first year of their marriage, while he attended graduate school in Los Angeles and Clair kept their student housing apartment in haphazard order, his maternal grandfather died. After years of one alcoholic illness after another, the old man—an artist, a crank, and a cauldron of unpredictable tempers—had finally yielded. His liver must have been a prune at the last, and his passing caused less mourning than ambivalence.

This was the lost, last summer of Watergate. Grimshaw typed the final draft of his dissertation—a comparative study of tax law during the Johnson, Grant, and Hayes administrations—while the daily soap opera of the hearings burbled in the next room. His mother, herself recently separated from her second husband, flew immediately to Birmingham to comfort her mother and to superintend the details of her father's burial; he and Clair left two weeks later, his dissertation finished and Nixon forced from office.

They arrived in sweltering August humidity and were met at the airport by his mother and grandmother. The older women had become sisters of widowhood, it seemed, both gray-haired, adorned in cotton print dresses and sensible shoes, both eager to please the young; one was simply more stooped, more shriveled by age than the other. At his grandmother's, he and Clair were ushered up the dark creaking staircase, then through a still darker hall to the master bedroom and the only full-sized mattress in the house.

"We can't, Mamaw," Grimshaw said, feeling their presence now in his grandmother's grief to constitute a kind of invasion. "We can't take your room."

"Don't be silly." The old woman stood before them, full of the sprightly good humor of the survivor. "I haven't used this room in months. Anymore, my legs prefer ground level."

"You have the whole top floor to yourselves," his mother added, noting that she too was occupying a room downstairs.

"Thank you," Clair said—the first words she'd volunteered without benefit of either prompt or question.

Without warning or preamble, his lively mother suddenly embraced his reticent wife. "Thank you both for coming," she said. "I know it's difficult to get away, you're both so busy."

"And still practically newlyweds," his grandmother added.

"Yes, that's true, isn't it?" his mother said, holding Clair's shoulders, measuring, it seemed, Clair's posture, her substance so rarely given voice.

He had never been able to explain to his family's satisfaction why he had married her other than sex, and embarrassed now that such innuendo should come from his mother and grandmother,

Grimshaw said, "Oh, I think we're beyond that."

They did not bother to hide their amusement.

"I just meant that we don't have to hang on each other all the time," he said. "Not like some."

"Thank you," Clair said suddenly, "for your bed. We very much appreciate it."

It was one of her most coherent statements.

"That's all right, dear," his mother said, stroking both of Clair's arms. "Quite all right."

"We're happy to do it," his grandmother said. "We're happy for you, Robert," she said, then winked.

And so it was that four hours later, at the stroke of nine o'clock, the two older women yawned, announced their fatigue, and proclaimed their intention of going to bed, leaving Grimshaw and his wife alone in the front parlor with his books and her magazines. The mantelpiece clock loudly marked the seconds. From nearby rooms came the soft dry sounds of his mother and grandmother undressing, then dressing for bed, then the sound of water running through the pipes before—with the squeal of old plumbing, old valves—it ceased.

"Bobby?"

Her voice had dropped an octave, and he was not so callous yet that such an overture—this one word, his name, spoken in such throaty tones by this different creature, this second wife—failed to stir him. He nearly stopped breathing. They began to shed clothing in the staircase, finding new purposes for the landing, discovering that wood, in sympathy with the animal kingdom, bends and breathes and, as such, speaks.

In recalling the first night of this visit, Grimshaw would remember the sensation as slapstick, pure vaudeville, as if the entire house, keeping time to their rhythms, were registering the wind-whipped moaning of a northern storm, especially when they had ascended to the top of the stairs, turned right, then right again to collapse into his grandparents' bed, only to find after the crash, the tenuous sound of splintering, that—no Hollywood bedframe—it too was wood: wood frame, wood slats, a mahogany headboard placed in unfortunate proximity to the bedroom wall. A laugh track would not have surprised him.

He would also remember whispering "Clair, Clair, Clair," over and over as a kind of fool's mantra against the noise and racket that they and this bed were making. She was even then looming above him, riding his hips, gripping him with thighs and pelvis, each of them slipping against the other in a fine film of sweat and exercise, and at each new direction their bodies took, she yelped louder and in increasingly higher pitch, a Charo imitation: *Ai, ai, aiyee.* He could only imagine the mutation of those sounds, echoing down hallway and stairs and chimney, traveling the length and breadth of studs and joists and headers, cascading through the opened second-story windows into the sticky Alabama night. He would have shushed her if it would not have seemed like such a silly prudery, like a horrible breach of the sexual contract. A betrayal of his wife's one true voice. He could not do it. Not at nine o'clock, not at midnight, nor at three, their coitus denoting cycles of life and death and regeneration in regular three-hour intervals.

That morning he rose unsteadily into cruel sunshine. Clair slept, the sound of her breathing a machinery hum. His mother and grandmother sat in the shade of the back porch, drinking coffee. They looked at him as he sat down, and the look they gave him was knowing, their faces showing the lines of their respective ages, their matching gray heads exhibiting a matching disarray, a matching fatigue underneath their careful irony.

"Sleep well?" his grandmother said.

"I'm sorry if we bothered you." He wanted to say that he and Clair were never like this when alone, but how could he? He might as well have accused his mother and grandmother of being responsible for Clair's sexual behavior as well as his own.

"We slept like babes," his mother said, somewhat fiercely, he thought.

"Heavens, yes," his grandmother added. "Babes."

From the back porch the three of them—for a considerable time—pondered the backyard in uneasy silence. In the force of the August sun, the grass appeared too green, too real, too insistent upon its own presence.

"Your house and yard are lovely." Clair stood behind them, brushing her hair, gazing into the same middle distance. Water from the shower beaded her forehead. Her blue bathrobe was loosely tied, and as she brushed her hair, it threatened, inch by inch, to fall open.

His mother stood and, in lieu of a hug, pulled the sides of Clair's bathrobe together.

"Good morning, dear," his mother said, giving her daughter-in-law a kiss on one cheek.

Grimshaw could not have said what she truly meant.

The apprehension of sexuality is never more acute than when suffered with one's own family, and Grimshaw felt this now keenly as he shared his mother and grandmother's discomfort. He watched his mother patting the lapels of Clair's bathrobe. He watched, too, as Clair smiled, and in that instant, he knew that he had been watching a contest all along, that Clair was now the only one with a husband, a partner with whom one could share staircases and kitchen tables and bathroom floors and most especially beds—beds of whatever description and volume. And he understood further that—on whatever level of consciousness—Clair knew that she had won this unadvertised battle; she had marked her territory, and all that she saw was hers.

Later that same day, his grandmother showed them in to each of the rooms in her disorderly old house, giving Clair her first official tour. At the back of the second story were his grandfather's studio and study, unused now and unchanged for the past ten years. The house, so noticeable for its lack of decoration, had collected all its adornment here: the walls of both rooms, those not made of glass, were covered with canvases and prints of his grandfather's work and copies of other artists from the ancients to the moderns.

"It is very beautiful," Clair said.

"It's a goddamn mess," his mother said.

"Well," his grandmother said, ignoring his mother, "if we looked even the littlest bit, I bet we'd find half a dozen bottles of bourbon at least, he loved his whiskey so."

"I meant that it is very beautiful," Clair said again, "that you kept it this way."

"Then I shall have to give you something to take before you go," his grandmother declared. "Something to remember your visit by."

"We'll need to dust first, Mother," Grimshaw's mother said. She turned and spoke to Grimshaw: "If you hear retching, that will be us."

"You shush," his grandmother said. "Clair, you shall have something special." It was a promise made in passing, and Grimshaw thought little of it until his grandmother produced a mailing tube just before he and Clair were to board their flight back to Los Angeles. She handed the tube to Clair. "I debated a long time, Robert, so don't tell me if you don't like my selection. You're welcome to anything else in Edgar's collection when you get settled in a place of your own."

They flew with the mailing tube riding above them in the overhead compartment. Then, after changing planes in Dallas, they carried it to their next flight, and a flight attendant stored it in the coat compartment of the crowded 727. They did not have a chance to open it until they boarded the shuttle bus from LAX to Westwood.

Grimshaw had expected one of his grandfather's lithographs; but instead of the fine straight lines, the precise circles and squares of his grandfather's *Flatland*-inspired prints, Grimshaw unrolled a badly reproduced poster of Brueghel's *Netherlandish Proverbs*. It was one of his grandfather's favorites, he knew; this poster had hung near his easel in a cheap black frame for as long as he could remember. During one visit to his grandfather's studio, he had been made to look at it for an hour or more while his grandfather traced the structural development of the painting's composition: the painstaking detail of one hundred proverbs brought to life.

Grimshaw was twelve years old at the time. His grandfather had been drinking as usual, and he was ashamed of the confusion that the old man inspired in him. Still, it was the sort of painting that a twelve-year-old boy could find infinitely fascinating, with its depiction of old sayings now archaic or unintelligible by language and culture—of devils and demons, pissing and shitting, nakedness and unaccountable sadism, a sort of scatological *What's Wrong with This Picture?*, a graphic illustration of chaos as the golden mean of human behavior. Now it seemed merely hideous and crude, full of medieval perversity, colored as it was by the memory of his grandfather and his grandfather's lecture.

"What colors do you see?" the old man had said. The question was rhetorical, for his role was but to listen. "All these muddy browns, the color of shit. Just a backdrop for the spots of blue and red. Which is precisely the point. Red is the color of sin, blue the color of folly. That's the lesson, boy, and you'd do well to learn it now instead of later. Where's Christ? Where's Jesus? A nickel if you can find Jesus," his grandfather had boomed like some sort of tent preacher gone sour. Grimshaw had looked, but the blank-eyed caricatures swam before his eyes, the clutter of human folly and sin too overwhelming. "You see here," his grandfather's finger had identified the figure of Christ in the right foreground, "here he is, sitting on a blue chair getting bearded by a monk in a red robe. Or over here," the finger jabbed the left center, "an upside-down globe, upside-down and blue it is. *Verkeerd*—the Nether-landish word that means both upside-down and wrong. And look at the little red son of a bitch in the window above the world. Got his pants down, giving it the moon. Just below that some fool biting a pillar, the Dutch equivalent of a hypocrite. And what do you think Herr Brueghel puts in the center foreground? Some dishy little slut in a red dress putting a blue cloak over the head of an old man with a crutch. Probably her husband. That's the way the proverb goes: *'Foukens die geern hier en daer den offer ontfangen / Moeten haer mans de blau huycke omhangen'*— 'The woman who gladly welcomes favors here and there / Must hang the blue coat round her husband.' She's putting one over him, you bet. And down at her feet, some fool filling a well after the calf has drowned. Our version of closing the barn door after the horse has run."

His grandfather had stood with him in front of the picture, muttering, "Stupidity and foolishness, deceit and despair." And then, before he poured another drink for himself, he pointed to one last figure: a man ramming his head against a wall. His grandfather had saluted the man with the water glass of bourbon. "Fucking life in a fucking nutshell."

He and Clair looked at the poster while the shuttle bus came to a complete stop on the San Diego Freeway. Traffic surrounded them on all sides while blue exhaust rose into the sweet, ocean-scented air. This poster held memories for him, but his grandmother had made it clear that it was a memento of Clair's first visit. What resonance could there possibly be for her? he wondered. She would look at the blue cloak and think a good deed was being done. What could his grandmother have been thinking?

"It's lovely," Clair said.

"What's lovely about it?" Normally he would never challenge his wife's innocent judgments, but cross as he was becoming with the discovery of this gift, he couldn't help himself.

"Everyone seems so . . . " For a moment her eyes looked frantic, as if she, his stolid wife, were about to cry. "Everyone seems so *busy*."

The news that Clair might envy the busy lives of Brueghel's fools did not entirely surprise him, but it did raise unsettling questions. For what unspoken dreams did his silent wife yearn? To what busy foolishness did she wish to commit herself? The thought that there might be some burning, transparent hole within his otherwise opaque wife occasionally struck him in the middle of the night with the force of nightmare and revelation— a dark window and a face illuminated by lightning—causing him to bolt upright in bed, his breathing rapid, his heartbeat erratic, only to discover once again Clair's body stretched long against his own, and the air humming with her placid and contented snore. His alarm was only a trick of sleep, an illusion of his subconscious mind. And yet, try as he might, his vision of Clair as a creature of plain surfaces would be forever altered, clouded by the shadow and presentiment of depths heretofore unsuspected.

Following his degree, Grimshaw took a teaching job at a small college in the state of Washington. He had hoped for a larger, more distinguished school, a university of ivy and tradition; in the end, however, he settled for prefabricated classrooms on an estate bequeathed by a chemical manufacturer with a bad conscience. His colleagues were frights, the administration tight-fisted. During a cocktail party in honor of new faculty, he was told by more than one person that the college had been in a steep decline for years.

And yet this was now his college and his position! Clair seemed genuinely happy to make the move to the damp darkness of the Northwest, and on the promise of his modest salary, they made a down payment on a cottage overlooking Lake Washington. So what if his college was second-rate and his department filled with monsters and buffoons? He could still take delight in this house and its view of waters and a setting sun. They quickly bought furniture and amassed debt like a talisman. How could they fire him if he owed so much money? Clair, although agreeable to all his selections, was adamant about only one item: over his objections, the Brueghel poster was framed and given a place of prominence above the fireplace. It was too morbid, he had argued, too cartoonish for such a display, and they had since received many originals of his grandfather's work; but all his arguments were to no avail. The poster stayed.

In his second year of service to the college, he and Clair entertained for the first time, a dinner for his department, and in the weeks before the party, Grimshaw imagined every conceivable horror: the salmon rémoulade transformed into Clair's meat loaf, discussion of Carter's domestic policy directed by Clair's views on fast food, or the worst scenario of all—that the colleagues who plotted against one another by day would openly despise one another by night. But by every measurement, the dinner turned out a success. He had not counted on the civilizing effect of flatware or the forgiveness that occurs by candlelight. A vinous haze seemed to bathe everyone present in a glow of courtesy and upright conduct; no one grew belligerent or combative, and at dinner's end there were no injuries—either physical or emotional—to repair. The only question was what to do with Dr. Elfred, the department chair, who had passed out in the living room during after-dinner drinks to the amusement of all except Myra Hendricks, whose shoulder Elfred had used as the most convenient pillow.

"Just turn the lights out, and let the old bastard lie," Myra said, "and pray he don't piss on the sofa." She was struggling to find the lost sleeve of her overcoat, the last residue of her party manners fading by the second.

"He can't drive, certainly," Grimshaw said. Through his open front door he could see the wet street and the older man's ancient Volvo. "We'll get him settled."

"Fine," she said, kissing Clair's impassive cheek. "Be it on your heads."

Together he and Clair draped a blanket around Elfred. A year away from retirement, he had once been an expert on Soviet affairs and Cold War policies, but following his wife's death during a supposedly routine hysterectomy, he had sunk into a torpor from which he had not recovered. His authority on Soviet tendencies had stopped like a broken clock, and he was prone to quote Joe Stalin as a contemporary source even in 1977; in his prime he had been known as a holy terror, an intimidator of callow students and junior faculty alike, but since his intimacy with tragedy he had turned into a pudding.

At first glance Grimshaw thought that he might have had a stroke—his skin was the color of veal, and his jowls were dotted with the blood of a less-than-successful shave—but no, his breathing was regular, his sinuses echoing. He was sleeping the sleep of the wicked, the incompetent, and the overly medicated. Grimshaw folded Elfred's liver-spotted hands underneath the blanket, and then he felt Clair's fingers massaging the back of his neck. Her teeth nibbled the ridge of his ear.

"Bobby." He could not even be sure she had given voice to his name, for her lips had merely moved. She might as well have kissed his inner ear with her tongue; she might as well have unzipped him while wearing feathers and a Merry Widow. So they left Dr. Elfred, leaving as well the dinner dishes and the glasses, but remembering the lights even as they grappled with one another.

What more needs to be said? For doesn't our lovemaking, so earnestly sought after, so anticipated, so eagerly plotted, run much the same course? Clair led her husband to their bedroom by her fingers and her teeth. What they couldn't know was their engagement with farce: that the concussions of their lovemaking would sound to Elfred's wine-addled ear like a fulfillment of the Red Menace—the world was coming to an end after all. He leaped to his feet from the sofa, and in the darkness and his confusion, entangled in the phantom embrace of the blanket, he sent a whole row of crystal wine glasses crashing to the floor even as he yelled out stage directions for the apocalypse: "This is it! Incoming! Here it comes, by God!"

Grimshaw reluctantly left his wife. Elfred stood in the middle of the living room, turning in circles. Grimshaw turned on the lights to survey the damage, then shepherded Elfred to the spare bedroom, giving the older man a pair of his old pajamas and a new toothbrush. The chairman was apologetic and contrite and did as he was told, too abashed to ask questions.

Back in their bedroom, Clair sat on the bench seat of the bay window, looking out into the dark night, looking for all the world like the mermaid of Copenhagen. Her composure was absolute. He would have gone to her, would have gladly resumed their labors, but for a heavy weight of desolation or sadness—like something remembered—that seemed to have flown from her, ballooning now within his own chest. He slipped back into their disheveled bed, the weight slipping away now too, ephemeral, so that he could not be sure it had ever been, and then he was asleep, not waking until late the next morning when he heard the murmur of voices—Clair's flat, uninflected alto, Dr. Elfred's cracked bass.

Clair was pouring coffee, Dr. Elfred eating a piece of toast, while she looked at pictures from his wallet.

"You have a lovely family," she said. "They all have such wonderfully straight backs. And good teeth."

"Yes. That was their mother's doing. Posture and hygiene."

"It is so important," Clair said, "and no one cares anymore, don't you think?"

Suddenly catching sight of Grimshaw in the doorway, Elfred stood. "I must apologize," he said. "Terribly embarrassing."

Grimshaw held up one hand. "No. No need."

"I was in my cups, I'm afraid." He had showered and was dressed once again in his customary attire—gray flannel slacks and a blue oxford-cloth shirt, frayed at the cuffs.

"We all were."

Clair opened the front door to retrieve the morning paper, and a gust of wet air rushed in.

"Your wife," Elfred whispered, "is lovely."

"Yes, I know."

The older man suddenly reached across the table, grabbing Grimshaw's hand in both of his own. "Since my wife died . . ." His hands were trembling, and he did not bother to finish his sentence. "I'm envious, son. God's blessings upon thee."

And then, Grimshaw evidently had not expressed enough agreement, for the old man grasped his hand again, squeezing it much harder than Grimshaw would have thought possible.

"God's blessings," Elfred hissed, "do you hear me?"

But the years did not spare the Grimshaws any more than they have spared the rest of us. Blessings or no. And if cruel time has stolen our vitality as well as our youth, why should it be different for Grimshaw and his lovely, low-wattage Clair?

He did not last as a professor of American political history—even at an institute with more money than self-respect. Denied tenure after five years, Grimshaw failed to procure another position. His résumé had grown thin and out of date; he was indistinguishable among battalions of Ph.D.'s; he was not so remarkable as he had once imagined. So then he tried his hand first at real estate and then stocks, and except that the market suddenly become bullish in the early eighties, he would not have had any success at all. As it was, he and his clients were wiped out in 1987 in the massacres of October, and then for a time, while his bankruptcy petition was processed, he sold Audis for a man who thought his vocabulary extraordinary and delighted in calling him Doctor Grim. If he had been chained to a wall, he would have rammed his head into it for the sheer pleasure of other pains.

Clair did not seem to be touched by the calamities of her husband's downwardly descending career. And yet, how heartbreaking it is to see what disappoints a simple mind! They were forced to move from the house overlooking Lake Washington to another, even smaller one, and then in the last stages—before they fell upon the mercy of legal protection—to a second-story apartment in an ancient Victorian in a questionable neighborhood. The rain fell in more mean-spirited fashion from clouds that loomed darker with more malevolent intent. Even the evergreens seemed somehow sickly and threatening. Their only child, a daughter named Sophie, was transferred from her exclusive girls' academy to public school midway through her second-grade year, and her inherited stoicism broke her father's heart. Their list of friends grew shorter and more distant with each new decline in their finances. He began to drink vodka with lunch and pick fights with his oblique-witted wife at dinner. And yet, with each new setback Clair remained singularly impassive, and Grimshaw thought that only two misfortunes had truly disturbed her Panglossian faith: when she discovered that their latest residence did not have a garbage disposal and when the movers tore the Brueghel poster into bits while moving their refrigerator out of the trailer. She had sat down on the outdoor staircase and wept. If Sophie had fallen off the Bremerton ferry and drowned, she could not have been more undone.

He could not have said why he had never looked elsewhere for companionship or romance. For a couple formed in the early seventies, the odds favored either divorce or extramarital dabbling. He knew full well Clair's limitations. He knew also that certain women—a bookkeeper at the Audi dealership, for instance—would not have ignored his attentions. There were many possible reasons: that he was not willing to risk the safety and security of the known, that to hurt Clair by some indiscreet infidelity would have crushed him, that he was afraid of all women smarter and more self-promoting than his wife, that since Sophie's birth his vision of women had been utterly transformed. That some nearly dormant moral impulse made such liaisons unthinkable. All of these were possible, and yet none of them seemed to be altogether true. All he could honestly say was that he was joined to Clair, and at the root of their conjunction was an enigma.

At the nadir of their troubles, they were visited by friends of Clair's family. The Pattersons—a retired plastics manufacturer and his wife—were returning to Ohio from a three-week tour of the Orient. They had found that by staying with missionaries they could travel frugally but in relative American comfort. Grimshaw, although normally opposed to such obvious freeloaders, thought it somehow fitting that their two-bedroom apartment would be the Pattersons' last stop before home. For Clair's sake he welcomed them and brought down the crystal wine goblets—*tokens of a palmier time!*—and asked leading questions about their travels. Inevitably they were as tiresome as they were cheap, and their gift of boring monologue no less intrusive than their habit of imposition. Grimshaw poured glass after glass of burgundy. He nodded at each of Howard Patterson's assertions that the missionaries in Bangkok were the salt of the earth and knew the best bargains in the open-air markets. And he smiled while Olivia Patterson spoke into Clair's habitually glazed-over stare, using a little-girl voice and the tones of the tourist who, speaking to a Japanese, believes that volume and a distortion of syntax are all that is necessary for understanding.

After dinner, while Clair cleared the dishes and then put Sophie to bed, Howard Patterson took Grimshaw aside. He put a meaty hand on Grimshaw's shoulder, and Grimshaw braced himself for the usual round of condolences about their recent difficulties. Would there be no end to it? Wasn't it enough that he had been bored to death by this philistine. Did he now have to be pitied as well?

"Listen, son, I appreciate all your hospitality, but I have to ask you for one more favor, if I might. I feel bad asking this, but we're old, we've slept in strange beds for twenty nights straight, and Olivia, well, she has a bit of a competence problem, holding it all night, you know, especially when the bed's not up to snuff. I'm looking around your place here, and I know you folks have had your share of problems, but right now I'm thinking we're going to wind up sleeping on some foldout with a bar right in the center of our damn kidneys. Am I right?"

The older man was fidgety, his hands hitching at his belt loops and pockets, and he was obviously pained by the necessity of his request; even so, Grimshaw seriously considered playing ignorant and dumb.

"Do we have a Hide-a-bed? Yes. But what you're really asking is, Would we mind if you slept in our bed and we slept on the couch?"

The plastics manufacturer blew out a long breath. "I hated to ask, son, but there it is. We come here like beggars, and all I can do is ask for more."

The rain that streaked the windows had traveled from the gulf of Alaska; Howard and Olivia Patterson had traveled from the grace of missionaries to be with them here this night.

"We'd be more than happy to switch," Grimshaw said, relishing the sound of the untruth. But the imagined sound of the Hide-a-bed's springs, their musical quality as played by his wife in her full hostess mode, he relished even more.

"We appreciate it, we really do."

Water dripped from the sagging gables and eaves; the world outside the windows was darkness and chill.

He helped Clair change their bed with fresh sheets while the Pattersons found their nightclothes and toiletries and repacked their luggage. "They're old and they're friends of your family, but they're also rude and pushy and cheap," he whispered while they stripped off the old bedding. "Imagine! Treating missionaries like innkeepers. I'll bet they promised each one of them a donation when they get back home. They probably made a killing on exchange rates and all the stereo equipment they could lug on board. 'We come here like beggars.' What a load of crap."

She shrugged but refused the opportunity to add further fuel to his diatribe. They moved to the living room and bade the Pattersons a good night and sweet dreams, and when the older couple had entered the Grimshaw bedroom, they firmly closed, then locked the bedroom door, the sound of the lock as clearly audible as Olivia Patterson's titter of little-girl laughter.

"Bobby."

He knew how to interpret his name, and before she could lay aside the folded bottom sheet which she was holding, he had bounded across the mattress of their couch to embrace his constant Clair.

"Baby," he breathed into the nape of her fragrant neck. He nibbled one of her perfect ears.

Her response, however, was a disappointment. She stood stock-still, rigid as a pillar. "Listen," she said, her free ear cocked toward their bedroom door.

At first he could hear only the sound of the wind in the eaves, but then quite clearly he heard the rhythmic sounds of his own mattress and box spring.

"'A competence problem.' More crap."

"Bobby," Clair said, "look."

Through the window, the pearly white eye of a full moon gleamed in an opening of the weather. A halo of mist surrounded it. They opened the front door and stood in bare feet on the damp upstairs landing. To the east was a faint rainbow projected of mist and moonshine and thrown onto the screen of a departing cloud.

"Lovely. Beautiful," Grimshaw said to the air. And he remembered the first time he had seen Clair. He had been eating breakfast in a coffee shop on Wilshire and trying to edit a paper on ethical reform within Harding's Cabinet. A rare summer rain was beating against the pavement and sidewalk, and everywhere people were running with briefcases and newspapers overhead while spray shot up from automobile tires and storm drains swallowed the rest.

Out of the corner of his eye, he had seen, without consciously registering their presence, a young woman helping an older man along the sidewalk. Then, a collage and a whirl of color as the young woman went sprawling onto the cement, her blue umbrella cartwheeling into the street and under the wheels of a Buick.

Normally not prompted by the misfortunes of others, Grimshaw had found himself outside in the stinging rain before he understood what he was doing. The transient was already a quarter mile away, Clair's purse flying in the air behind him like a red tail.

"He didn't mean to hurt me," she'd said as he helped her from the ground. "I didn't have any money."

He had steadied her, then dodged between two lanes of cars to rescue her battered umbrella. They were both drenched, and when he returned and saw her flat blue eyes, he had felt gallant and foolish and had trouble getting his breath. Something seemed to have lodged itself against his lungs. "Thank you." She had taken the broken skeleton of her umbrella from him, fumbling with the fractured ribs, the ripped cloth, and then turned to move away.

"Don't go. Come have coffee with me," he had pleaded. "You're soaked."

"Bobby," his wife now said. "Come inside. It's wet."

Inside the living room, the lights had been extinguished, and she was just a voice in the darkness. He felt his way toward the couch, bumping his shin on the metal foldout frame.

"Bobby," Clair breathed, "I'm here."

He dropped his clothes in a pile on the floor, and the springs of the Hide-a-bed squealed when he slid under the sheet and blanket.

"I'm coming to get you," she said. The blanket rose up above them as she made a tent to cover them from all that was outside and inside—folly as well as sin.

Tabloid News

Jeanette, Parker's sister-in-law, came through the jetway door dragging her two-year-old daughter, and he thought for a moment that he would have to carry them both to the car. Jeanette's face, normally olive complected, looked pasty, blotchy, as if she'd used the five hours of flight time to cry, while Bonnie, his niece, hung from her mother's hand like a doughy piece of carry-on baggage. She was parroting the same phrase over and over—"Bunny wet, Bunny wet, Bunny wet"—and making her best use of a two-year-old's passive resistance.

"Hey, sis. Over here," Parker said. He waved his hands above his head. Myrna, his wife, was at work—she was always at work—and he had been named chauffeur.

"Parker." Jeanette dropped her carry-on, and the passengers behind her began to bunch up in the narrow alley between the gate and the jetway. He hurried to get the bag and the baby, trying to move Jeanette over to the side next to the railing. "Sorry," she said. "It was a bad trip. Little Bun-Bun here did gymnastics in my lap the whole way, and I think I probably owe about six people for dry-cleaning bills." Parker caught the smell of gin when she spoke.

"An hour and we'll be home, you can put your feet up," Parker said, aware that he was using his father's voice. His father's trumped-up good humor had been his favorite device for mollifying irrational women such as Parker's stepmother and Parker's wife. Parker was only beginning to realize that there were certain things about his father that he didn't like. A recent revelation, it made him feel as though he were starting all over again as a son. "Anyway, it won't take long," he said, trying to make his voice sound less jolly, less rah-rah.

"Sure."

Together they moved through the terminal. Bonnie grabbed Parker's hand in her wet, warm ones as they stepped onto the escalator leading to the baggage claim. Jeanette leaned against his shoulder. He could feel her body begin to shake. He set the small bag on the next lower step of the escalator and held his sister-in-law around the shoulders. Her arm went around his waist, and he imagined that to anyone in the terminal they looked like a tired family just returned from a vacation to the Grand Canyon or Colorado Springs. Jeanette moved against him. "I'm sorry about your dad's mess," she said.

"Thanks. I'm sorry about Vic," he said in return.

"Fuck Vic."

At the bottom of the escalator, a few dozen people were already standing around the two baggage carousels. The silver wheels moved around and around. A couple of suitcases, refugees from previous flights, circled endlessly. Inside there would probably be someone's underwear, socks, dirty laundry, toiletries, maybe a souvenir for a loved one. Parker wondered what could have happened to the owners of the suitcases since the time that their belongings had been lost. He could imagine the carousels continuing to circle in the dark even early the next morning with the two suitcases still unclaimed.

"I didn't mean that," Jeanette said. "I'd like to say 'Fuck Vic' and mean it, but I don't. I can't. Not yet anyway. I get mad at myself when I don't mean it, though."

"Give yourself some time, sis," he said. *And in an hour you'll have your feet up.* Sometimes Parker wished that there were a clamp he could buy for his lips so his father couldn't leap out. "I mean, you don't get over these things in a day or two," he finished lamely.

"Thank you, Brother Thom." Jeanette's mouth turned up at one corner. The color was beginning to come back to her face. "You are an inspiration, I'm sure."

He knew he'd sounded stupid, but what was he supposed to say? *Whyn't ya buy a sharp knife and cut your husband's balls and pecker off? Why'd ya marry the bastard in the first place?*

"I was just wondering," she said, "why your last name is a first name and your first name a last?"

Parker shrugged. "For the first three years of grade school I thought my name was Tom Parker."

Jeanette put her head on his shoulder. She was laughing or crying again. It was impossible to tell.

"Bunny wet."

Parker and Jeanette looked down at Bonnie, who was now dangling from Parker's arm. A thin brown trail descended one leg while a bloom of smell drifted upward. Jeanette sighed, pulled a disposable diaper from the bag, and led her daughter off in the direction of the restrooms. Parker watched the baggage carousels with their two orphan suitcases. He thought up lives for the owners of the suitcases while he waited, and although he imagined victims of espionage or crime, he couldn't think up predicaments bizarre enough to be satisfying. Leave that to the tabloids, which, in a strange search for comfort, he'd recently taken to reading. He thought of taking one of the bags as if it were his own, living from its contents for a day or two, trying on another's life, as it were, as a way of gauging whether or not his own life and expectations were simply fantasies.

And though everyone waited, standing at attention, from the small door with the rubber flap, nothing appeared.

Life, Parker believed, was not supposed to be this way. His wife's family must be rubbing off in some mysterious, unpleasant way. He had grown accustomed to Myrna's ritual when dealing with letters from home—a water glass of wine, then the mail. Myrna's three sisters, all younger than Myrna, seemed to have married for misery. Grace's husband, a computer programmer, whom Parker remembered only for wearing thick, black-framed glasses, was diagnosed as schizophrenic three months after the wedding. Ingrid had eloped with an operator of heavy construction equipment, who died two years later when his earthmover turned over on him in an area of heavy mud. When his will was read, it was discovered that Bob had had a male lover in a highway town in Idaho. Now Jeanette, the youngest of the four, had discovered that Vic had fathered at least two illegitimate children previously and that number three was in the works, each by a different woman. Number three's mother was suing him for paternity, and while Vic did not deny his involvement, he could not afford to mortgage his franchised spa outlet any further than it already was. He had come to Jeanette on his knees, one letter reported, in a greasy sweat, swearing that it would never happen again, he would get counseling, he'd never loved anyone but Jeanette, etc., etc. When Jeanette seemed to be weakening, Myrna bought the plane ticket and ordered her sister to the airport.

Parker had liked to think that he was somehow the buffer between his wife and such soap opera. They had been married twelve years; he had always been faithful, he held a steady job—he was a high school social studies teacher—and he took pride in the fact that he and Myrna had, quite rationally, decided not to have children of their own. Children meant constant demands and threats to any couple's established peace. They were an invitation to disasters of all kinds. He was Myrna's single, still point in the midst of her chaotic family, and two days after they were married, they had moved to California from Oregon and away from the family's soup kettle of poor choices, bad luck, and intrafamilial gossip, rivalry, and alliances.

Parker had also liked to indulge the notion that such things happened only in Myrna's blue-collar family and not among his tribe of pudgy, soft-fingered white-collar relatives, that her family's misfortunes were entirely the product of their class and a deficiency of virtue rather than circumstances beyond anyone's mortal control. But now that his own father could be counted among the names of the family's headlines, he was having to acquaint himself with the stew of compromised, melodramatic life.

His father, sixty-seven years old, had been charged by Parker's stepmother, Lydia, for spousal abuse. She'd recently been to a seminar on that very subject, and she had identified her experience. Evidently, jolly good humor was not enough. When the police came, following her phone call, Lydia told them that her husband had beaten her that very morning, that he had beaten her for twenty-two years, that she was through taking it, he was cheap and unforgiving and violent on top of everything else, it was no wonder that his first wife had run away. She did exhibit the makings of a very nasty bruise on her right cheek, evidence, according to Parker's father, of where she had fallen into the bathroom counter the day before, but in the end, he ducked his head into a squad car, beginning the long tunnel toward fingerprints and pictures and humiliation.

Parker bailed his father out that night sometime after midnight. His father had aged ten years, his stepmother had become a stranger, and he realized with an unpleasant jolt—for the first time since his mother had abandoned his father and him, for reasons his father would not or could not explain—that he too could become the victim of chaos and human unpredictability. *What was going on?* Either his stepmother's arteries were beyond reclamation or his father was a monster with Toastmasters' training. *And what could possibly be next?* He had visions of himself blurrily pictured in the back pages of the *Star*, and underneath the caption: "Man Performs Abdominal Surgery on Self." As if there were some vestigial organ, some appendix of moral ambiguity. He would operate with a butter knife. Let his expression of grief be the subject of supermarket scrutiny.

When he complained to Myrna, she outwardly sympathized, but he suspected that in her eyes he saw a glimmer of satisfaction and triumph: *So now you know what it's like, kiddo. Join the rest of us.* They had often fought on something like this very ground.

She held the view that her family, in all its extremes, was very much the social norm; it was his own expectation that was wacko, according to definition. She had told him on more than one occasion that he couldn't demand the world to march to his own drumbeat of propriety, and she seemed to see Parker's father in their spare bedroom as a small price to pay for the proof of that lesson.

When Parker brought Jeanette and Bonnie home, the dogs across the street, Alaskan huskies, were howling even though it was only eleven-thirty in the morning, and Parker's father was standing on the front lawn howling back. The dogs had been howling for two weeks, ever since their owners had separated and filed for divorce. Even after Parker had unloaded their luggage and they were inside the house eating lunch, the howling—as if the San Joaquin Valley were winter tundra and the sun a full moon—was audible.

"Doggies," Bonnie said, "doggies cry."

"Someone should shoot those miserable animals," Parker's father said, "and put them out of their goddamn misery."

"They're just unhappy," Jeanette said. She seemed to understand the wellspring of Parker's father's anger, and she laid one hand on his arm.

"All the more reason," his father said. "I never did anything to that woman, but because she's unhappy with herself, I wind up going to jail. Is that fair?"

"Cut it out, Pop," Parker said. He had hoped to keep the conversation out of this particular groove, to distract his father by means of lunch meat and bread and mayonnaise. "Don't start, okay?"

"Twenty-two years, and suddenly I'm a sadist. She's that unhappy, she should kill herself. Leave me out of it. My first wife, maybe she was unhappy too, who knows? At least she had the decency to disappear. No fuss, no scenes."

"Time doesn't mean a thing," Jeanette said. "If there's one thing I've learned it's that people invent themselves every day."

"I don't believe that," Parker's father said.

"Vic thinks I've abandoned him and stolen his daughter. Can you believe that?"

"Vic's a special case," Parker said, bringing out a plate of sliced tomatoes. "He ought to be castrated, then institutionalized."

Tears squeezed themselves from Jeanette's eyes. He could tell he'd said the wrong thing. Again. Shit. His father was looking at him now with an expression that could only be labeled Reproach.

"Cry all you want," Parker's father said, patting Jeanette's back, moving his chair next to hers. "Number-one son here is a bit of a clod sometimes. Let it out, you'll feel better."

Parker remembered such advice from when he was in grade school and had not been included in some activity, a friend's birthday party, perhaps, or a trip to the public pool. After his mother's flight to nowhere and before Lydia's arrival, he had turned to his father for comfort and consolation; he'd always felt better afterward, but he also remembered feeling that it had been at the expense of his own honesty, that he'd needed to make the situation much worse, more dramatic than it really had been, that in order to warrant such paternal attention, such fatherly solicitude, he'd diminished his own life in proportion to the fantasy of trauma he'd constructed.

Jeanette's shoulders were heaving now, and Parker wondered to what extent they were heaving for Vic or for Jeanette herself, for her marriage or for Bonnie. Or whether she was merely crying to keep her own need for sympathy fresh.

The dogs continued to howl. Bonnie beat on her plate with a spoon.

"You might not believe this, Jeanette," Parker's father was saying over the din, "but he was nice when he was a boy."

"I was not," Parker said. "I was rotten. It was you; you were so rotten, I seemed nice by comparison."

"But I never beat you, not even when you were a lousy teenager," Parker's father said.

"I can't believe this is happening to me." Jeanette's voice was a low moan.

"There, there, girlie. It happens to everybody. Sooner or later." Parker's father continued to pat Jeanette's back, as practiced as a mother.

Myrna slid into bed about one o'clock, and Parker, feeling the bed shift, rolled over to her.

"Sleep," Myrna said. "I need to sleep."

She had come home at eight-thirty, long after dinner was over, with apologies long and sincere. The computers had gone down at midday. A report, absolutely essential, had to be prepared. Her boss had practically threatened the entire staff.

As soon as the litany concluded, the two sisters closed themselves into the spare bedroom, leaving Parker and his father alone in the den. Bonnie slept in a Port-a-crib in the living room, and everyone crept from room to room in a pantomime of quietness and stealth. Parker put sheets on the sofa bed while his father alternately dozed and watched a too-quiet television. At ten he turned off the television and handed his father a pair of pajamas. The indistinct sounds from the spare bedroom had not abated. There was nothing to wait up for. He was suddenly, irredeemably tired. Exhausted by the number of people now inhabiting his house.

But then Myrna had come to bed and some internal alarm had sounded, his mind and heart a speeding collage of fear and potential horror. He rose to check doors and windows, and hearing a sound from the darkened guest bathroom, he snapped on the light expecting an intruder with a cartoon robber's black mask but finding instead Jeanette, naked, sitting on the edge of the bathtub, hugging herself, her breasts pinched by her arms, her legs crossed around the black triangle of her pubic hair, her body rocking to some ancient rhythm of grief.

"Sorry," he whispered, fumbling, not fast enough with the light switch, a burlesque of speed and dexterity. "I'm sorry."

"It's okay." Her voice was as dry as sand. "I should have closed the door."

"Can I do anything?"

He detected movement in the darkness, movement that he interpreted as negative.

"You're a good guy, Parker," she said. "Myrna doesn't know how lucky."

"I'm no bargain," he said. "Just ask Myrna." He was embarrassed by the sound of his own thoughts expressed by someone who barely knew him. A surprise to know that the disguise had worked. "I'm glad that you could come; I'm just sorry about everything else."

"Thanks. I'll make it. I always do."

"Get some rest."

"Sure."

He felt his way through the dark hallway, listening for any further disturbances, though his heartbeat of alarm was now stilled. He slipped under the covers beside his wife, as deft now as any cat burglar could hope. Eyes closed, he ambivalently wished for sleep, the earlier dim collage now replaced by a single snapshot: the flash of his sister-in-law's skin against the white porcelain of the tub, an image, he discovered, that he did not wish to remove. Although to dwell on it for long would be to lose some truth of that image of himself—*a good guy!*—so carefully constructed for public view.

July fourth: Parker promised Bonnie that the family would go to the park, to see fireworks and eat hot dogs, this in spite of Jeanette's reservations concerning two-year-old girls and stomachaches and the fear of loud noises. Myrna rolled her eyes when Parker made his announcement, but to his surprise she packed the picnic basket and organized everything that they were to take. "Colonel Fun has spoken," she said.

At the park, they found a spot near the lake in the tentative shade of three pine trees. Myrna and Jeanette set the table and unloaded the Tupperware containers of potato salad and coleslaw while Bonnie ran after the paper plates and napkins when a breeze kicked up. Parker grilled the hot dogs and hamburgers, supervised by his father, who reminded him to keep the fire low; otherwise the only thing left would be the rat toes and the other beef byproducts. Parker's father said that Lydia had become a vegetarian ten years ago, and he still couldn't rid himself of her descriptions of how hot dogs were made.

After a dinner consumed quickly and in a silence punctuated only by the table etiquette of those unused to eating together, Parker's father took Bonnie down by the lake to feed the ducks with leftover hot dog buns. Jeanette and Myrna turned over onto their stomachs and began to talk in adolescent whispers and giggles, two sisters who had discovered, after the fact, that they had always liked each other. They reminded him suspiciously of those fragrant girls in high school who had never spoken to him except in mockery, so secure were they by comparison with himself.

Alone, Parker suddenly couldn't remember why they'd come; it was the Fourth of July, but beyond that the motive now seemed blurred. They were in this park, he decided, because it was the Fourth of July, and eating hot dogs and watching fireworks seemed like the things one was supposed to do if memories of family were to be made. He could pretend that the surface of their presence here was the truth: a father, a wife, a sister-in-law, a niece, himself—each person with clear head and pure heart, genuinely pleased to be with one another. Not thrown together by some third-best accommodation to pain and injury.

Bonnie and his father were running up the hill from the lake, his father jogging just behind Bonnie in that pretense of not quite catching her that Parker remembered from his own childhood.

"Doggie bite," Bonnie announced. "Doggie bite Bunny."

Jeanette rolled over on the blanket. "What?"

Bonnie raised one hand, which showed no visible wounds. She started to sniffle, then to cry, then to wail with total abandon.

"Baby," Jeanette said, "show me. I can't see anything."

"Dad," Parker said, "what did you do?"

A flicker of embarrassment crossed Parker's father's face. "Nothing," he said. "It was just a dog. Just a hungry old poodle on some old biddy's leash. Bonnie stuffed some bread in its mouth and her finger got in the way a little, that's all."

"Finger hurt," Bonnie said.

"The skin's not even broken," Jeanette said.

"She'll be okay," Myrna said, patting her niece's back. "She's a big girl, isn't she?"

"Sure she is," Parker's father said. "She's a little trooper."

"Dad," Parker said, unwilling to let the old man off the hook so easily, "can't you be more careful? She's only two years old, for Chrissake. You don't let a two-year-old do something by herself when she might get hurt. There's all kinds of things, rabies and distemper and . . . You know that."

He was being unreasonable, he knew. There had been no bite,

no tragedy. Only a parody of accident and injury and pain. He was just tired. No longer able to differentiate between the real and the imagined. Tired of listening to his father's false humor and its pretense of order and authority. Tired of being embroiled in the failures of others, no matter how slight or trivial.

His father had visibly become an inch taller. "Contrary to popular opinion, I seem to remember raising one son who survived, and I'm not senile yet. She ran all the way back here, and she didn't even think about it until she saw she had an audience. And who made you the expert on child care, Mr. I-don't-want-to-have-kids-because-I-don't-want-to-be-bothered?"

"That's not it," he said, suddenly unsure. *Why was it that he and Myrna had never . . . ?* He couldn't remember a single coherent argument among the dozens they'd discussed.

He could imagine with equanimity any conceivable demise—flood, earthquake, fire, dismemberment, drowning, disease—so long as it had to do with his own person. Such things were the cost of living, such things were to be expected; to expect them was, in some way, to control them. But as he watched Jeanette impassively comfort Bonnie, he knew that the dream of controlling such pains was an outrage—that there was an entire world of natural disaster and human calamity and chaos lying in wait. Much more serious than the gumming nibble of an ancient poodle. A dry-cleaner's bag. A wading pool. A can of Drano. A hot dog. Another person. There was a story of disaster and self-recrimination inside everybody and every object, and there was no control for such things. You could go crazy trying to find it or make it. And the best reminder he could offer himself was of Keith Myers's mother and his own role as the agent of grief.

The memory thirty years distant was still fresh. Even now, it had the capacity to make him squirm. After his mother left, particularly sensitized to the possibilities of pain and loss, he had come with his father to this town of dust and cotton fields and vineyards, and as the new boy in the third grade, he had been anxious to please, to establish himself, to impress the dumb, gullible farmers' children. Another boy, even newer than himself and a year younger perhaps, came to the school a week later. Parker had watched with delight. Frail, holding his mother's hand as he ascended the concrete steps, this newer boy seemed an easy target: he wore stiff blue jeans that cracked at the knees, a red and white striped shirt with a button-down collar. A tartan plaid beret covered his head. Ridiculous. Parker had waited until the mother turned reluctantly away, descended the concrete steps to her car, blown a kiss to her stolid son. Then, he swooped down, screaming something wild and inarticulate, and tore the tartan beret from the boy's head. He had run, still screaming, hearing in his own mind his audience's laughter and approbation, but instead, whirling around to find that yokel audience standing stock-still, frozen, slack-mouthed in some bovine expression of horror. The boy's head, so pale as to look blue, had been shaved some time before; it was now covered with fuzz, only a wispy imitation of hair. A pink line of scar parted the right side of his skull. Parker had nearly fallen to the sidewalk under the weight of his own shame. The boy licked his lips with a nervous tongue.

"You asshole," Keith Myers said. "Asshole."

Parker would always be grateful for that—that Keith Myers had cursed him, had not damned him further to that shame by some inhuman expression of forgiveness. No . . . that job was done when he saw the car still standing at the edge of the curb with Keith Myers's mother in it—obviously she had seen the whole thing—her head buried in her arms above the steering wheel, Parker watching the dumb show of her tears, realizing that she had chosen to let her son brave the perils of a cruel world alone.

It had been the closest thing to an out-of-body experience he had ever known. Not only had he sworn in that instant that he would never place himself in such a compromised position ever again, but he had also seen Keith Myers from his mother's eyes, recognizing the incalculable cost of loving a child. And from some nameless organ of outrage, he had felt his own anger that no one, not even his father, would ever suffer so for *his* pain, anger that his mother could have betrayed him like this.

And now, he imagined Bonnie, on her back, choking on a piece of hot dog, a hot dog that he, Parker Thom, had cooked and encouraged because it fit in with his own vision of family memory, and hovering nearby some woman wearing all white, a specter that seemed to have taken its shape from the nurse of his grade school, a woman who had scolded and lectured about the dangers of sneezing without a handkerchief at the ready; she was clucking her tongue about what fool would feed a two-year-old a whole, windpipe-stuffing hot dog. Didn't he know the horrible statistics?

And too, he saw himself, recognizing his kinship with Vic—that he wasn't somehow immune to the tugs of sexual desire and conquest; if he had been faithful, it was due more to his own aversion to the entanglements and deceptions of infidelity rather than any devotion to virtue. Jeanette's brown legs had appeared in more than one twilight fantasy in that world between wakefulness and sleep. The thought of being even less adept with the light switch fogged his mind at odd hours. *What about Myrna?* The question was sudden and insistent. The hours she had chosen to spend at work when it wasn't necessary, in a job for which she had never concealed her loathing. Why, when she could be home with him, did she choose to stay away? Was it out of need of independence? Some other reason? *Of whom did she dream?*

He was dreaming this with his eyes open, sweating not from the July heat but from some nameless ache that was emanating from somewhere deep in his bowels, wishing that he could gather his loved ones in, protect them all from accident and trouble and tragedy, which was when the fireworks began, rising into the deep blue of the summer sky, rising with their dangerous and deadly and gloriously beautiful sparks.

He was lying on his back staring at the ceiling, Myrna on her side with her back next to him. The windows above the bed emitted a faint drift of warm air, the clear, writhing sound of husky heartache, and from other backyards, the muffled explosions of illegally obtained firecrackers. A full moon sailed across the sky with its pulse of white light. Grace poured into the room. From the next room, he could hear the sound of the rocking chair and Jeanette's low singing. Bonnie, awake to the low hum of darkness, was protecting every second saved from sleep. From the den came Parker's father's predictable snore. Parker reached for Myrna. She brushed his hand away from her breasts, then her belly, allowing him to settle for her hip.

He would settle gladly. He would play nurse and counselor and foil for his father and sister-in-law and niece, and he would do what he could to keep his wife happy. Even a child if she wanted that—if he had somehow bulldozed her, using her family's history as well as his for his own purposes—if they weren't now too old to make such a change. If she hadn't, without telling him, already left. He would accept the risk that accompanied the choice, the risk that in making room for tragedy and error, he might lose his own manicured self, become a victim of compromise, ambivalence, and pain. *Those brown thighs!* He felt himself floating above the bed, seeing himself and Myrna as his mother might see them, two aging children resigned to making accommodations for each other, seeing also Jeanette and Bonnie and his father, his benevolence toward them buoying him up as if he were riding on top of a balloon, and he held his breath—fearful of this moment and all its attendant risks—praying that his love would hold.

A Blessing

We are not, as a family, robust breeders. My mother had three miscarriages before I happened along, and then I was a solo act. For years, my wife said that this was the whole problem: I had been so much the object of my parents' attentions as well as affections, they had lived so long with the fear of losing yet another child that, even after I had grown up, moved away, and married, they still could not let go. And neither could I. For the effect on me has been real. Constantly bathed in the lime-light of my parents' expectations, I performed my role of the dutiful, successful son—at school, in athletics, at church, as a child, and now as an adult—with a desperate guilt and obligation, as if some sort of repayment for their overweening affection needed to be made, as if upon my shoulders rested the burden of my parents' other disappointments, as if my life could somehow recover for them what had been lost.

But there was something else. Although an only child, I somehow knew, even before my mother listed for me the durations of her many failed pregnancies, that I was not the *oldest* child. Even at the age of three I distinctly felt as though I were occupying a place that by all rights belonged to others. I came to believe that I had two brothers and one sister, three older siblings who were simply on vacation, a conceit that I shared with my kindergarten teacher one morning and for which I received a spanking that afternoon.

"How could you lie like that?" my mother said when we were home, her voice fraught with concern and grief in equal measures.

I stood mutely before her, consciously aware of having told what was apparently untrue, although the certainty of my siblings' presence was as palpable as toast, their aroma, as it were, overpoweringly strong.

Later, my mother told me about the miscarriages and her grief in language she deemed appropriate for a five-year-old. She said that the other babies had been sick, that she and my father had prayed and prayed, that each time they had been crushed by sorrow until I had come along, and that was why they loved me so much and wanted only the best things for me. Because I was their *only* child.

"God sent you to us," my mother said. "You were a gift we'd nearly stopped hoping for."

It is disturbing to a child to be so complete a monarch over his parents' emotions, and it seemed to me, even then, that I had enormous leverage—I could ruin them if I wished. I could have told them several stories. How I knew that my sister would have loved dancing—she would have loved Chubby Checker and the twist in its day—and yet I also knew that, had she lived, she would have been fat and sadly disappointed by the cruelties of life. How I whispered with my brothers in the front hall closet, a place comfortable in its darkness and the fusty smell of aging wool coats, a boys' club in which I confided my longings and fear. When my parents, concerned by what they perceived to be my loneliness, asked about what I could possibly be doing in a front hall closet, I mutely showed them the comic books and flashlight that I had had the foresight to bring as props. And they, who could hear my whisperings, chose to believe in my creativity, that I could conjure up imaginary playmates for myself, not realizing that my visions of family were appallingly literal. Until I turned twelve, I could have told them stories of my brothers' comings and goings and my sister's heartbreaks, when one day without warning or fanfare I knew that I would not be seeing my brothers or sister again, that in the growing importance of my own life (and in my need to shine brightly for the sake of my parents) their outlines had dimmed. I could have told my parents everything. But I did not. For pathos has its powers as well, and cognizance of that power doomed me to goodness. To crush them would have crushed me also, and even though at odd moments, I felt the presence of my brothers and sister hovering on an axis just slightly different from my own, I never spoke of it again.

Until I met Janice, who was from a family of seven children. When I said that I envied her childhood, surrounded as it was by chaos and vitality and the literalness of family life, she snorted at my naïveté.

"Don't be stupid. We lived in a two-bedroom house. My parents had babies in their bedroom for eight years, while my sisters and I shared the other bedroom and my brothers slept on couches and chairs. We're talking *Tobacco Road*, not *Life with Father*."

"Still," I said, unwilling to let it go, yet unwilling to speak in anything but the most elliptical terms, "you *have* brothers and sisters. I'll never know what it's like. Not the way you do, anyway."

"I see them three times a year, and we get along. Back then, I would have killed a couple of the others just to get more room."

I trusted Janice, and I trusted her familial experience as being broader than my own; and frankly, I had begun to doubt my own memories of twenty years before. So when we decided to get married, we also decided that children could be put on hold. Janice had endured enough family to last several lifetimes; my fascination with family could be classified as less than empirical. We had become part of a trend, one described on the covers of national newsmagazines: Double Income, No Kids—DINKs. We didn't like the label or the self-satisfied, self-gratifying consumption its image conjured up. But even less did we like the children of friends, little monsters who turned their parents' conversational abilities into distracted preoccupation, shrill argument, or the saccharine of psycho-pedia-babble. Still, our list of single and/or childless acquaintances was shrinking and the names were getting younger. We both admitted to a certain degree of selfishness, a selfishness that frightened us but a selfishness we protected with the jealousy of an *amah*. We had a right to our adult privacy. We didn't have to defend ourselves to anyone else.

And then Janice came home one evening after a routine appointment with her gynecologist. He had informed her that her biological clock wasn't just ticking—the mainspring was playing crack the whip. She came home from her appointment and stood in front of the bedroom mirror. "I'm too fat to get pregnant," she said. This was not true; Janice has never been remotely overweight, and yet when I said something to that effect, she turned on me with a look of withering mockery. "You're not the one," she said, "you're not the one who has to become a blimp for a year. Or wear clothes designed by Ahmad the tent maker." In the space of a sentence, the world had tipped. We had gone from sterility to fecundity. Tillers of human soil.

And yet time wasn't all that we had to worry about: physiologically, Janice was one of those women who, if she had lived one hundred years ago, would in all likelihood never have gotten pregnant in the first place. So we became participants in that divine prank whereby an act that seventeen-year-olds routinely perform as horseplay in the humid backseats of Volkswagens (and which, just as routinely, yields unwanted issue) is reduced in thirty-year-olds to something resembling a Mr. Science experiment, with just as much passion and just as much success. It is a phenomenon illustrative of our time, I suppose—so much concern with the avoidance of reproduction, only to result in the frantic application of technology, forcing the body to do what it was primed to do all along.

Others have extolled the absurdities of temperature taking and ovulation charting, the careful selection of one's underwear and a whole host of other indignities; I will not add to it.

Fourteen months later we were pregnant.

"Congratulations," Janice's gynecologist said. He patted her on the knee. He shook my hand. He is the forty-year-old son of a

Polish ship worker, and he has seven Catholic children of his own. By his own admission, he is not yet finished fulfilling his personal command of fruitfulness and multiplication. "So happy, so very happy."

Janice did not begin to cry until we were alone in the car. "I'm pregnant," she sniffled. "I'll have to quit my job. I'm going to get as big as a house, have varicose veins, and have sudden strange desires to wear polyester stretch pants and keep soup-can curlers in my hair until noon every day. I'll lose my waist, and then my patience when he throws all your underwear into the toilet and tries to flush it."

I had no idea to which problem I should respond. "He won't do anything like that," I said.

"You don't know anything," she said. "You don't know anything about kids and what kids do to parents, especially mothers. The only kid you've ever known was yourself, but you were born old, and you've even forgotten that."

I half expected those ghosts of my childhood to visit in confirmation, but the air behind Janice's head was still, uninterrupted.

"I wanted you to be happy," I said.

"I am," she sobbed. "Don't be dumb."

"No. I won't be dumb."

We drove the rest of the way home in silence, slipping past vineyards dotted green with leaf.

When we went to bed, Janice wore a flannel nightgown and a quilted robe. "You've done enough." She rolled over onto her side, her back to me, and when I put my arms around her, she snored into her pillow.

You might, I suppose, think Janice unreasonable. And you might think me more than a little ignorant of the irresistible demands of estrogen. I can honestly say that I conducted more than one secret conversation with myself, that I often dissected the strange logic whereby Janice and I had suffered fourteen months of uncomfortable copulatory arrangement leading to a pregnancy she now said she never wanted. And which was all my fault. I harbored the illusion that I had done no wrong, that Janice had gone off center. I could take comfort as the aggrieved party. And I would, of course, be wrong.

We endured one week of *détente*. Then, one dark morning near dawn, I became aware that Janice was no longer in bed, that the aggrieved wings of her shoulders no longer pointed in my direction. Light seeped from beneath the bathroom door. I heard sobbing. Convulsed, choking, stifled cries, a wilted bouquet of tears. Janice was sitting on the toilet, her knees pressed together, her arms around her abdomen.

"Sweetheart," I said, not entirely sincere, not then. "Cupcake, tell me about it."

"I'm bleeding." She held for my inspection a wad of red-streaked toilet paper.

"You're bleeding," I repeated.

"Bleeding. That's what I said." She had stopped crying, and her voice was clinical, detached, the bearer of facts, albeit unpleasant. "I'm going to lose the baby."

"You don't know that," I said. "You're not a doctor."

"No. I'm just a hormonally imbalanced woman." She looked at me. "I've heard you talking to yourself. And don't tell me you haven't. Talked to yourself, I mean."

I stood mutely in front of my wife, accused and convicted.

"Go back to bed," Janice said. "You're not doing me any good by staring at me."

What can I say of the anguish suffered for those who die before birth? It is as unsatisfying as it is unsettling, as if the burden, although weightless, still buckles the knees, a shadow without object; there are no funerals, no ordered rituals of grief. My brothers and sister had come before me, and I had never known mourning except at that distance. It is not enough, by way of consolation, to say that no name was lost.

We drove to Dr. Wozniak's office at eight the next morning. Recognizing the signs, the nurses quickly ushered Janice into an exam room; they helped her out of her clothes and onto the harsh paper of the exam table with that solicitude reserved only for other women, a connection denied to men. One nurse, a stout woman in a flowered uniform top, smoothed Janice's cheek with the backs of her fingers, saying, "Sh, sh, there, there," cooing and clucking her comfort. For her part, Janice began to cry musically, a lullaby cry of sniffles and restraint. She blew her nose into a proffered tissue. "Post-natal drip," she said, laugh-weeping into her Kleenex.

A second nurse, an older woman wearing glasses with no-nonsense steel frames, shooed me away. "There's nothing more useless," she said, "than husbands. Lucky for you she's strong." I sat in a corduroy-covered armchair and looked at the back issues of *Sunset* and *Parents* and *People* spread out in neat fans on the waiting-room coffee tables, unable to pick up any of them, unable to break their happy symmetry.

Half an hour later, Janice tottered from her room. She was holding a piece of paper. "We have to go to the hospital," she said. "I have a prescription."

We did not leave the hospital until the hour before dawn of the next day. An orderly wheeled her out while I brought the car from the parking lot. Stars littered the sky in useless celebration, and I thought of the past twenty-four hours: of pregnancy and miscarriage, and the surgical investigation into my wife's ability to conceive and carry. Dr. Wozniak had spoken to both of us following Janice's recovery from the anesthesia.

"There's nothing wrong, thank God," he said. "Nothing to stop you from getting pregnant again. But not right away, okay? No—" and here he used a phrase that sounded like hanky-panky, a Polish-sounding euphemism for sex, lovemaking, intercourse "—no *nifky poofky* for three weeks. Use your contraceptives until three periods have gone by, and then we'll get busy, okay?" I did not stop him from using the inclusive pronoun. "It will work itself out, you'll see. Babies will come if you want them. I feel sure of that." Good Catholic optimism. "In the meantime," he cautioned, "no big plans. You'll maybe feel sudden urges to change your life—a new job, a new house, you might even look at each other and think, Do I know this person? Very normal, very typical. But don't dwell on these. Live your life as before. Get rested. Eat. Drink. It will get better, trust me."

And so we were in the car, driving away from the hospital, trusting Dr. Wozniak, trying to forget the bloody, blue rope of tissue that had come from between Janice's legs during our drive to the hospital.

"I'm sorry," Janice said. "I wasn't sure, and I lost the baby."

"The fetus wasn't healthy," I said, "and that's not your fault."

Before we left the hospital, Dr. Wozniak had said this, so I felt that I was on safe ground. "This early," he had said, "to lose the baby is a blessing."

"It was sick," I said, aware as I said it of my daughter's presence and my mother's own words, "she was sick and she would have had a horrible life."

"I wished it to be sick."

"You can't blame yourself."

She sat with her hands in her lap, tearing at her cuticles, and I wished that I had bought her something in the gift shop, something for her to hold.

"Don't go home," she said. "I don't want to go home. I don't want to rest right now. Just drive."

We followed the highway that followed the river, tagging along as it rose into the foothills. Ground fog had begun to rise, blotting out the accusations of the stars.

At a bend in the highway, Janice ordered me to stop and pull to the side. To our right was the riverbank, strewn with river rock, sand, and empty beer bottles in this the fifth year of drought and hopelessness. To the left, two ancient horses stood observing us from the center of dry pasture. A barbed-wire fence leaned halfway to the ground.

Our shoes made sounds unnaturally loud in the dawn fog as we crossed the highway. "Here horsey, horsey," Janice called, a whispered shout. "Come on, baby," she said.

Neither animal stirred.

Hiking her dress up to her hips, she put one leg over the sagging wire.

"Janice," I said, "what are you doing?"

"Nothing new," she said. "I used to pet horseys all the time, but lately I haven't had the time."

I held the wire down for her, then followed. The two horses watched us as we approached. Janice touched one, then the other, on the neck and in the spot between the eyes. "Poor horseys," she said, "*you* don't have much time, do you?" They ducked their heads, their eyes well acquainted with grief. "If I had some sugar, I'd give you some." She stroked their patchy coats.

In my pockets I could find only a stray packet of hospital Sweet 'N Low. "What can I do?" I said.

"You could not ask dumb questions." Her voice broke, as brittle as pressed flowers.

I held her then in the presence of aging creatures, aware of an increased chorus of souls, their lives uninterrupted by birth.

Reflected Music

Cunningham's father enlisted in the navy in 1944. He was seventeen, newly graduated from high school. The navy seemed like a safer bet at the time; he was sure to be drafted anyway, and who in their right minds would go into the infantry as a matter of choice? He trained in Virginia, and then, because it was something he'd always been interested in, he applied and was accepted into radio school. He was three-quarters of the way through the course when Germany surrendered. He was certified as radio-competent three days after Hiroshima was incinerated. He never went overseas. He never saw sea duty. He counted his blessings and waited for his release from service, his return to civilian life, his future secured by others. He spoke of the two years as good training for his career as an electrician but boring as hell.

As a boy, Cunningham was always vaguely disappointed in his father and in his father's inability to mythologize his memory of World War II; in the history books, this last good war was rife with drama and symbolic significance. Good and evil so clearly defined. But for Cunningham's father, the war had begun only as an inconvenience when he was a sophomore in high school; he'd found out about Pearl Harbor when he couldn't find anything interesting to listen to on the radio, the war preempting schedules all across the band. His high school years from then on were lived in the shadow of that which loomed after graduation, the nervous certainty of the draft, the possibility of death on some incomprehensible foreign shore. But as it turned out, his military service had been marked by even more banality than peacetime.

The only story Cunningham's father could tell his son, one that conveyed anything at all, occurred after the war on both fronts had been safely concluded, a month before he was released in the fall of 1946. His father had gone to mass that morning, had experienced again the disquieting sense of taking Holy Communion in summer, in a uniform of blue dungarees, the day full of heavy, muggy heat—a ritual overcome by the extremities of weather and context—and now he was asleep, along with nearly every other man, in his barracks on a late Sunday morning. Flies buzzed against the screens. The barracks was quiet with the low tones of men sleeping away their exile, their boredom measured not by the watch but by the calendar. Someone turned on the one phonograph and began to play at full volume the sound track of *Oklahoma!*

Oh, what a beautiful morning . . .

Cunningham's father rose, groggy, gluey-eyed, and told the offender, a huge Polack named Nowiki, a former steel worker with a history of belligerence and assault, to shut the goddamn thing off. Nowiki, still drunk from his trip to Richmond the night before, told him to smoke it. Cunningham's father stood his ground. Nowiki slid down from his top bunk and without preamble swung at Cunningham's father.

I've got a wonderful feeling . . .

What happened next Cunningham's father couldn't say. He came to himself in the latrine of another barracks. There was no one else about. He faced his multiplied reflection, his image fore and aft reflected and reflected, then reflected again, each time progressively smaller, in the opposed rows of mirrors. He was leaning against a sink, pressing a thin piece of steak to his eyes, the skin around which was already puffing into tropical blooms of discoloration. He had no idea how he'd gotten there, who'd taken him, why. The next week he saw Nowiki from a distance. Nowiki's hands were bandaged—evidently he had ducked enough by instinct that Nowiki had connected with the metal posts of the bunk behind his head—and either Nowiki did not see him or else he simply wished not to acknowledge his latest sparring partner's presence. His father was quick to point out that he had nothing against Nowiki except his black eye, and he blamed that on Nowiki's hangover rather than on Nowiki himself; one could not carry grudges against people when they were not themselves.

A small story, but one that Cunningham found compelling—the very thought of his mild-tempered, open-faced father giving orders to a lurching drunk, the subsequent fight, the discovery some hours later of having been transported by unknown hands to another place, the awakening alone, the reductionism and multiplication of the Manichaean mirrors, the curious wives'-tale detail of the steak. His father's curiously impersonal forgiveness. The cheery music, founded on that false bedrock of goodness. It was his one true transmitted memory of World War II, and it was enough when, in 1972, Cunningham's lottery number was twelve and he would have surely been drafted except that the draft had been suspended the year before; it was enough to know when he was eighteen years old that his father had fought but only in this most peripheral of ways, and that his father had no desire for his son to fight the battle he had missed, no desire to march side by side with his son in some out-of-step Fourth of July veterans' parade. His father hoped, in fact, that his son could avoid even the temporary trouble caused by a Broadway show tune. This despite the usual father-son troubles, the usual father-son arguments of older and younger generations, when Cunningham wondered what had happened to that forgiveness so casually extended to a relative stranger. So, instead of going to a battlefield in the steaming rice paddies of Southeast Asia or the guerrilla war of family life, Cunningham, without remorse or hesitation, bravely went away to the mist and fir trees of peaceable Oregon, to a college neither he nor his parents could afford, to work out the ever-widening counterpoints of his life: he took art classes and business classes; while he worked part-time for the campus police, he tried pot and, for a brief time in wide-eyed innocence, sampled a small smorgasbord of uppers, downers, and LSD; he joined a fraternity of premed and prelaw majors, let his hair grow to his shoulders, and by the time Watergate erupted and Saigon fell, he felt nearly safe.

"You look like shit." Carole Hibner stood in front of him, a frank look of distaste crossing her lens-distorted, myopic eyes. One leg crossed over the other, a prim picture of the elementary school teacher she one day hoped to become, she held the ring of master keys in both hands, uncertain, it seemed, about relinquishing the keys—and with them the safety of such cherished halls—to such a wreck. Cunningham collapsed onto the couch.

Having spent the last six hours in athletic, sweaty endeavors with a sophomore from Kansas named Mary Klyne, a heavy-breasted girl who was somehow able to give off the hot odor of August wheat fields even while standing in the dorm showers at three in the morning, he ached with love.

"I ache with love," he groaned.

"It's too disgusting, I'm sure." She wrinkled her nose as if she, too, could detect wheat fields and the dank mushroom smell of sex. "You'll be all right? You can make rounds?" She placed the keys on the desk.

"I can make rounds."

"You won't go to sleep in the golf cart again?"

"I promise, Mother." It was annoying to have his first hideaway exposed, but he would think of something else. Maybe. Maybe it didn't even matter.

"You're sure?" She kicked the leg of his couch.

"Squeeze Roger for me."

Her physicist boyfriend. Who did not always recognize her, especially in the rarefied light of his lab. Whose name summoned a flush to her face in the most mottled designs he'd ever seen, a crochet pattern of blood starting at the base of her neck, moving upward along her throat, to her chin, her cheeks, the roots of her mouse-brown hair.

"I'm going to study—" giving his couch one final kick "—and as for your filthy animal mind, I'll have you know that not everybody thinks that sex is something you pick your teeth with."

Then she was gone, her bulging backpack the last object he saw. How could he tell her she had it all wrong, that sex was neither toothpick nor after-dinner mint—no dessert of any kind—but a main course to be served and savored in large, voraciously consumed mouthfuls?

With the door to the security office still vibrating on its hinges, he staggered into the bathroom and, facing the mirror without the benefit of his glasses, rubbed the face that seemed a stranger's.

While her roommate was away at the coast, Mary Klyne had invited him to her bed in the women's dormitory, meeting him at the door like some vision sprung from his own imagination—in black garters and stockings, the lingerie and her practiced, expectant air at odds with the bland innocence of her farmer's-daughter face. With his bottles of tequila and lime juice still carefully cradled underneath his parka, panting and eager, he had unraveled. This was so far removed from their most recent backseat fumblings as to make them seem like the horseplay of children. And he'd been afraid he wouldn't learn anything in college! He had found surprise upon surprise—her whispered suggestions, her improvisations new to him, her evident enjoyment of the act, her busy tongue. Her unconditional insistence, whispered into his blood-deafened ears, that he wear the rubber that she proffered.

"We don't want to overpopulate the world," Mary Klyne had murmured, "or little Mary's insides, now do we?" She had straddled his legs and unrolled the sheath down over him with a little snap that seemed electric.

This first time in such domestic surroundings—*an actual bed!*—the premeditation of margaritas and condom, he had felt so transported around this new bend in the labyrinth of sexuality that he could not remember—and it did not seem important, after all—who was the seducer, who the seduced.

Now, putting on his glasses, he discovered that the stranger's face in the mirror was puffy around the eyes, the skin droopy as if it were a rubber mask left out in the sun too long. Cunningham ran the sink full of cold water, dunked his head, and pulled his hair back into a rubber band. He had four hours of work to avoid, preferably in some manner that would not result in outrage on the part of the campus police, the underpaid professional cops who looked upon their student assistants—*fucking hippies*—as rich-kid turds with ticket books. Retrieving the master keys from the desk, he took one last look in the mirror before going out into the predawn gray. Things did not look good. He'd lost himself within the Bermuda Triangle of love and lust and infatuation; anyone with eyes, he was sure, could not fail to recognize his translation.

––––––––

For two hours he made the rounds of classrooms and labs and parking lots, checking doors and windows and illegally parked cars, the underpowered golf cart bouncing across the uneven cobblestones, but the only thing Cunningham could think of was Mary Klyne's skin in the flickering light of her sand candles. And while dawn announced itself as a reluctant, weary lightening of clouds and mist, for Cunningham it was full of such potent glory as to make the muscles of his stomach and throat constrict.

At six o'clock, he ran the golf cart into the hedge of fir trees behind the women's dorms. Before he fell asleep in the shifting camouflage of the branches, he watched as half a dozen male subjects retreated from the rear entrance, their gaits weak-kneed, their eyes lost in the shadow of smug fatigue, while on the second floor, in the corner room, two naked women, sisters of the moon, rose from a single bed and embraced in front of their opened window. So moved was he by all that darkness offered that he could not have said whether or not they were beautiful, whether their embrace fascinated or repelled him. Night's work was being done. With or without him. And of this he was absolutely certain: the vision was private, intended only for him.

The question, of course, is this: *who could possibly take this boy-man seriously?* Who can possibly believe the intensity with which any twenty-year-old explores his own ego? To insist on the primacy of his own discoveries! He is laughable. As though sex and ideas, the pleasures of mind and body, had been invented for him, as if he had been the one to experience such things for the first time. He is himself a creature of his own fantasy, so entirely indifferent to any thought of ambivalence or moral disorder, that every sentence his mind can think to form begins with the word "I," and in his own ears it rings with the resonance of perfection.

He woke just in time to unlock classroom doors. In front of the organic chemistry lab, three of his fraternity brothers, the premed students, stood smoking cigarettes, ready to give him shit.

"Give us the keys, Cunningham," they said. "Then you can sleep all you want." The smoke from their cigarettes rose, then fell in the suspended mist.

"You'd blow the place up," he said. "I'm saving the free world."

"You're a riot. You're killing us."

One of the brothers, Gary Davis, stopped him. "Someone's looking for you."

"Who?" If it was the police lieutenant, he could kiss this job good-bye.

Davis shrugged. "I told him to look in the shack around eight. That there was no telling where you were hiding before then. Don't worry," he said, "it wasn't your boss."

"Thanks, Gary."

"A key, Cunningham, that's all I ask."

He tried to think who it might be—who he might want to see—but he had no ideas, only the sudden, irrational notion that his father had chosen this very morning to materialize. The idea was absurd, but the very absurdity of it made it all the more possible. And all the more frightening. The idea of having to represent himself when he felt so spent.

But when he returned to the office, there was no one waiting,

no one sitting on the bench outside the locked door, no one prepared to judge the way in which he was conducting his life, and
after having filled out a rounds report that was once again a product of wishful thinking and invention, about to leave, he heard his
name spoken in a whisper:

"Cunningham. Brother Cunningham."

Standing in front of the desk was the flower of some eastern
prep school, older than himself by three, maybe four, years, attired in clothes current to the previous decade: wrinkled, loose-
legged slacks; a white dress shirt, equally wrinkled, the sleeves
rolled up to the elbow; a skinny black tie. The hollows of his eyes,
the pale cast of his cheekbones, seemed to hint of soul-tormenting
dissipations, the pretense of debauchery cultivated for effect.
Fashionably depraved.

How he had opened and closed the door without his hearing,
Cunningham could not understand.

"I was told you could help me." Still a whisper. He half-fell onto
the couch, one leg over the arm, a loose-limbed posture that seemed
to carry with it the images of lacrosse and squash and privilege.

"Who told you that?"

"The boys at home." He dipped his head in the general direction
of the fraternity house. "I need a place to stay. I'm all done in."

"Stay at the house."

"I would," and here his eyes closed as though he'd suddenly
become immensely tired, "I would but I'd prefer not to have a lot
of attention. I need peace. I need quiet." The eyes blinked open. A
stare directed into his own. "I was told you could help me. That
you might know of some unused space and that you might have a
key to fit."

"Maybe."

What in Christ's name was this, anyway? Who was this flit and
why was he looking for some hole to crawl into and why did he
have to come today—today, when he himself could barely think
for fatigue and preoccupation?

"There's a storage area behind the music department where
they keep stands and risers. Junk like that. The last concert was a
week ago."

"Perfect."

"I still don't understand why you don't just stay at the house. The couches are decent." The dull pressure in his skull was reminder enough. "I ought to know," he added.

"I've lived in groups as long as I care to." He was whispering again.

"Commune?"

The other shook his head. "Army. The goddamn army." It was a confession. "I was in the goddamn, sadistic army."

His voice was bitter, and Cunningham heard the echoes of helicopter blades and the roar of a jungle burning.

The other man's head lolled against the back of the couch. "My name is Randy Joyner, Cunningham, but everyone calls me R. J. Talk to Frankie—" the chapter president, Frank Blanchard "—he'll vouch for me. He told me to ask you."

R. J. held out his hand, and Cunningham, always embarrassed by the childishness of the gesture, returned the fraternal handshake.

"It's all right. Come by the house at seven tonight. I'll have a key for you."

"Great. You're saving my life. Really." He waved his hand to stop Cunningham's protest. "You just don't know."

He passed a key to R. J. that evening, and he watched an evening later—in the presence of music stands, the stacked collapsible risers, a scarred harpsichord, and billowing plumes of dust—as R. J. unrolled a sleeping bag and set out the contents of a small duffel bag and toilet kit. Frank Blanchard had told Cunningham that, appearances notwithstanding, R. J. deserved all the help that a fraternity brother could get; he was a goddamn war hero, for Chrissake, and he had come home to a roast. Who wouldn't be a little nuts? Who wouldn't want a little privacy?

After that Cunningham saw R. J. infrequently, sometimes in the early mornings when the gymnasium opened, the toilet kit and towel under one arm, or occasionally in the cafeteria, eating alone, a book propped open on the salt shakers. And he would think that he should ask him how it was to live in a room with props, with such dust and one's own knowledge of horror, but the other man's concentration seemed so single-minded—on a book, on the imminence of a shower—that he refrained. And then, as the semester began to draw toward a close, with his own attentions directed elsewhere, he forgot him.

Mary Klyne's roommate, understandably uneasy with a third presence haunting their room, volunteered to move, to take the place of a girl who, during the frenzy of a panty raid, had fallen down the circular staircase, fracturing her leg in three places and dislocating her hip. She had elected to recover at home. With the roommate gone, Mary Klyne welcomed him into her fragrant arms upon their return from the library or study groups. He found, in those hours of thrashing with Mary Klyne, reserves of energy he'd never known. He had found that, yes, it was possible to study until one in the morning, be passionate until four, and create new ways of dodging work until eight, when it was time again for class and study, in the belief that no one had ever thought these thoughts, no one had lived this life before.

No surprise, then, that when the thought inevitably came that Mary Klyne, for all her energy and invention, was, outside the boundaries of her candlelit dorm room, boring and moody and more than just a little childish, he pushed the thought aside with the devotion of a true believer. And while her tempers, previously hidden, showed themselves within the security of their "relationship" and a great deal of their conversational life was concerned with how good they were together—how well they understood each other—Cunningham could only think guiltily of the summer, when Mary Klyne would wing her way back to Kansas. When he would have a break from her, with the fraternity house to himself, working as he would be, playing junior G-man on the day shift, and maybe even filling out his first entirely truthful report.

And then one night, as Mary Klyne tickled him in yet another prelude, he discovered an even more disquieting thought: that he might not even mind a break from this constant, all-consuming eroticism, how tired he'd suddenly become of it, of Mary Klyne's Frederick's-of-Hollywood version of it, a thought as quickly dismissed as it appeared. For, after all, what could this possibly say about him—*to fade so quickly!*—as if to call into question his own sexuality, that in the last analysis, under fire as it were, his own maleness was shown to be wanting?

And so Cunningham did not immediately remember R. J. when the latter appeared early one Sunday morning at the security office door. Seconds passed. Cunningham jiggled the set of master keys in one hand, ready for another abortive set of rounds. Illuminated by the yellow light above the door, R. J.'s already mournful face was tragic, bordering on the consumptive. Dark shadows haunted his temples. Mist coated his hair.

"Brother Cunningham," he whispered. His voice was hoarse. "I need another favor."

The favor was a simple one: a key to the house once the spring semester was over, once the other brothers were gone, cleared out. R. J. was in bad shape. A cold that he couldn't shake. The dust was driving him wild.

At first, Cunningham had had his reservations—to share such splendid solitude with a stranger, especially one about whom he entertained more than a few doubts and questions. But once the semester had ended, he was glad enough for the company. The end of the spring brought with it nothing like that sense of rebirth poets were always celebrating. Instead, the last week of finals began in the midst of the last burst of rainfall; then graduation, and then this fragmenting of friends to various states and countries. Each semester, but especially spring, seemed more like the dissolution of a society, the last gasp of an era, albeit a renewable one. Thirty-five fraternity brothers left in the space of three wet, alcoholic days, and Carole Hibner was gone too, taking her disapproval home to Cincinnati and leaving behind Roger and his perfect indifference. Cunningham wondered if he even knew she was gone.

The day after graduation, Cunningham took Mary Klyne to the airport. She wore a white India-cotton top, her straight yellow hair dropped like love's pendulum to the small of her back, and for the first time, when she kissed him at the gate to her flight, the smell of perfume mingled with the wheat. He suddenly knew that, despite all his misgivings, he would miss her far more than she him. Which, upon the arrival of her second letter, proved to be the case. In the middle of a breathless paragraph about her older brother Bill, she asked whether she had mentioned about going to a Grange Hall dance with Bill's best friend, Hank, who was nothing really, just a sweet, sweet farmer's boy, and didn't Cunningham think that while they were apart for three months that to go out with other people, well, wouldn't that be best? The world was a very crazy place, and they each needed as much experience with other people as possible. There would always be the fall to look forward to, and then they would get back together again and be all the more in love with each other for having gotten to know other people, didn't he think? Cunningham had a thought, but it was not one he felt comfortable expressing either publicly or privately. He did think about other women, but those in the college's summer programs were generally forty-five-year-old English teachers with short, prematurely graying hair, and he had not as yet developed any manner for meeting women outside of a classroom.

As for R. J., Cunningham felt his presence more than he saw it. He evidently had his connections, and he had been very quickly hired by one of the local radio stations; he was doing a jazz program from midnight to six in the morning, introducing himself for some inexplicable reason as Jo-Jo. Cunningham saw his towels and shaving gear in the bathroom. He heard him come into the house at seven in the morning, just as he was thinking of getting out of bed, and once on a Friday night, while regret and rage and relief over Mary Klyne mingled in about equal measures, he listened to Jo-Jo's Jazz Shop for the entire six hours while deliberately consuming a fifth of Frank Blanchard's Crown Royal. The music, possibly because of the alcohol, seemed to start out fuzzy—studio groups trying to make the crossover between rock and something close to jazz—but then, as the hours went by, the music became clearer even as it became more complicated, a parallel to his memory of Mary Klyne, which Cunningham could not ignore—that their sexual encounters had taken their place in his mind only as a blur of sweaty, good-natured, extremely pleasant but exhausting workouts. The one particular he remembered, on the other hand, was the way her straight yellow hair swung as she tilted her head toward him, a masquerade of undivided attention as he spoke, a gesture that Cunningham (he realized it now) had found as irritating as it was endearing. He also realized now that until the semester had actually concluded he had somehow assumed, his exhaustion notwithstanding, that it would be he who would find another exercise partner, and that he would be the one to write the bright and breezy note. So, who could know?

At seven o'clock that morning when R. J. came in, he was sitting in the one good leather armchair, the empty bottle of Frank's whiskey between his ankles, silently crying, unable to stop the backwash from flooding his nose and pouring down his lips and chin. R. J. briefly looked in, left, then returned to stand in the center of the living room, quietly observing.

"Drinking alone," he said. He pulled Cunningham from the chair. "Come on, Ophelia. Next time you plan to raid Frankie's hootch, you let me know."

R. J. was shoving him up the stairs, Cunningham thinking what an extraordinarily nice thing this was that he was doing, this brother, this prince of a brother, who obviously understood about the way of things, about the treachery of women and the dangers of living alone when one is bereft and forgotten, neglected and ignored.

"You're not so bad, not so flitty as I thought," he managed to say. Even drunk, he wondered about the proprieties. "I can't tell you enough," he said. "Really."

That afternoon he would remember R. J. guiding him first to the bathroom, where he threw up in great stomach-convulsing heaves, then putting him to bed, much as he remembered his mother doing when he was sick with the flu. The covers were pulled back, the sheets smoothed. His shirt and pants somehow removed, his glasses folded and set aside on the desk. R. J. had tried to pull the broken window shade, then abruptly gave up.

"You're a pitiful thing, Cunningham," he had said. "You're sentimental, self-absorbed, and melodramatic." He sniffed. "And you smell like a wet couch."

Cunningham had agreed with him then. He agreed with him now.

"I'll be here if you need anything," R. J. had also said.

When the sunlight of four o'clock filled his room—it seemed a visitation, this light, as if it had mass and substance—his head was throbbing with the concussion of self-reproach, and the taste in his mouth was rancid. But there was music of a kind he'd never heard before emanating from the walls, as though plaster and wood and wire could breathe out their own identifiable tones. He called out for someone, anyone, to enter into this light and listen to the glory of this complicated sound, but R. J. was already gone.

That sound obsessed him for a week or more, those notes that seemed just out of reach of his hearing. But later, it seemed so distant as to be the memory of a dream, a scrap of imagination.

And after that R. J. disappeared, and curious, Cunningham listened to Jo-Jo's Jazz Shop as first one, then another, substitute announced the titles in their characteristically bored voices. I'm telling you this, they seemed to say, even though you already ought to know the names.

One morning the doorbell rang, and two men in gray suits filled the doorway. "We're looking," one said, "for a friend of yours, Randy Joyner. You seen him?"

Cunningham shook his head.

"You haven't seen him." The agent's voice was bored. "You haven't seen him at all."

"No." What was he supposed to do? What were the rules?

"Not for a while."

"Not for a while."

"He was here, but now he's not."

"Oh? And where did he go?"

"I don't know."

"But he was here. He was here living in this house."

"He was staying here for a little bit, but now he's gone and I don't expect him to come back. He was talking—" a name popped into his head "—he was talking about Kansas, about going to Kansas."

"Kansas." The agents looked at each other.

"Son," the other man said, "let me make sure I have your name correctly."

"He said he'd always wanted to see wheat fields and prairie dogs."

"Just for our records, son."

They left soon after with his name and their disbelief. The second agent had handed him a card with instructions to call if R. J.

should reappear. There were two phone numbers—one for a Portland office, the other for Washington, D.C.

"He's got a little problem," the first agent had said, "and he needs to clear it up."

From an upstairs window, Cunningham watched as the two men sat in their car. They seemed to be making notes. He half-expected them to sit in front of the house all day, and he wondered how he might leave without being seen, but five minutes later he heard the car start, and he watched as it quietly rolled away.

They did not come back, and Cunningham, relieved, chose to believe that they were simply one more strange summer fruit.

By mid-August the campus was deserted. The few summer classes were finished; the sports camps had run their course. Cunningham's job consisted of keeping everything locked, a job he could perform well enough, his early morning deceptions no longer necessary: he was getting plenty of rest. He had also found it curiously satisfying to break out whatever small, incon-spicuous windows he found. So far, no one suspected him as the perpetrator, and in fact, the police lieutenant, a linebacker for the college in the late fifties, had told him that he'd be given a raise starting the first of September.

"You're okay, Cunningham," the lieutenant had said. "Your hair's too long and you look like a girl, but you're okay. When your head's not up your ass to your elbows."

He had chosen not to argue. What evidence could he raise in his own defense?

Mary Klyne's last letter had come as well; she had announced that, yes, it was sudden, but she had decided to stay home and get married to what's-his-name from the Grange. She supposed that at heart she really wasn't so adventuresome after all, but they had had some fun, hadn't they? She was sure that he would be happy, etc., etc., etc. Cunningham wasn't entirely surprised. Sur-prised that she should choose another lover? Absolutely not. That she should choose to marry? The world was a goddamn strange place, wasn't it?

To have once fostered such illusions about his own magnetism—that was the true surprise. Looking in the mirror each morning, he saw himself as though wakened from a coma. Who was this long-haired, unkempt stranger? Why was his face possessed by such a scowl? And why was he looking at himself with such intensity, and what secrets did he expect to uncover? If his father and his father's generation used violence to cover their own inhibitions about sex, was it possible that these strangely weak reactions to Mary Klyne's rejection would open him up to some bizarre expression of violence?

For moments at a time, he saw himself revealed, but then he clothed himself again in that costume of delusion that we all reserve for ourselves—that which allows us to be strong and beautiful, fair and generous, touched by light, approved by men, and beheld by the eyes of God. He now found the tailoring, however, more than a trifle ragged.

And then, just as Cunningham began to believe that he might have to face this stranger on something like honest terms and just as he began to believe that R. J. was truly gone for good, he heard his voice again on Jo-Jo's Jazz Shop, and the next morning at seven o'clock the front door opened, then closed. Footsteps moved up the stairs.

R. J. stood in the hall.

"Hey," Cunningham said. "I didn't expect to see you."

"I didn't expect to be seen." R. J.'s mouth twisted. He rubbed his eyes. "I was going to Canada, but some arrangements fell through."

"Listen," Cunningham began, "some guys were looking for you."

R. J. opened the door to his room. He shook his head as if this were old news. "Don't worry about it. It's no big deal."

No big deal? What was this guy thinking about? He had talked to the fucking FBI.

"A misunderstanding," R. J. was saying. "I'll straighten it out."

"From Canada?"

R. J. shrugged. "Don't think about it. It's my worry."

"They wanted to know where you were," Cunningham said.

"And you didn't know anything to tell them."

"I told them Kansas."

R. J.'s mouth twisted again in something like a smile. "Well, Dorothy, did they believe you?"

He remembered the agents' faces. "No," he said. "I don't think so. I don't think they bought a word of it. Even when I was telling the truth."

That night they drove to a house near the peak of Council Crest in the section of low-profile millionaires' homes. R. J. parked behind the detached garage, then opened the side door of the garage with a key on the same ring as his car keys. He turned a light on from a switch near the door. The garage had been converted into a stereo room. Racks of components lined one wall. Other racks, for albums and boxes of tapes, stood nearby. A daybed was the only other item of furniture.

"Who lives here?" Without instruction, Cunningham's voice had automatically lowered to a whisper.

"I used to. My parents still live in the house. They keep the garage like this, hoping I'll come back."

"But you're going to Canada."

"I'm going to Canada."

"When arrangements are made."

"Yes." R. J. stopped, as if listening to another, more familiar sound. "But there's something else."

He led Cunningham outside. In another part of the yard stood a chain-link enclosure, a dog run. R. J. quietly opened the gate, and a quivering, panting form wiggled out from the darkness.

"Come, Sasha, come, girl," R. J. was whispering. He held the dog by its collar, and together they walked in front of Cunningham back to the garage.

Under the overhead light, Cunningham saw what looked like a miniature greyhound. Its short-haired, nearly naked body was squirming in R. J.'s arms, its tongue darting out of its needle-thin muzzle to lick his face. Its finely muscled legs chattered on the floor as neatly as a deer's.

"Have you seen," R. J. said, "a whippet before?"

Cunningham shook his head.

"They are incredibly sensuous animals," R. J. said. He was stroking the dog's head and shoulders, cooing to it as to a baby or a bird. "Look at her eyes. Beautiful eyes."

Cunningham saw brown irises dominated by a dog's black pupil. A dog's eyes.

"Why don't you stay here?" Cunningham asked.

"Because I'm going to Canada," R. J. whispered. "I have to go."

"You went to Nam. You're a hero."

R. J. snorted. "That's Frankie's story. I went to Texas and lasted all of six weeks. I went over the fence at about two o'clock one Sunday morning. My parents think I'm in Mexico."

"Why? Why did you go?"

"Because I didn't want to stay. Isn't that obvious? I woke up in the middle of that night as if I'd slept sixteen hours and would never need to sleep again, and I thought to myself, 'How in the hell did you get here? You don't want to be here.' I left in my underwear, and I stole some laundry from someone's backyard. The stars were out and I could almost touch them. I hadn't felt anything the whole time."

R. J. put the dog on the daybed and pulled a spool of tape from one of the shelves, threading it onto the reel-to-reel. "You'll like this. Miles Davis, John Coltrane, Newport, 1958. 'Bye, Bye, Blackbird.'"

First a piano, then a trumpet, muted, touched its few notes. They suggested a melody familiar yet utterly changed. Cunningham manfully followed the trumpet, but the sax lost him for good. It made no sense. Incomprehensible. He was dead sober. His ear followed a note or two, and then it became lost in a language he had never learned.

I don't understand, he thought, I don't understand a goddamn thing. He shook his head.

"Give me a hug, Cunningham. I've fucked up my life."

R. J.'s arms went around him. Sasha whimpered from the daybed. The saxophone bounced its impossible tones around the room. And Cunningham, as he felt his back stiffen to the other man's touch, knew that the complications of intimacy were only just beginning.

Trailing
Clouds
of Glory

The
Children's
Crusade

Although on principle they believed in public education, Mr. and Mrs. Breeland transferred their daughter to private school during her sixth-grade year. The experiences of their friends' children had cautioned them, and none too soon it seemed. By the time a child entered junior high, the schools were filled with gangs, graffiti raged across the walls like warnings of the apocalypse, and it was not uncommon for the administration to issue edicts barring the wearing of certain colors on certain days.

The dangers of this world are well documented and their threat increasingly clear. Even more troubling, however, to Frederick Breeland's ear was a certain toughness, a coarseness even now overtaking his daughter's remarks. At the breakfast table, she was apt to speak of her friends using names such as Rat and Stinky, and her teacher, the redoubtable Mrs. Farragut, had been immortalized, he knew, as Miz Bloody-gut for a regrettable incident involving a leaky sanitary napkin. He and Amanda had listened to such talk but had disagreed on the severity or necessity of response. Amanda tended to believe that childhood was marked more by cruelty than kindness and that this was merely an inevitable stage of development; having recently joined the all-woman sales force of Trixie Love Properties, she tended to express her views with a certitude he found unsettling and remote. And although such pessimism troubled him, Freddy yielded to the force of his wife's conviction. But then, speaking during another morning hour about a convicted murderer's impending execution, his daughter—his kind, sweet daughter, whose bottom he had once diapered, with whom he had once played Candyland and Trouble—this same daughter had said, "Give the scumsucker the juice." Appalled, he cautioned her loudly and at full throttle, lecturing her about the sanctity and frailty of human life, even that which belonged to scumsuckers. Where, oh where, had the garden of childhood gone? His daughter had nodded her golden head above her cereal, clearly abashed by the extent of her father's displeasure, but it was just as clear, Freddy thought, that this period of moral tractability would not last forever. She would go to St. Martin's-in-the-Fields, the elementary school connected to their church, damn the expense. And Amanda, for once, agreed.

In the months following her transfer, the Breelands noted several changes in their daughter, not all of which they approved. True, she now sat quietly with her hands folded in her lap, her table manners had improved markedly, and her school uniform was crisp and clean. When she responded to their queries, she said, "Yes, sir," and "No, ma'am," as if she believed in their authority as fact. Before meals, she recited a traditional grace—"Bless us O Lord and these thy gifts which we have received through thy bounty in Christ our Lord"—and on her lips the words were not rote phrases but rather an incantation, her compact with an ancient and alien power. At such times, she asked that he and Amanda join hands with her and close their eyes, but despite all good intentions to the contrary, his own never failed to open halfway through, and his peeking would be met by the ironic gaze of his wife, an expression alternately bemused and horrified.

"Look at her," Amanda whispered through clenched teeth. Dinner was over and the dishes had been cleared. It was an evening in April, unseasonably cold. Their daughter had refused what had been prepared for dinner, accepting only the few uncooked vegetables that Amanda could find at the bottom of the refrigerator. And now she stood on the patio, staring into an aquamarine sky. A bitter wind skated across the backyard, kicking up leaves and paper, but their daughter faced into it in the thin white blouse and plaid skirt of her uniform, in what Freddy assumed was further mortification of the flesh. The evening star blinked above the rooftops. "She's turning into a little grubworm, Freddy. A grubby little nun, a Christmas-bucket bell ringer. Her skin will turn pasty, and her hair will go flat. After fasting, what's next? Giving our ill-gotten gains to the poor?"

Freddy sought to console his wife. It was Lent, and the ideals of youth should be encouraged, but Amanda was adamant in her blame, for whose idea had it been, after all?

She had been transferred at midyear during the semester break. And as luck would have it, the first Monday of the new semester was Valentine's Day. He had stood with his daughter in the graveled courtyard of St. Martin's, attempting to quell the second thoughts and misgivings of a parent determining his child's future. The school, a U-shaped adobe building roofed in Spanish tile, presided over three-quarters of the courtyard. The fourth side was dominated by the church itself, a bilious monstrosity that reminded Freddy of the hull of a freighter—capsized and sinking stern first—but the courtyard was lined with fruitless pear trees, and whenever a stray breeze frolicked among the branches, their delicate blooms threatened to bless the ground with snow.

He had resisted the impulse to take his daughter's hand, and he had fought the lump that formed in his throat when he looked at her amidst these harbingers of spring and new life, remembering with fondness his own days in school, when no stronger perfume existed than the combined odors of wet coats and steam heat, modeling clay, fresh notebook paper, pencil shavings, and mucilage. There had been no limitations then; one could be anything. A line of poetry—he could not have said from what or where—came unbidden to his lips, and he mouthed the words silently: "We ourselves flash and yearn." So he thought then, too, reluctantly of the inevitable unhappiness of childhood, even one spent in the best of circumstances: the unintended insult, the ever-shifting alliances—copied from adults—of friendship and rivalry, the feeling of being helpless, unwanted, and unloved. The sense that life moves at a snail's pace, that one can be anything precisely because at present one is nothing, nothing more than a cipher, as pliable as a piece of Play-doh.

He had sent his own daughter off to a new school on Valentine's Day, for godsake. Who had been there to love his daughter, his little girl, when no one would even know her? In her public school classroom she would have been treated to valentines and an understood affection by Rat and Stinky, but at St. Martin's she had to have been no more than an orphan—an object of pity—in the midst of family not yet her own. He remembered that, at the door of the principal's office, he had hesitated and nearly turned away. Her language had been common and her view of the world marked by cynicism and distrust, but what models of his own had he ever tried to impart? He had overreacted, that much was obvious, and he regretted his failure to heed that inner prompting. Only the most heartless autocrat could have exiled his daughter for the sake of his own offended propriety, but now the joke was on him: he had been so worried about his daughter's adjustment that they now worried whether she hadn't adjusted too much and too well. Each week they had seen new signs of troubling devotion.

Amanda stood at the glass door to the patio, her arms crossed, flattening her breasts, and Freddy took a position behind her while their daughter paced the windswept patio, her lips moving soundlessly, her posture and attitude penitential and ridiculous and heartbreaking. To see them this way, the two unequal feminine poles of his life, nearly overcame him. Freddy opened the door.

"Sweetheart," he called, "sweet pea. Come here, please. Your mother and I would like to talk to you."

"Yes, Daddy."

The girl moved like a mother superior, her head and hips gyroscopically level, her hands clasped at her waist.

Freddy cleared his throat: "Sweetheart, Mommy and I are a little worried about your new school, how you're getting on there. I know that changing was not something you wanted to do at first, but we thought it was in your best interest."

He cleared his throat again.

"Father Oldham taught us a new song today," their daughter said, "and I think I know it now."

She sang in her high, clear voice:

> I sing a song of the saints of God
> >   Patient and brave and true,
> > Who toiled and fought and lived and died
> > >   For the Lord they loved and knew.
> > > >   And one was a doctor, and one was a queen,
> > > >   And one was a shepherdess on the green:
> > > > >   They were all of them saints of God—and I mean,
> > > > >   God helping, to be one too.
>
> > They loved their Lord so dear, so dear,
> > >   And his love made them strong;
> > And they followed the right, for Jesus' sake,
> > >   The whole of their good lives long.
> > > >   And one was a soldier, and one was a priest,
> > > >   And one was slain by a fierce wild beast:
> > > > >   And there's not any reason—no, not the least—
> > > > >   Why I shouldn't be one too.
>
> > They lived not only in ages past,
> > >   There are hundreds of thousands still,
> > The world is bright with the joyous saints
> > >   Who love to do Jesus' will.
> > > >   You can meet them in school, or in lanes, or at sea,

In church, or in trains, or in shops, or at tea,
For the saints of God are just folk like me,
And I mean to be one too.

"That's very nice, dear." Amanda's voice was level, although Freddy had seen the muscles on either side of her jaw bunch up like tiny squirrels when their daughter had sung the line about the fierce wild beast. "Very nice, but I'm not sure that so much church is quite . . . healthy."

Freddy rushed in, ignoring the warning signs of Amanda's squirrels. "We're not saying it's bad, you see, just that too much of it can be bad like five pieces of pizza can be awful if you eat it too quickly and then you have to drive for miles and miles on narrow mountain roads. Although one or two pieces is just fine, five pieces is not good at all. You see what I mean?"

"Daddy," she said very seriously, "Father Oldham said that nowadays women can become priests. It used to be that they couldn't, but now we can. He also said that I have a particular aptitude for matters of the spirit. He thinks I have a calling for it. Isn't that wonderful? Did you know that when Jesus used the word 'spirit' it was the same word as 'wind'?"

Her broad cheekbones were shining in the weak light of a purple sunset, and he had not the heart to contradict her, for how can a parent hope to oppose virtue in a child?

But Freddy knew what such sentiment would do to her mother, and Amanda was true to form; she went to their bedroom and locked the door, and no amount of coaxing could induce her to come out and talk. His only recourse was to live the evening without her, pretending as he sometimes did—when Amanda was at a city planning meeting or showing property to clients—that they were poor and he a single parent whose innocent child trusted him with her future. He helped his daughter with her homework, rejoicing in the orderliness of fractions and the elegance of their multiplication and division. At nine o'clock, his daughter readied herself for bed, and he tucked her in, marveling at the speed and violence of the change now overtaking her: that he kissed her not under the gaze of Michael Jackson or Tom Cruise but beneath Jesus sweating blood in Gethsemene and Mother Teresa, who blessed the heads of dying children. Then, after dousing all the lights of the house but one, he drank beer and read an endless novel by Michener until he fell asleep in his chair about midnight. He immediately began to dream of his wife from the first of their marriage when they had truly been poor and her chief form of activity in times of trouble and confusion had been to strip naked and run the vacuum over the floors of their tiny second-floor apartment. She was vacuuming now in his mind, and he waited for that moment when she would lift the vacuum from the floor onto the cushions of the sofa. Her skin would be flushed with the exertion and he would thrill to the combination of her strength and her indifference to her own nakedness.

The dreams of early sleep do not last, overshadowed as they are by the deeper slumbers that follow and then by early morning's chaos of symbol and nonsense. They do not last unless one's sleep is interrupted by a phone call or the sound of dogs barking, cats trysting, or an angry voice traveling along the corridors of night air, and even then, such dreams may leave no memory except the faint fear of loss or trouble. But when Amanda woke Freddy at two, the impression of her vacuuming was still so distinct that he rose from his chair intending to grab her roughly about the waist, squeeze her good breasts, and breathe into her ear.

"Don't be stupid," she said. "We have a problem."

"A problem," he said. He was still advancing on her, confused by the presence of her bathrobe and the absence of her vacuum.

"Stop it now." She flipped on the lights. "I did not endure nine months of pregnancy, twelve hours of labor, and a caesarean only to give the world some low Baptist missionary who cannot afford decent shoes."

"But, Amanda," he said, aware of some disjunction, "we're Episcopalians."

"Precisely," she said, "precisely my point."

She was a lovely woman still—broad shouldered and broad hipped—whose energy and temper had not abated through the years. She had borne a child, and she was unyielding in her opinion of what was and was not appropriate for that child.

"Who is this Father Oldham? And what sort of line is he feeding her?"

"He's the chaplain, I believe, and I'm sure she just misunderstood something."

"You're sure of that?"

Can one be sure of anything? He touched her shoulders, hoping to draw her in. But not for nothing had she played basketball in her youth; she avoided him with the ease of a point guard eluding the dangers of a half-court trap.

"Don't kid yourself," she said, already free. "You'll see this Father Oldham tomorrow. I'll make the appointment myself."

Amanda had offered him entry to their bedroom, but her half-hearted gesture toward the door and some odor upon the night air let him know that the invitation was less than sincere. He slept the rest of that night on the sofa, and he slept badly. His kidneys felt swollen from beer, the button on the middle cushion seemed the size of a softball, and a draft from a poorly glazed window had targeted his feet. He was slow to shower and slower to dress. Amanda smoked three cigarettes while he and his daughter ate breakfast, and the bitter smell became confused with the taste of his bacon.

On the way to his office, he drove his daughter to school. From the car, he watched as she crossed the street, went through the gate, and disappeared from his view. She had walked past several groups of children. She had not been spoken to, and she had acknowledged no one. Her apparent friendlessness caught at him, and tears threatened to fill his eyes. He drove around the block once, hoping he might see her in some more optimistic light, but evidently the bell had rung sometime before he turned the last corner, for the playground was empty.

At work, he pushed papers from one corner of his desk to another, waiting for Amanda's call. Just before lunch, his phone rang, and Amanda gave him the news. "Oldham will see you at three." Her voice was raw as though from crying. "He doesn't have an office, Freddy. He lives at the parsonage, but he's not even officially on the staff."

She had talked to Dr. Wainwright, the school's principal. Yes, the school often asked Oldham to talk to those children who had found it difficult to adjust. And every day before the final bell, he conducted singing and devotions for a different class. No, Father Oldham was merely a volunteer; technically he was retired, but he had never learned to wear a shirt with a civilian collar, so the saying went. He had been an Anglican missionary in the Philippines for forty-three years. He had practically been elevated to sainthood on Mindanao for his devotion to children, his savvy for farming, and his staunch anti-Marcos politics, and he would have stayed on for death but for an elderly daughter who forcibly persuaded him to return.

"Dr. Wainwright was very forthcoming," Amanda said, "I will say that for her. And she didn't think I was strange to be concerned. She said Father Oldham could be very compelling, but that he wasn't any sort of problem. I don't believe it for a second though. She has to say that for liability's sake."

A wave of static passed between them, and then the unintelligible sound of another conversation mixed with the recorded music that Freddy associated with mall department stores.

Amanda's voice emerged from the surface of such aimless noise. "I still want you to talk to him. And if you don't, I will."

"I'll talk with him."

"You tell him that our daughter is not a missionary project. You tell him that we've raised her to lead a normal American life without so much as a shred of guilt. I'll hire a lawyer—I guarantee it—if he even tries to show her a picture of a mud hut."

"I'll tell him."

"You better."

A picture of Amanda and his daughter occupied one corner of his desk. The photograph had been taken a day after his daughter's birth, and although Amanda was smiling widely for the camera, Freddy was inevitably startled by the impassive forbearance of the baby's face. There had been something otherworldly and ancient about her from the start. So maybe her current piety was not the anomaly it had first appeared.

"I'll tell him," he said again. He could imagine Amanda sitting at her shared desk, the fuchsia realtor's blazer hanging from the back of her chair, while she bit her nails throughout the conversation. "I'll tell him that you'll suck his blood until the only thing left is a pile of sand."

"Thank you," she sniffled.

He hung up the phone feeling as though he'd taken a contract to kill someone. He looked at his watch. The day seemed spent, wasted by anxiety. He rose from his desk and told his secretary that he had become ill, that he was going home to lie down with the phone unplugged.

He took his coat from its hook and went to lunch, and in the shop next door to the diner, he played with the newest computers and their demonstration software. Then he went to the barber shop near St. Martin's, where a new girl, one he'd never seen before, cut his hair and giggled. Could he believe this weather? No, he could not. The day was indeed fair and breezy after weeks of cloud and wind and rain. The girl stopped for a moment, thinking, still with a clump of his hair in one of her hands.

"Do you think," she asked, twirling her scissors around her index finger, "do you think that weathermen get fired if they're wrong too many times? I sometimes wonder about that, whether weathermen have a sort of quota, and if they're wrong three times a season, they're history. Like I sort of see a trap door in front of the map, and if they say clear and sunny and it turns out windy and cold, then this door opens up and *zap!* they're outta here. Do you ever think about that? About weathermen? I've been thinking about what weathermen do ever since the sun came out."

She could not have been more than a year out of high school. Short hair dyed the color of plums. A bulky, loose-weave sweater, the long, gauzy print skirt, and the bangles of a child whose most fervent desire was to visit Woodstock and whose deepest regret was that time is not, in fact, reversible. She was an exotic flower, the child, he supposed, of parents who fought and whose boyfriend occasionally beat her—she moved and spoke as though she were bruised underneath the skin—but she was trying to speak to him at some level he could understand. And although the attempt seemed silly and charged with the awkwardness of childhood, it was nonetheless generous and—from such a delicious little armful—flattering.

He watched her movements behind his head while he thought glumly of his next appointment. What could he possibly hope to accomplish? Convince an ex-missionary that preaching to children at a church school was inappropriate, a violation of decorum? How much better it would be to pay for a shampoo now that his hair was already trimmed, a manicure that his nails did not need. So what if her talk of weathermen was silly and inane. For her, wind was wind. The fate of a mediocre weatherman could be decided by the touch of a button, the movement of a lever. Her life—no matter the shape of its actual contours—would be no mere symbol for some other truth. His daughter, however, had taken up residence in a world fraught with meaning behind meaning—how frightening to imagine something of the trouble she was sure to encounter.

"... good hair," the girl was saying. "Thinning, but holding its own, you know what I mean?"

When she was finished, she brushed his shoulders and ears and forehead. She touched the back of his neck with her free hand, a gesture that seemed to confer upon him a blessing of the physical, no matter how superficial, no matter how grave the flaws. He paid the girl and overtipped her, grateful, before stepping out onto the sidewalk and into the brisk breezes of spring.

Through the open window of his car, he heard the high, sweet sound of children singing. *Savior, like a shepherd lead us, much we need thy* . . . The door to the parsonage was open, welcoming this laggard spring, and he could see that the front room must be filled with children. Two forty-five. His head fell back against the headrest and his eyes closed. *Jesus loves the little children, all the children of the* . . .

The parsonage was a puddle of adobe surrounded by scree at the farthest, most desolate edge of the blacktopped parking lot. The screens sagged and the roofing tiles were cracked and sliding toward ruin. Usually vacant, the house was now used by the diocese to house newly retired ministers and missionaries before they moved on. The condition of the building was often enough to encourage new horizons. What incongruity was there between the appearance of this pile and the lovely, innocent sounds now drifting from within?

He waited until there was silence following the hymn. He heard a murmur not unlike prayer, and then children slowly began to file out, his daughter among them. Her golden head was bowed in thought, her hands clasped at her waist. She walked with a girl who could have been her reciprocal—where his daughter was tall and thin and blond, this other was short and stocky and brunette. He called to her, but his throat seemed to constrict and close, his voice a mere whisper; her connection with this other girl while she was yet unaware of his own presence had undone him more than her solitude of the morning. She would walk to Mrs. Petcock's, where the genial old woman would feed the after-school children milk and cookies, and his daughter would watch television among the nodding heads of other abandoned schoolmates until Amanda picked her up at five. The other girl looped her arm through his daughter's and pressed her head against his daughter's shoulder as they walked across the parking lot and disappeared behind the sinking freighter of the church. He twisted in his seat to follow their progress.

"You must be Breeland."

The voice was high and nasal—as though the speaker had endured the trials of a cleft palate in his youth—but not unpleasant. Freddy turned again in his seat. Father Oldham stood next to the car window.

"Your daughter is a remarkable child."

"Her mother and I think so."

"You think so because she's yours." Oldham opened Freddy's door. "I believe she's remarkable because she's alive."

He had to be in his seventies, but the retired priest looked twenty years younger. This impression of youth was in part due to his attire, or so Freddy believed; Oldham was wearing a pink polo shirt, blue jeans, and a pair of running shoes. His skin was brown because he had gone out into the world to do the manly work of the Lord, and although he was nearly bald, a few strands of dark hair crossed the glossy dome of his scalp with precision and order. He was short, no more than five feet two, but unlike grim Napoleon, Oldham seemed happy to share a world filled with taller men, and as he waited for Freddy to disengage himself from his seat belt, he bounced on the toes of his running shoes. As Freddy had suspected, his face held the scars of childhood surgeries, clumsy by current standards; his upper lip seemed foreshortened and jaggedly put together and his nose poorly molded clay.

Is there any greater challenge to an individual's perception than marriage? From Amanda's description he had expected Ichabod Crane and a voice of doom, but instead he was looking at this honking dervish dressed in boys' sizes.

He followed Oldham up the steps and into the front room. "You'll have to excuse the condition of this place," Oldham said. "It's temporary, and I can tell you I've never lived in such a mess, not even my years overseas."

The front room was bare of furniture except for a short wood stool on which the priest must have sat during the recently concluded devotional. Gum and candy wrappers littered the floor, testimony of the room's recent occupants.

"I give them the candy," Oldham explained, "and I tell them to throw the paper on the floor. Why not? They've been listening to rules all day long as it is. And if the diocese really cared one way or the other, they could have found—" The priest stopped abruptly. "Come on. I'll make coffee."

"About my daughter," Freddy said, following him into a kitchen more cheerful, cleaner certainly, than the front room.

"Yes, you have a daughter, of course, and you've come here to accuse me of having a low forehead, haven't you? Well, what do you think? Am I a danger?"

The older man was inviting his inspection. "I think," Freddy said, "that you're just about all forehead."

Oldham clapped his hands, startling Freddy. "There you have it. Have a seat, Mr. Breeland." He indicated the Formica-and-chrome dinette set against the back wall of the kitchen. A small stained-glass cross had been affixed to the window above the sink with a suction cup. Red-stained light bounced about the room while Oldham stood at the stove, putting water on to boil.

"'Out of the mouth of babes and sucklings,' Mr. Breeland. Children. Jesus loves the little children. But what is man or woman that God should be mindful of her when she's still a little shit, right?"

How could he possibly respond? "All I know," he said, stammering to bring this conversation back on track, "is that my wife and I have been concerned for some time now about her behavior. And some things she's been saying."

"Her behavior. What's wrong with her behavior?"

"Actually nothing. Honestly, I'd have to say it's much better. Her language, too. But we're worried because she seems so *detached* from everything."

"Maybe you should be more worried about attachment." He brought to the table two white crockery mugs of instant coffee. "Why shouldn't she be detached? Attachment is precisely where we lose our souls. 'He that findeth his life shall lose it,' Mr. Breeland. The great paradox of the faith: finding is losing. And attachment to the world is, not surprisingly, detachment from God. I should think you might worry more profitably about greed or promiscuity or intemperance."

The coffee was hot and bitter and tasted strongly of soap, but Freddy drank it down from embarrassment and courtesy. "We hope she'll recognize excess in all its forms."

"You hope."

"Of course. But we'd also like for her to have a normal childhood. We have no interest in her becoming a junior Joan of Arc."

The priest's brown face turned mahogany. "You want her to play tennis and dream of hollow-eyed actors and gossip with girlfriends on the phone and worry about the color of her socks."

"Actually, yes."

"Too bad, too bad," Oldham cried. "Too, too bad." Under the duress of his emotion, his voice sounded like the bleating of a sheep under the shears: "Too bah, too bah, too, too, bah."

"We want only for her to be happy, not haunted."

"Happy in surfaces, you mean."

"I'm not sure that some depths are meant to be plumbed."

Oldham jumped from his chair and retrieved a manilla envelope from another room. He opened the clasp, then spilled out hundreds of black-and-white photos, many old and yellowing with pinking-shear edges, onto the table. They were pictures of children, in groups and alone, posed formally in church attire or nearly naked at play.

"Forty-three years of children, all cripples and orphans. I can no longer tell you their names, but I know their hearts. They have all understood the hidden form of God—far better than their parents, far better than my so very brilliant colleagues. The simplest child at play knows the comfort of the invisible.

"I have been called many things, Mr. Breeland: gnostic, Manichaean, and heretic. Simpleton, dimwit, and fool. But look at me. Harelip. Horror. Who could possibly see through my appearance and into my heart but a child? My wife worshiped in the same church as I did for a year before she could bring herself to talk to me. Matter is nothing when one worships in spirit and in truth, and children must train their eyes for the unseen before adults persuade them differently. 'I have known you,' God said to me, 'ever since I misformed you in thy mother's womb—that through your disfiguration you might lead others to an appreciation of the spirit and revulsion of the flesh.' If I believed otherwise, how could I love a potter who makes such sloppy ware?"

"Father Oldham, please."

He was pacing, his face had begun to shine with sweat, and his scars had turned to ivory. How to make him stop?

"The children are the usable ones. Adults are generally lost causes. The child is father to the man, and the girl is mother to the woman of God. The spiritual is all around us, can't you see? We, Mr. Breeland, *we* are the shadows. There are angels so close to you that the feathers of their wings could make you sneeze if you had any sense. Your daughter still hears the chords of immortality, and if you deny her those frequencies, you will deny her true beauty, true love, for the sake of counterfeits and illusions."

Oldham talked on and on, his voice threatening to lose the final consonant of every word. While he spoke, his hands referred to this or that picture, pointing out virtues impossible to see with the eye. At first, Freddy tried to follow the priest's monologue, wondering if it were possible that through his daughter he might have stumbled onto something far greater than the sinking freighter of churchly ritual, but soon afterward he found himself considering the only other alternative: Oldham was crazy, deranged, over the line.

Wasn't he?

Later, as he pulled away from the parsonage, Freddy was reasonably certain. Oldham had lived too long in a world of clearly defined opposites; his physical misfortune had unhinged his thinking, and he had invented a shadow play to replace a reality he had found too cruel. What sense could he possibly make of the breeze on a spring day? A lover's touch or the accolades of friends? In a world consigned to flames, these were meaningless, Freddy understood, mere tokens, distractions from that which is true and eternal. Still, was the material world so opposed to the spiritual that, as Oldham had claimed, to derive pleasure from one was to be divorced entirely from the other?

He drove home, fearing a loss of contact with the road and remembering with chagrin his one brush with such piety—an extended and embarrassing episode when he was fifteen, one that involved a girlfriend, the girlfriend's mother, and more than one pentecostal prayer meeting. The girl had been forbidden by her mother, who watched her like a hawk, to date him. But she could see him at her church. Strange that, although his infatuation with her had once bordered on the obsessive, he now could remember so little! He could remember neither the girl's name nor what she looked like. He could remember only the sight of the church itself, more like an auditorium than a sanctuary, an expanse of heavy red carpets, theater seats, and electrical wires for the sound system and the amplifiers. He could remember too how happy he had been to hold her hand between their balcony seats, hidden that her mother might not see, and the sly curve that came to her lips whenever he gave that hand a squeeze. He attended for months. He went forward at altar calls, gave his testimony when asked, and shouted amen during the pastor's sermon. He spoke in tongues at prayer meetings, using—when imagination failed him—the words from "Wooley Booley," "Louie, Louie," and "Obladih, Obladah" as a last resort. Following one such meeting, the girl had pulled him along through the darkened hallways of the education wing, where they kissed and pulled at each other's clothes for fifteen minutes or more, ending only when her mother discovered them and pulled them apart. Then, shouting the word *animal* over and over again, she slapped her daughter until the girl's mouth bled. He could not tell now which had been the more despicable act, her mother's abuse or his own pretended zeal. And if his own daughter were truly caught up by images of the divine and the transcendent, who was he, that he should act as judge?

And yet, with every turn he took, he saw the signs of advancing spring. Bare branches had given way to blossoms and leaves. Pansies dotted every yard. The odor of wood smoke had been transformed into the perfumes of warm earth and mown grass and the bouquet of opening flowers. Children were at play on every street, and their cries reverberated up and down each block. It was not possible, he thought, that these experiences could not be counted as good.

He drove in confusion; he came home to chaos.

He was not so boorish to believe that, after working all day, Amanda should have candles burning and the dinner table laden—he did not demand a beer for his hand and a footstool for his feet—but neither did he expect to find a fuchsia blazer in a heap on the couch and his daughter's plaid skirt, rust-stained and crumpled, on the hallway floor. He was about to yell something irritable and insensitive but then heard the sound of his daughter's moans echoing from within her bathroom.

"It hurts, oh shit, it hurts. Goddamn, it hurts, oh shit." Her voice was raspy and adult in register, a metronome of pain all too earthly in its nature, and he would have rushed in but for the sound of his wife. "There, there," Amanda crooned. "It's a bitch, I know, a terrible bitch."

He backed away from the door and picked up his daughter's skirt and his wife's jacket. The stain had already stiffened the stiff cloth and was roughly the size and shape of home plate. He studied the skirt, feeling as though the message it had to convey were somehow eluding him. His daughter, it seemed, was too adept at traveling from world to world, each one more foreign, more ancient, more potent than the next.

"Hang my jacket up, please."

He had not heard her leave the bathroom. Amanda stood in front of him, eyeball to eyeball, a posture she had adopted more and more since going back to work—standing too close and generaling the person in front of her. She wrinkled her nose in something like disgust and satisfaction. "You can throw the skirt away."

"It's too early for this."

"Not for the women in my family. I was ten. We take our fertility seriously."

"Is she—?"

"She's okay, considering she sat in a puddle of her own goo for most the afternoon. Mrs. Petcock will have a reminder on her den floor for quite some time to come, I'm afraid."

"Ah."

He told her then about his meeting with the priest, how he had looked and lectured, and how at the end of their talk, Oldham had said that their daughter would rise above the ashes of their indifferent lives, but Amanda seemed not to hear. The priest didn't matter now. Even when he said that his last sight of Oldham had been of the old man pawing through his pictures of damaged children, many of whom he had undoubtedly returned to earth.

"She'll need another uniform skirt, I suppose," Amanda mused. She did not look displeased. "I don't have a clue about dinner. She'll be hungry in a bit, our little saint. You can order us pizza while I go tend to her."

The
Summers
of My Sex

━━━━━━━━━━

I. IN MY FATHER'S POOL

California is a state largely devoid of water, and so its citizens are obsessed with the subject. It is the presence of water that turned the desert into the most fertile land on the face of the planet. Water had reclaimed paradise from the ravages of the sun; any threats to paradise are not taken lightly, and you will find that the rare, native Californian is no more vociferous than the hordes of resettled easterners. They understand the issue, and they quickly take it for their own.

My parents, both Ohioans, were no exceptions. My mother, a staunch, conservative Republican, was horrified when Goldwater threatened to block California's access to Arizona's portion of the Colorado River. After getting clobbered in 1964, the old fascist probably figured he had no one left to offend. But offend my mother he did, and she never forgave him.

My father's obsession took a different form. Once a swimmer in college, he built swimming pools in the backyards of each of the houses that my mother and he owned. Those first pools, built before I was born, were nothing out of the ordinary, their only distinctions being size and rectangular shape. They were meant for laps, for diving, for the exercise of the water. They were not pools for splashing in or for landscape decor or parties sporting a Polynesian tiki torch theme. But in their last house, he built no ordinary pool. An engineer with little patience for the purely decorative, he later attributed that last pool to my birth; conception and my mother's delivery had awakened a sense of creativity that he didn't completely understand.

He started with the same basic rectangle—ten feet deep at one end, three feet at the other, fifty feet long, twenty feet wide. The pool had been dug by backhoe, smoothed, then surfaced in concrete. The concrete was painted white, blue tile lined the top of the concrete, and a beige coping block formed the lip above the tile. Two diving boards, one meter and three meters in height, rose above the edge at the deep end.

The shallows were something else again. Beginning near the patio, my father built a narrow channel that encircled the main pool, looping behind the diving boards, then emptying back into the shallow end. A waterfall began the flow, the water falling ten feet at a high pressure, tumbling over rocks and logs. The channel descended another five feet, and the current was remarkably swift. A pump, constructed from my father's design, piped the water back to the falls. In between the channel and the main pool, a series of small hills were landscaped, a horseshoe of humps and hillocks, each covered in a variety of tropical foliage. There were bottlebrush, bird of paradise, and camellia bushes. Azaleas and palm trees and guava. River grass lined the channel. A system of clicking sprinklers kept the vegetation watered. When the sprinklers were on, shooting wide arcs of spray, the hills seemed a rain forest—wet, humid, warm.

Just after my first birthday, my father outfitted me with an orange life jacket, one so overlarge and overbalanced underneath the arms that there was not even the possibility of my face getting wet. He would set me down at the top end of the channel, just below the falls, and let the current take me, bobbing like an orange cork, a cocoon of kapok and canvas. I could not get enough of it. And summer afternoons were spent with my mother or father starting me at one end and lifting me out at the other. I had gone from the womb back to the amphibian without much intervening time spent on solid, unvarying ground. Later, as I became better able to swim and walk, the life vests became smaller, and my parents' transit duties declined. But the channel remained the place of water and movement for me, the main pool merely where life ended, signaling the time to get out and start again.

One day during my fifth summer, I was paddling upstream amid the river grass while my mother, wearing sunglasses and reading Arthur Hailey, watched from a lounge chair. She wore a skirted swimsuit, but she also wore a sun hat; her nose had been painted white and a towel covered her legs. I suppose you might say that she had a love-hate relationship with the sun. She burned easily and feared diseases of the skin, but her feet occasionally appeared from beneath the towel to trail in the pool's chlorinated water, as if for reassurance of its continuing presence.

The doorbell had just rung, and my father had gone to see who the visitors might be. Now he came back outside. As he opened the sliding glass door, I heard him say—uneasily—"If that's what you want, sure. I guess so."

He too was wearing a swimsuit, a pair of knit trunks with a small ornamental buckle in the front. He was compactly built, smoothly muscled in the way of swimmers. Because the season was new, his skin was white, with the exception of his left arm, which—when he drove to and from work—dangled out the window of the car.

He was followed outside by another man, and a woman followed him. The man was older than my father. His hair was wavy, combed straight back, but graying at the temples and in streaks at the top of his head. He wore a terry-cloth shirt-jacket, one that did not hide the rounded paunch pushing at the buttons or the gray chest hairs curling over the top button of the placket. He was smoking a cigar and the ashes scattered across the patio.

My father was saying, "It takes a while for most people."

"I'm a natural," the man said. He held the cigar between his lips and the lighted end brightened to red.

The woman was much younger than the man. She was also much younger than my mother, and when my mother saw the two visitors, she scrambled from the lounge chair, tossing away the towel and the sun hat. One hand fluttered near her nose but refrained from scraping away the zinc oxide.

"Laura," my father said, "this is Bud Johnson, from the office in Washington. And this is . . ."

"Eileen," the young woman murmured, "from an office in Pacoima."

"Pacoima," my father said.

My mother shook hands with the man while looking at the woman. Her hair had been cut very short, and my mother thought that the man named Bud might recently have spanked her.

"Mel here tells me," the man said, "that he can teach me how to dive."

"I can start," my father said.

"The basics—swan dive, jackknife, half gainer."

"I'm sure he can," my mother said with a worried expression around her eyes and the white nose.

"But in an hour," my father said, "I'm not sure how much . . ."

"Lovely!" Eileen said. She had edged away from the group and was now dipping the toes of one foot into the water of the channel. "It's moving!"

"There's a pump," my father said.

"How cute!" Eileen said, seeing me in my orange vest, dog-paddling against the current, remaining in virtually the same position despite my effort.

"My son," my father said.

"Our son," my mother said.

"Let's hit the boards," the man said. "Whaddya say?"

"Sure," my father said, "okay. You want to get used to the water first?"

The man named Bud ground out his cigar beside a blooming

camellia bush and stripped off the shirt-jacket. His belly was even rounder than expected, and my father wondered how he could ever hope to do a somersault in the air.

"Can I come in?" Eileen asked me.

"Sure," I said. When I turned to answer her, I stopped paddling, and the current swept me backward down to the main pool. I climbed out, arms and legs and knees on the coping. "You have to do it like this." I grabbed her hand and pulled her to the base of the falls, then jumped in rear end first, arms and legs in the air, letting myself go the full circuit of the channel.

"I'm not sure," she said when I had climbed out again from the main pool. "I'm not sure whether I can do it like that. I think I'm too big."

"Try," I said.

"Well . . ."

"She'll have to swim a little, I think," my mother said. "Big people have to swim."

My father was telling Bud that one of the most important parts of a good dive is a good approach to the end of the board. Most people don't get good height, and then they look like bricks when they're in the air, he said.

"One, two, three, up with the arms and legs, down, then push for as much height as you can get," my father said, demonstrating on the lower board.

The man named Bud squinted at my father as he took his steps and jumped. "That tall one," he said. "Time I leave here, that's where I'm going off."

"It's more dangerous than you might think," my father said.

"Not to worry," Bud said.

Eileen was unbuttoning her blouse and jeans.

"We have some swimsuits," my mother said.

"That's okay," Eileen said, "I'm always prepared."

In the late fifties, two-piece bathing suits were rare, bikinis unheard of. So when Eileen stepped out of her jeans and threw her blouse off, and when she was not wearing anything but what looked like a set of polka-dot underwear, my mother gave a little gasp, thinking, *This bitch. This twitching piece of, of, of* . . . her mind momentarily blank, at a loss for the proper concept, which was, of course, sex. I didn't think anything of it at the time. But now I know that Eileen was one of those rare bodies, totally without self-consciousness. It seems surprising to me now—in this age, tolerant of nearly every form of undress and nudity—that most women while on public display still walk as if every pair of eyes were riveted on each erotic and private zone. They walk as if afraid that they are about to lose their drawers. They square their shoulders so straps won't slide. Eileen had none of that. She did not hook her thumbs underneath the elastic of her bottoms, making sure that her bum was covered; she did not make minute adjustments to her halter. She dove head first into the channel, a tricky little maneuver since it was only two and a half feet deep, a skimming little dive that carried her halfway around the circuit. She did not take her first breath until she reached the shallow end, water beading on her skin, a mythical creature in the flesh. My father caught her act at the apex of his latest demonstration jump, and he wondered if he would ever come down, if he would live to meet the water. My mother's hands twitched at the ruffle of her skirted swimsuit. Bud reached for his shirt-jacket and the cellophane of another cigar. I paddled against the current.

My father came up from the main pool.

"Where did you find her?" he whispered to Bud.

"Friend of a friend." He winked. "You gotta have friends in a strange town, you know."

"Wow!" Eileen sat on the coping of the shallow end. "That's great!" She waved to my father, who grinned and frantically waved back. "I've been on slides before but this is great."

"Thanks," my father said. He smiled as though accepting an award.

My mother offered Eileen a rubber bathing cap, a blue one with rubberized yellow flowers on the side. "You probably ought to wear this," she said. "Mel gets upset when long hair clogs up the filter."

She smiled, pulled at the close-cropped hair, now wet and lying flat against her skull. "It's not so long," she said.

My mother juggled the cap in her hands for a moment, then threw it into the lounge chair behind her.

"Now you go," Eileen said to me.

I jumped and yelled, sending the water up in a concussive spray, the water clear and flashing bright in the California sun. Eileen laughed and clapped, and my mother clapped along with her.

"My turn," Bud said. "What you want me to do?"

"Just get a feel for the board," my father said. "Take a few jumps, that sort of thing."

"What kind of dive?"

"Just dive. Don't worry about style, yet."

"I'll do a swan," Bud said. "They're the easy ones."

"They look easy," my father said.

"No sweat."

Bud took his three steps and jumped, coming down as the board was coming up—he did not hit it well at all—his height not much above that of the board itself, his posture in the air sloppy, and when he entered the water, his legs spread apart and his knees bent as if he were squatting upside down; but he seemed pleased with himself.

"Whaddya think, huh?" he spluttered. He thrashed his way to the ladder. "How about that?"

"Fine," my father said, "but you need to work a little on that approach."

"Eileen," Bud yelled, "you see that, huh?"

"I'm sorry," she said, "I was watching the kid."

I was coming up in the shallows.

"Well, you watch me the next time. You came to watch me dive, right?"

"Right, Bud."

My mother lifted me out of the pool with a towel. "Time for a little nap, don't you think?" she said.

"No."

"Yes."

"Longer."

"You have ten minutes."

My father was back up on the board, and Bud was pestering him to the higher one. "C'mon, let's see your stuff."

Reluctantly, my father climbed down from the one-meter and ascended the ladder of the three-meter. He looked very alone. From that height he could see over the hedge of pyracantha shrubs into our neighbors' backyard and their kidney-shaped pool. Plastic lily pads floated near the skimmers. My father measured the distance to the end of the board, secure in the knowledge of his superior layout and design.

"Fuck the approach," Bud said, "I wanna see something with some balls on it."

My father took his steps. His jump was a high one, and he got good height from the spring of the board and his legs. He went up, and at the top of his time in the air, he grabbed his ankles in the pike position and went around once, twice, and then half again, opening out, hands forward, reaching for the water. When he hit the surface, he raised hardly a splash, and he knifed down to the drain at the bottom.

"Oh, wonderful," Eileen said, clapping her hands.

"Your feet came over, just a little bit," my mother said. "Don't you think?"

"No," my father said, "I think I hit it just about right."

"I could do that," Bud said.

My father kicked one leg over the coping blocks. "It's not as easy as it looks."

"What else can you do?" Eileen called.

"There's only a couple more," my mother said, "but that was his best."

"He's got lots of dives," I said.

"Five minutes," my mother said.

"Do another one," Eileen said.

This time, my father stood on the end of the board with his back to us. His toes were his only connection with the board itself, his arms forward, perpendicular to his shoulders for balance. Water dripped from his suit with the ornamental buckle to the end of the board and fell in the sunlight. When he was set, my father brought his arms down to his sides, then scissored them up, then down again, to get the board going. He went up, and throwing his head back, he did the first somersault tucked in a tiny ball; then he opened out and did the second one in a layout, hitting the water feet first, hands pressed tightly against the sides of his thighs.

Eileen was clapping again, and my father was smiling, although he was embarrassed because he was a modest man.

"Well, now we know that you can do the same thing backwards that you do forwards," Bud said.

"That was terrific," Eileen said.

"Real nice, honey," my mother said.

Bud was climbing the three-meter ladder.

"Thanks," my father said.

"You watch this," Bud said.

"Careful, Bud," Eileen said.

Seen from such a height, his stomach was a marvel. When he took his erratic steps, it jiggled and swayed, and when he went up, it went up with him, but independently. He tried to do a one-and-a-half pike, I think, but he couldn't reach to grab his ankles, and he never got all the way around. My father said that he pulled his head out of it, and where the head goes, the rest of the body follows, no matter how big the stomach. Bud fell ten feet in what my father called the cat position, arms and legs clawing the air. When he hit, he hit with the sound of clapping, if the hands responsible for the applause are cupped, the air rushing out, the sound sharp and hollow at the same time. He hit face and belly first, and water sprayed out in all directions. Waves broke against the blue tile.

My father jumped into the pool. Bud was spluttering, trying to get his wind, and Eileen was saying, "Oh. Oh. Oh, my."

I was laughing, and my mother was too, but she covered her mouth with both hands.

"Goddamn," Bud gasped, "goddamn it to hell. I almost had it made."

"Shit," my father said, "you're lucky you didn't rupture an organ."

"You could have hurt yourself," Eileen said.

"Shut up," Bud said, "shut your ass, Eileen."

My mother grabbed my hand and pulled me away from the pool, saying that it was surely time for my nap now, no matter the amount of elapsed time. I struggled, but I didn't resist. She carried me into the house through the sliding glass door, into the cool of my bedroom shaded from the sun. She brought me a glass of water to drink; then she told me a story about a cow and the moon, and how she got hung up one Saturday night. I went to sleep, and then my father was waking me. He let water drip from his hair onto my eyelids.

I didn't know that the man named Bud had told Eileen that she was nothing better than a two-bit floozy from a cheap bawdy house in Pacoima, or that he'd also told my father that he wasn't worth a tinker's dam as an engineer. Eileen said nothing, pulling her blouse and jeans over her wet swimsuit, so that as she sat, the outlines of the bikini became visible through her clothes. My father said he might not be much of an engineer in Bud's eyes, but then Bud wasn't much of a diver in his. My mother made drinks, strong ones, and when Eileen and Bud departed, it was peacefully, if not amicably. There was no way I could have known that a week later my father would lose his job, only to be snapped up by another firm at double the salary (for those were the good days of engineering, when engineers were at a premium, seemingly destined to be society's next philosopher-kings). Neither could I have known that twelve years later the San Fernando earthquake would rattle and shake the house, crack the pool, and ruin the pump of my father's design. The pump was never repaired, and the falls dried, a hill of cement, rocks, and railroad ties. By that time, my father had given up swimming and diving—he had developed his own middle-aged belly. And after I moved away, my father's pool became just another swimming pool on the backside of a Californian's house.

I didn't know any of that then, when I woke to the dripping water from my father's hair. He was lifting me out of bed, then down to the pool. Bud and Eileen were gone, and the sun angled into our eyes from the west. He strapped me into my jacket, and together we played our game—my father holding my feet in the cradle of his hands, then catapulting me out of the water and over his shoulder so that I did my own kind of dive, at his mercy, in his control, over and over again, my mother sitting on the coping blocks, her legs in the water, watching, the water flying into my face, my eyes and mouth and nose full of the chlorine and the afternoon sun, over and over again.

II. BLUEBEARD, BLACKBEARD, LIGHT, AND *LITTLE WOMEN*

Every other year my parents and I traveled by train to Ohio. My mother's family was there, three women living in a cavernous old house on the edge of downtown Cincinnati, one German house among hundreds of other German houses. When I was a child, I believed in their lives only on the occasion of our visits. There was my grandmother, whose husband had died of an appendectomy before my mother had finished grade school; my aunt, married and divorced in the space of one year, living again with her mother; and my cousin Maddy, six years older than myself, the product of the terminated marriage.

Cincinnati meant women without the company of men, and when my father entered their door, he shifted the barren feminine scale into temporary balance. He mowed lawns, installed electrical fixtures, repaired appliances. He collected the check for everyone's dinner in a restaurant. He opened doors and stepped aside, waiting for every other person to enter before he did so himself. On vacation in Cincinnati, I heard the continual chorus: "Thank you, Mel"; "That's so nice of you, dear." And as the only other male member of the party, I basked in his masculine glow.

When I was four years old, we had taken the El Capitan from Pasadena to Chicago, a route distinct only for the absence of scenery. The train rolled through Los Angeles and the curtain of smog, then immediately onto the rock and sand of the Mojave Desert and the deserts of Arizona, New Mexico, and Texas. In the wee hours of the morning, we stopped at towns with names like HardCrust, BakedBrains, and OutOfLuck, the two or three passengers waiting dourly beside their cardboard suitcases underneath dim yellow lights and the bugs battering themselves senseless. At dawn I watched when the train slid by the outskirts of towns too small, too dead to warrant a stop, always two or three pickups waiting at the crossings, the blue exhaust billowing into the pink sunrise. Yucca trees, Joshua trees, telephone poles, and rangeland fences flashed by, near and far. We passed diners in silver trailers, the portable signs flashing EAT and CAFE. In the parking lot of one such place, I watched one overalled farmer as he removed himself from his spring-flattened, windshield-cracked station wagon. Tossing his cigarette away, he stretched in the cold desert air of morning, in the same instant tossing the train a look, the look the Indians must have given trains a hundred years before.

But then, maybe I didn't remember this until it was no longer possible to ride in a passenger train from Pasadena to Chicago via the dry and dusty deserts.

For a four-year-old, the train meant two days of scurrying up and down the steps of the double-decked El Capitan cars, getting cups of water from the dispenser near the bathrooms, and pestering my parents for coloring books and soft drinks. During the day, one or the other of them would sit with me, playing card games or telling me stories. We took our meals in the dining car, served by waiters in white jackets. At night we moved to the observation car, and there—underneath the dome of the world, the stars shining all around us, the moving planetarium—I fell asleep, to waken the following morning in the seats we'd reserved two cars away.

In Chicago we changed trains. Then, instead of the majestic El Capitan, we moved our bags to the overhead racks of the Riley. The only line from Chicago to Cincinnati, it was a bitter, half-day disappointment. No dining car. No observation dome. The cars were single level, stuffy and airless, and full of passengers who smelled of travel. Stewards carried trays of sandwiches that were mostly white bread and wax paper. I was told to be quiet and not allowed to run. My father sat with me and read a paperback mystery, glancing at me every now and then to make sure that I was coloring Huckleberry Hound and Yogi Bear and not the arms of the seat. Gradually, my crayons no longer held my attention. I watched the scene from our lurching window. I asked my father, "What makes green?"

If the Riley was a comedown from the El Capitan, at least the view was better than those forlorn stops at two o'clock in the morning in ToeJam, Arizona. Trees, vines, and green grass grew thick and lush not ten yards from the tracks. Cows grazed in their meadows. Alien pictures for the child born and raised in the irrigated desert that is California. In California, we are told, everything is illusion, starting with the movies and extending even to the grass that grows in the front yards of suburbia—dichondra, not a grass at all but a perennial herb, a one-leaf clover, a Martian's carpet. And then there were the other suburbanites, too lazy or efficient, who filled in their front yards with concrete, painted it green, and called it good. In California the only things green are kept so out of curiosity, for novelty's sake, like tigers contained in the heart of an urban zoo. To keep the tumbleweed and cactus at bay.

My father put down his Agatha Christie and answered my question as well as he could. Without losing me completely, he gave me a condensed version of the role of chlorophyll in the process of photosynthesis. This is not to say the why of green, only the how, for who can say why green is green except God? I peppered my father with the why's of a four-year-old, yet for the first time they were not the careless, indiscriminate pesterings of a child uncaring of the answer he receives. My father was aware of that, and our discussion was sober, educated, a dialogue between two adults.

"I like talking with you," I said.

"I like it also."

"You don't mind if I ask you questions?"

"Only so long," he said, "as they're not silly ones."

So we rode on through the green fields and forests of northern Illinois and central Indiana, until the time when we entered the confines of the Cincinnati Terminal, that shell-shaped WPA project that echoed with the sounds of returns and farewells. My grandmother and aunt were there to meet us and so too my cousin, Maddy. While the adults went to collect the baggage, Maddy demonstrated for me the terminal's acoustics. Standing at the opposite end of the main floor, she whispered, "I'm glad you're here." The words traveled along the high arching ceiling and landed, *plop*, in my ear.

"I'm glad, too," I giggled.

"Where's your mommy and daddy?" Maddy waved to me from her position, fifty yards away. I saw her only briefly through the hurrying bodies of other adults, each carrying some kind of luggage, a coat over an arm.

"Where's yours?" I said.

"Mom's with your parents and Grandma's at the baggage truck."

"Where's your daddy?" I said.

"I don't have one."

I insisted. "Everyone has a daddy."

"No."

Maddy worked her way through the crowd, back to where I stood.

"I don't have one," she said, "that's all."

She held my hand as we waited for the adults to reappear. Later Maddy and I played cards, seated at a small table in the pantry of the huge house. We ate potato chips and she showed me a new game called Crazy Eights. We played Crazy Eights, Go Fish, War, and Old Maid until I fell asleep, carried to a bed by unseen hands.

But, the summer I was six, our trip was very different. My father came home early from work with the announcement that he would not be able to go as planned. Work pressures. A proposal that had been delayed. Problems in a system. He had to stay.

It was late in May and the days were lengthening. My father pulled his station wagon into the garage, lowering the heavy door with a bang. In the vacant lot next door, I was sitting with my legs over the edge of the second story of a tree fort, perched high in a eucalyptus. Joe Shay and I drank Cokes straight from the bottles, and we pretended that we were pirates, plotting strategy. Joe was singing a dirty song about girls' underwear that he'd learned from his older brother. The sun touched the top of the foothills, and my mother opened the kitchen window, calling me home for dinner.

In the kitchen, my father was undoing his tie. "It doesn't have to be done this very minute," he was saying.

My mother didn't answer.

"This isn't intentional," he said.

I opened the door. "What's to eat, wench," I said, still in my pirate's world.

"Talk to your mother respectfully," my father said.

"Your father's not going with us, and we're going to Pasadena," my mother said. "To cash in his ticket."

"Something for work came up."

"Even though we've planned this trip for over two months now," my mother said. "But that's just the way your father is—he's very dedicated to work."

"I wish that I were going to be going too."

"Of course you are, dear," my mother said. "I know that. We'll just go to Pasadena, cash in your ticket, and then next week, your son and I will board the train together without you. We'll call you when we get to Cincinnati, and you can pray to God that nobody tries to talk to us in the Chicago train station because I'll die if they do, I can promise you that. On the spot."

"Nobody will bother you in Chicago."

"Since when were you a woman walking with a small child in a downtown area?"

"Don't be ridiculous."

My father was taking things out of his briefcase. My mother was grinding hot dogs in the meat grinder for the sandwich spread she made for our lunches. I was edging toward the door that led to the garage.

"And where are you going?" My mother pointed at me with half of a hot dog.

"Outside," I said. "We attack Bluebeard's fort at dawn."

"We're attacking Pasadena and getting a refund for your father's ticket because work is more important than family."

"You've got it all wrong," my father said. "Blackbeard was the pirate. Bluebeard married and murdered six wives."

My mother gave my father The Look that said, You see, you see how things are? You know that I'm right. My father and I ate hot-dog-spread sandwiches and looked at each other guiltily. Bluebeard's castle was safe for another day. My mother sat at the table with us and spelled words on the tabletop with the toothpicks.

In those days, the railroads were a different proposition. The impact of the commercial airplane was still to be felt; the great vaulted ceilings of train stations still echoed with the sounds of businessmen and their leather soles on the marble floors, the agonies and joys of leave-takings and arrivals. Nowadays, train stations are haunted places. Many have been torn down or consolidated with a bus depot. Trains run only once or twice a day. In Cincinnati passenger trains no longer stop, and the terminal has been turned into an arcade of gift stores. But then, to get anywhere without the prohibitive cost of flying, one took the train.

That fact plus the iron-clad guarantee given to railroad workers and their unions produced employees we recognize today as typical civil servants. Paid well, they also had an airtight job security, which meant they needed to serve no one. At the ticket desk, one could count on snarling inefficiency, which explained the man with the mole above one corner of his mouth and the pencil behind his ear. My mother and father waited in the long line. I stood next to their legs, chattering away about the strengths and weaknesses of Bluebeard's fortifications. My mother listened to me absently, wondering how she would handle me in the Chicago terminal without my father, knowing as she did that we would be accosted by someone rude, either a porter selling dirty postcards or some out-of-town salesman asking if he might possibly buy her a drink. My father held on to the tickets, still not completely certain what the fuss was all about. Together they stepped to the window. The man with the mole above his mouth yawned.

"I need to get a refund," my father said. "We bought this ticket, and now I can't go."

"So?" The man yawned again, this time enormously. The dark hairs protruding from the mole waved in the air like the feelers of some sort of bug. "I'm sorry about your travel plans."

"We already paid for the ticket," my mother said, "and since we can't use it, we'd like our money back."

"You can't do that here. You got to go to LA."

"Downtown?" my father said. "Why can't you change it here?"

"Didn't I tell you I was sorry? It's a rule, no refunds from intermediate stops."

"It's a stupid rule."

"What can I tell you, lady? Life is full of stupid rules."

The people behind us in line were shifting impatiently. I heard whispered comments about my parents. "All I wanna do is buy a ticket," one woman muttered. "I don't want no money back, for godsake. You travel, you go from here to there, you don't get you a discount, you don't get no refund. Criminy if you don't."

My father tried again, thinking that reason would surely prevail. This was only a minor misunderstanding. "You must be able to give refunds here," he said calmly. "You sell tickets here, don't you? If you sell tickets, then you have to be able to refund tickets also."

"Listen, bud. If I sold you a ticket, then five minutes later you change your mind, even if you never leave the station, you get to make the trip to LA. You got it?"

"I never heard of anything so ridiculous," my mother said.

"So there's a first time for everything."

"Absolutely ridiculous," my father said.

"Well, now that's two of you," the man with the mole said. "Next?"

We drove to Los Angeles. My mother kept saying that the whole thing was ridiculous.

"What do you expect me to do?" my father exploded. He had turned halfway around in his seat while doing sixty-five on the freeway, and my mother said that keeping his eyes on the road might do for a start. So then we drove in silence, except once my father asked me about school, about what I'd learned that day. The only thing that I could think to tell him was that Laurie Baldwin wanted to marry Keith Zimmer, but that Keith thought Laurie was stupid. Mrs. Ninnis had had to stop Laurie from kicking Keith at recess because she loved him so much. Other than that, Bluebeard was the subject of my discussion, that treacherous pirate. He had double-crossed Joe Shay and me, and we were plotting his revenge.

"Blackbeard," my father sighed, "his name is *Black*beard."

In the LA terminal, my parents presented their case to a plain woman who wore the uniform shirt of the railroad company along with a string tie. They explained to her what the man with the mole had said in Pasadena, how they had been directed to her window. She put her hands on the counter and laced the fingers together in order to look properly intense.

"He told you to come here?"

"Yes," my father and mother chimed.

"He couldn't have done that," she said. "Let me see those tickets."

My father brought out the tickets from an inside coat pocket, and the woman began to read. She slipped on a pair of schoolteacher's half-glasses.

"Oh, huh. Uh. huh. You see? You see this, here?" She was jabbing at several lines on the ticket slips. "This says that your trip originates from Pasadena terminal, and you refund all tickets from either the point of origination or the location of purchase. Where you purchase these at?"

"Pasadena," my father said.

"Well, then. You drive right back there and you tell Mr. Mungo that you got double the reason—origination and location—and don't you let him pull that kind of stuff with you."

"Couldn't we, I mean," my father started, "couldn't you refund them here so we don't have to go through this again?"

"No sir," she said, "I couldn't do that. It'd be against the rules." She straightened up with righteous indignation. "And it's just like that Mungo too, I got to tell you, making you poor folks drive all the way out here for nothing, like he done. When you go back to Pasadena, you give him an earful, just like I told you, and maybe that'll stop his rude and uncourteous behavior. Pasadena issued the ticket, Pasadena issues the refund."

My father turned on his heel. My mother grabbed me by one wrist and we hurried to catch up. In the parking lot, he stood next to our car, taking deep breaths of the metallic LA air.

"Well," he said finally, "I guess it's back to Pasadena."

"The whole thing is insane," my mother said.

"I know it is, but what do you want me to do?"

"Talk to a supervisor," my mother said, "or a manager or a conductor or an engineer. Somebody ought to be able to do something."

"*I* have an idea," I said. A lovely little fantasy played itself out in front of my eyes. Joe Shay and I, each bearing flintlock pistols and cutlasses between our teeth, boarded the chicken-wire ticket cages of the LA train station. In my daydream, Joe captured the plain woman, who now wore the clothing of a gypsy. A Spanish comb held her hair, which had likewise changed from blond to brunette. Meanwhile, I backed Bluebeard into a corner, pushing him with the point of my cutlass against the drawers of a filing cabinet. I threatened him with dismemberment and disgrace if he would not meet the satisfaction of my parents. The hairs on his mole waved and wiggled in a disgusting display of fear and cowardice.

"Bluebeard—" I began.

My father turned in exasperation, thinking that it would have been easier to quit his job than it was to get a railroad refund. He told me to be quiet, swatting me with the back of his hand as he would a fly from a fence. I dropped to the ground, too stunned to remember to cry.

In the following week, my father was very careful. He bought roses for my mother twice, and I received a curved sword, the kind that a pirate would wave above his head while cursing the enemy. On the night when he brought my mother the second bouquet of roses and me the sword, my mother said that he could stop trying to buy his way out of trouble.

"I still haven't forgiven you for not coming in the first place," she said.

"Me, too," I said, cutting the air with the plastic sword. "Die, Bluebeard," I yelled. I jabbed my father in the stomach with the tip of the sword before he grabbed it from my hand.

"We don't kill people," he said. He handed the sword to my mother, and when he wasn't looking, she raised it above his head.

On another night, my parents drove back to Pasadena to face the taciturn Mr. Mungo. The plain woman from the Los Angeles terminal had called, and he grudgingly counted the money into my father's hand. My mother waited in the car. I lay with my head in her lap, telling her of my final day in school for that year. There had been punch and a cake, and because Keith Zimmer had decided that he really liked Debbi Arnbruster, Laurie Baldwin had poured her punch over his head and jammed her cake into his ears.

"She loves him," I told my mother. "They're going to be married soon."

"Oh, I don't think so. They're a little young, don't you think? But," she sighed, "you're right about love."

Three nights later, my father took my mother and me to the train station. He carried all our bags from the car, and at the ticket counter, he made sure that our luggage would arrive in Cincinnati when we did. Then we waited for the train. My father stood while my mother and I sat.

"You take good care of your mother," he said to me. "And when you're in Cincinnati, be polite because you'll be the only man there, okay?"

"Sure," I said.

"And if we get through this proposal, I'll hop a plane just as soon as I can," he said to my mother.

"Sure," she said. "You do that."

When the train pulled in, he kissed my mother and he kissed me, and then he kissed my mother again. "Call me," he said, "as soon as you get in."

He helped me step up into the car, lifting me over the gray step that the conductor had set on the ground. "I'm sorry I hit you the other night," my father said. "I didn't mean it."

My mother and I found our seats. Below our window, my father was waving to us. He was wearing his suit because he had just come home from work when we needed to leave for the train. He had loosened his tie and his shirt was unbuttoned at the neck. The platform was filled with people saying good-bye, but my father was the only one who was by himself. My mother and I waved back. I started to cry, which made my mother start to cry, which made me cry even harder.

"Don't do that," my mother said. "I won't be able to stop if you keep that up."

"All aboard!" The conductors picked up their steps from the platform. Everyone began to wave even more vigorously. The train started to pull away, lurching and gathering momentum. My father didn't run after the train as some did. He waved and we waved until neither one of us could see him. The conductor came down our aisle punching tickets, and my mother had to stop waving in order to find ours.

That night was the most difficult. Neither one of us slept very much. We watched the names on the sides of the depots change as the train rolled into town after town on the desert. In the seat next to the aisle, my mother dozed, then snapped awake while I tried to color a coloring book in the dark. We were not riding in the observation car because she didn't think she could carry me in case I fell asleep. But then, neither one of us fell asleep until dawn. The train was plowing into the sunrise, and then I was asleep and then I heard my mother groaning. Her head was moving from side to side and she was clutching a pillow to her chest. I shook her by one arm.

Her eyes opened. Outside, the rangeland extended to the horizon. Fence posts and barbed wire. I shook her arm again.

"Hmm?" she said. "Oh. I was dreaming."

"You woke me up."

"I'm sorry." She patted my hand. Her head rested against the back of her seat. "I was dreaming."

"I'm hungry."

"Then we'd better get something to eat, hadn't we?"

We walked to the end of the train before we came to the dining car, passing through five other cars in the process. It was still early, and people were sleeping underneath blankets with their mouths open and their hair mussed. Each time we went through the knuckle between the cars, I expected that the doors wouldn't open and we'd be stuck there while the floor shifted underneath our feet.

In the dining car, we were among the first to be served. An older steward brought me eggs and bacon and orange juice, and for my mother he brought coffee and toast. He seemed especially cheerful and his jacket was white and stiff. "Good morning, good morning!" he said to us. "Wonderful morning, isn't it?" The day was bright and clear, and the sky as blue as the underwear in Joe Shay's brother's song. I started to sing but then thought better of it when I saw my mother look at me.

"I should have known I'd have that dream," she said. "Every time I get mad at him I have that dream, and it makes me even madder. There he goes, running down the street, followed by a pack of beautiful girls ten years younger than I am. I never do any better than seventh place."

"You woke me up."

"I told you I was sorry. It's a nightmare; I never catch up. Your father enjoys having those girls chase him. He likes the attention."

Another train passed us, going in the opposite direction. For a moment the dining car flashed bright and dark, as if we were in an old movie. If I blinked, I could pick out details on the other train, another passenger train. I blinked and saw a number on the side of one car. I blinked again and saw a man's head on a woman's shoulder.

"It's so frustrating," my mother was saying, "because he's never running that fast."

The other train burst beyond our window, speeding toward Los Angeles, and the bright sunlight flashed through the dining car. On the ceiling were the reflections from my mother's wristwatch. When she drank her coffee, the flickers of gold jumped from the ceiling to the steward's white jacket to the nose of a gray-haired woman across the aisle. The beam of sunlight broke into pieces in the glass of water in front of me and fell out colors on the other side.

"Tell me," I said, "about light." Here at last, I thought, was the purpose of a train trip—to have mysteries explained. But my mother disappointed me.

"Light?" she said. "We have light during the day when the sun's up, and when the sun goes down, there's no more light until the next day."

"I know that. What *is* it?"

"It's . . . light," she said. "It is what it is. Have you finished your breakfast?"

I received many new coloring books and even some comic books. Prior to this trip, I had always imagined that they were forbidden and somehow wrong because I'd never before had one. Superman and Lois Lane fell in love several times, and Lex Luthor came close on several occasions to spoiling the fate of the free world. Each time I finished a comic book, I asked my mother for a new one. Finally, she bought me five of them all at once and said it was her final offer.

We slept better that second night, and that morning we were in Chicago. In the Chicago station no one bothered us. No one talked to us. No one seemed remotely interested in us at all. Then we were on the Riley, and then we were in the Cincinnati Terminal, looking for my grandmother, aunt, and cousin.

"There they are!" my aunt called.

My grandmother kissed me so that I felt the hair above her upper lip. My aunt kissed me, and Maddy kissed me politely on the cheek. She was twelve years old and twice my age, and she said, "Where's your father?"

I started to cry, but I caught myself. "With yours," I said. So then we were even.

At home, Maddy played Crazy Eights with me to make up for joking about fathers. My mother and grandmother and aunt talked.

"At least he didn't kill you," my grandmother said. "Your father would have killed me if I'd given him that kind of lip."

"I thought he was going to kill me once," my mother began.

It was an old story, one from before my time. After my parents were married, their honeymoon consisted of moving to California. My father didn't have much to pack, but one item worried my mother considerably. My father had an anvil that he'd forged when he was in high school, and because he'd forgotten to include it in the items to be shipped, he dropped it into the trunk of their car without giving it much thought. My mother couldn't understand why her husband would need an anvil on their honeymoon. They hadn't known each other that long before they'd gotten married, and after the ceremony she had second thoughts; she imagined the anvil as the pivotal instrument in some perverse sexual rite, or else as 'the blunt object' in a courtroom discussion of her homicide. After driving all day, my mother's fears were somewhat allayed. That is, until they went swimming in the motel pool that night. My father had been a swimmer in college, but my mother had neglected to tell him that her only knowledge of swimming was how to grab the side of the pool. If you held three fingers up above the water that meant you were drowning. In fun, my father dunked her, pushing her head beneath the surface of the water, and my mother came up spitting. Between the anvil and the dunking, she figured she'd survived two attempts on her life.

"Our marriage didn't get off to the smoothest of starts," she said.

The phone was ringing, and my aunt went to answer. "It's your husband, the psychopath," she said to my mother, "and he wants to know where in the hell you been, and why haven't you called?"

My father flew in to Cincinnati three days later. He took a taxi from the airport and surprised my mother, who was very surprised indeed. I was in the attic at the time. Maddy had written a play adapted from *Little Women*, and she was finding old clothes for me to wear so I could play the part of Amy, the youngest sister. When I asked her why I had to play a girl's part, she said it was because the boys' parts weren't very big. She had put a wig on my head. I wore one of her old dresses and my grandmother's shawl. I heard my father's voice downstairs, but Maddy was putting on my lipstick and she wouldn't let me move. But when he came upstairs, I jerked away from Maddy and tackled my father's knees.

"Bluebeard!" I bellowed.

"Avast, me hearty!" My father bellowed also, letting my mother know which side of the family my mouth came from. He was dancing me around the attic, my feet on his feet. "Home at last!" he shouted.

"Bluebeard!" I yelled joyously.

The floorboards creaked and groaned, the attic became the deck of Bluebeard's ship *Repulse*, my father and I laughed and danced a jig to his successful invasion while—without our knowing—Maddy made her way down the stairs, joining the company of the other women.

III. O. HENRY AND THE HAREM

It was the summer when my mother's cousin's husband died, and we were driving from Los Angeles to Cincinnati so we could take my mother's relatives on vacation. I was ten years old. In order to keep me entertained, my mother had given me a deck of cards and a one-volume *Complete Sherlock Holmes*, as well as the usual staples—comic books, paper, and pencils. I didn't always understand the Sherlock Holmes, and then when I did understand, it sometimes scared me; after reading "The Case of the Speckled Band," I imagined that I too might be bitten by a treacherous snake, one that slid down an imaginary dumbwaiter rope. But when I didn't understand and was tired of asking my mother and father questions, I practiced shuffling the cards. Across the flat reaches of Arizona and New Mexico, I shuffled the cards together end to end—*thib-i-thib-i-thip*—and then practiced bending them into each other the other way, so that they were shuffled and squared with a convincing sense of authority and ease. Previously, whenever my good friend Joe Shay and I had played Go Fish or Old Maid or Crazy Eights, he'd always said that the way I shuffled cards—corner to corner and then pushing them together with both hands—was the way a girl would do it, and I was determined to change my image. I also practiced shooting the deck from one hand to the other, riffling the cards in a line through the air the way a magician or a card shark might. This took me longer to learn, and I spent much time picking the cards up from the floor of the backseat. Frequently my father asked if we maybe couldn't get a little respite from the *thib-i-thib-i-thip* of the flexing cards, and then I went back to the Sherlock Holmes; or else I played games with my parents, such as looking for numbers on license plates and calling out the names of the different states, or we would take turns thinking of the names of cities, the last letter of the city corresponding to the first letter of the next player's choice of town. The great trick of course, was to use such names as Phoenix, Monterey, and Martinez, making my parents use such names as Xenia, Yreka, and Zamora. If I grew tired of the game, I tried to use the names Fairfax or Colfax. Then the game would be over because none of us knew another town that began with the letter X. If we had played all the games that we knew and if my father still asked that there be no more card shuffling, or if I felt a little carsick from reading the comic books or the Sherlock Holmes, then my parents had one last suggestion: "Watch the scenery," my mother said, while all around us the unchanging desert landscape disappeared into the horizon.

On the second day of our trip, we stopped in Colorado in Mesa Verde, and we hiked along with the park ranger as he told us the story of the ancient Navajo Indian nation, the way that they had lived at the top of the high plateau in their highly organized though primitive society of apartment dwellers. We walked in their steps, and we looked at the bowl-shaped depressions in the red rock, made from their cooking fires. We saw the outlines of their houses, and the ranger said, "You can almost feel their spirits still hovering in these places, can't you?"

Everyone on the tour nodded their head and no one said a word, visitors in someone else's house. I didn't say anything either. If I closed my eyes about halfway, and if I caught the light just right, I could see Indians making their dinners or sharpening their arrows. And then if I closed my eyes almost all the way, I could see Carl, my mother's cousin's husband, sightseeing along with the rest. I did not tell my parents. Instead I took pictures with my Brownie, and when we went back to our car, I went back to shuffling cards and rarely looked out the window.

My father drove the last eight hundred miles in a flat run. We ate in the car and stopped only for gas. My mother had said, "We could stop in Indianapolis and have an easy drive in the morning."

"Gotta get there," my father mumbled, and he drove the last two hundred miles in a driving rainstorm, arriving in Cincinnati just after midnight. My grandmother, my aunt, and my cousin, thinking that we would not appear until the following day, were in their beds, asleep. My mother rang the doorbell several times, and we heard their collie barking. My father brought our bags to the door, then lay down in the porch swing.

"They're probably in bed," my mother said a time or two. She was pressing the doorbell continuously and the dog's barking intensified.

I sat down on my father's legs, and he gave me room on the swing grudgingly.

"We could've stopped in Indianapolis," my mother was saying, "and gotten a good night's sleep. Now we're waking everyone up, and Celia probably thinks we're burglars."

Celia was my aunt, my mother's sister. She was highly strung, with a habit of installing extra locks on triple-bolt doors. One night she saw a black man standing on the sidewalk in front of her house. She assumed that his intentions were evil, his motivations perverse; she called the police, who told her she assumed too much—the man had only been reading a city map by the light of the streetlamp opposite her front door—but that did not allay her fears. When dead bolts went on sale she bought cases of them.

Now the dog was barking wildly, and we could hear her front paws hitting the door as she jumped.

"Maybe we should get a motel room," my mother said.

"You wanted to get here," my father said, "we're here."

I worked myself into a corner of the swing and got it moving back and forth. With the recent rain, the summer air was thick and damp, and even when the air was moving, it was uncomfortable.

"Come to the East in the summertime," my father was saying to himself, "and you come for the weather." He was unbuttoning his shirt as he spoke, and he was very nearly asleep.

Then the porch light came on and the curtain in the door was pulled back, and my grandmother, seeing my mother's face, opened the door.

"We didn't expect you till tomorrow," my grandmother said. She stood in the doorway in her bathrobe, her gray hair flying away from her head.

"It is tomorrow," my father said, looking at his watch.

"Sorry, Mom," my mother said, "Mel didn't want to stop."

"He better change his tune going in the other direction," my grandmother said. "With all these women in the car, he'll be stopping every damn mile, won't you Mel?"

"No man," my father said, yawning hugely, "no man in his right mind fights with his harem."

The next day, my mother's cousin and my mother's cousin's daughter drove across the river from Kentucky. Janie, the daughter, was fourteen and very friendly to me, even though I was younger. I wanted to tell her I was sorry about her father, but I wasn't sure how to do that. A couple of times I rehearsed myself, saying things like "I feel deeply over your loss," things I'd probably heard on the TV or in movies, but when it came time to say something I chickened out and said nothing; but then no one else said anything either, at least not in my hearing.

Because there would be eight of us in the car, my mother had talked my father into buying a roof rack for the station wagon. My father, in turn, gave each of us instructions. No one was allowed to bring more than one suitcase into the motel at night, and no one was allowed more than two bags total. This was not difficult for me since all of my clothes were in my mother's bags, but my father told me that it would be tough on the women. "If we let them, they'd have eight overnight bags apiece," he said. "We'd have to take a second car just for the luggage."

We left Cincinnati, driving due west, rather than returning south and west, the way my parents and I had come. My father drove and my mother occasionally spelled him at the wheel, with my grandmother sitting with them in the front seat. My cousin, Maddy, my aunt, and my mother's cousin sat in the middle seat, and Janie and I stretched out in the rear, where there was no seat, just stray articles of luggage that my father couldn't find room for in the roof rack.

We drove through Indiana, Illinois, and Iowa in what seemed like no time at all, though it took a day and a half. Janie and I played card games, giving me a chance to show off my newfound proficiency at shuffling. We also waved to people we passed on the highway, counting the numbers of those who waved back. Most everyone did. When we passed big trucks, we pulled imaginary ropes above our heads, signaling to the drivers that we wanted to hear their air horns. Not as many truckers blew their horns as there were people who waved, but by the time we hit South Dakota, Janie and I had counted sixty-seven wavers and twenty-eight toots. And just west of Sioux Falls, we waved at one man who spit a stream of brown tobacco juice out his window and into the next lane of traffic. So, we also counted one spit, though it was probably just coincidence.

Janie also like to read. While I struggled with the Sherlock Holmes, she was reading O. Henry, the collection of stories called *The Four Million*. I had never heard of O. Henry, except as a candy bar. Janie was shocked. She read to me such stories as "The Cop and the Anthem," "The Love Philtre of Ikey Schoenstein," "Mammon and the Archer," and "The Gift of the Magi," explaining to me the technique of the stories.

"The expected happens unexpectedly," she said, quoting something that sounded like a high school textbook. "They all have twist endings."

I didn't entirely understand this talk of "expecteds" and "unexpected happenstance," but I began to sense a vision of life that was something far different from what we had been led to assume. We were driving west, through the southern tier of South Dakota, and my mother and my aunt and my mother's cousin requested that my father take the scenic loop through the Bad-lands. My father refused, citing time (we were heading toward Mt. Rushmore), weather (it had begun to look like rain), and economy (we were driving about nine thousand miles as it was—who needed side trips?). My father really had little interest in a lot of funny-shaped rocks. But two hours later, when my father needed to take a little nap, my mother took the wheel, and she headed the car onto the scenic loop despite my grandmother's protests.

"He'll be furious," she said, "when he wakes up."

"It won't take long," my mother said.

So, we drove through the jagged rock outcroppings and the arid, hostile plateau, observing the brilliant colors and scenery that was truly worth watching. And when my father woke up again, we were back on the highway heading on our original course.

"We ought to be almost there," my father said, looking at his watch to gauge the time that he'd slept and the miles that we should have covered.

"Not quite," my mother said. "Another seventy-five miles. We visited the Badlands while you were out. It was pretty educational for the kids."

My mother was stretching the truth somewhat, since we hadn't even left the car and we could have gotten the same thing from a book or a postcard. Meanwhile, my grandmother had turned in her seat, on pins and needles over what my father might say.

My father scratched his head, yawned, and put his arms around my mother and my grandmother. "Oh," he said. "Fine." Then he slept the rest of the way to Rushmore.

In the back Janie and I giggled and whispered "O. Henry" to each other for my father's sake as well as my grandmother's.

The next day we also said "O. Henry" when the fog had socked in Mt. Rushmore. It was so bad that we could scarcely see the great men's chins, and then the joke was on us, because we had wanted to see the stone heads quite badly—and all our pictures would come out as blank rectangles of gray. So then we bought postcards and told each other we'd been there, even if we hadn't exactly seen it.

The focal point of the trip as designed by my parents was to be Yellowstone Park. This trip was retracing the honeymoon route they'd taken twelve years before. My mother told us about Old Faithful, and my father told us about the Paint Pots. It was possible, they said, to see bears at every turn. We left Spearfish, South Dakota, the morning after our visit to the foggy Mt. Rushmore. We ate big breakfasts—pancakes and eggs and ham and juice. There was a pot of strawberry preserves on the table, and I constructed a red mountain on top of my pancakes while my mother eyed me with suspicion. Four hours later we were in Buffalo, Wyoming, getting gas and taking restroom breaks. My father said that we would be making better time except that we had to stop every couple of miles for the ladies to go to the bathroom. If you didn't announce every pit stop seriously, they'd ignore you until the next freeway off-ramp, and then they'd be all over your neck.

"Men can hold it," my father said, and I believed him, even though something—the flip-flopping of my innards—told me that men are not always so tough, and that it is sometimes easier to be an idiot than to admit that sad fact.

We drove through Sheridan and then through Greybull, and in both places my mother asked if maybe we shouldn't get more gas, but my father said, why should we when we still had a good third of a tank? We were all singing in the car at the time—"Row, Row, Row Your Boat" and "The Blue Ridge Mountains of Virginia"—even my grandmother. But when we passed Emblem, Wyoming, my mother said, "The needle is almost touching E."

"I've got enough to make it to Cody," my father said, and then he started us singing "Ninety-Nine Bottles of Beer." But of course, we only made it to the seventy-third bottle before the car started to knock and miss and my father was swinging over onto the shoulder and my mother was saying, "You ran out of gas," and Janie and I said, "O. Henry."

Fortunately, there was another car directly behind us on the highway, another car full of tourists and luggage, and they pulled over onto the shoulder in front of us.

"Okay," my father said, "you can say I told you so."

My mother said nothing, staring straight through the windshield.

"She told you so," my grandmother said.

"Be quiet, Mom," my mother said.

My father sighed and got out of the car, walking toward the other car.

"He should've listened to you," my grandmother said, "but he probably figured you were just another stupid woman."

"So now what?" my aunt said. I imagine that she had already concocted several gruesome scenarios, ones involving blood and mayhem, or at the very least, starvation in the inhospitable plateau.

In front of us, the driver of the other car was walking back toward my father, and then the two of them were shaking hands. Then my father walked back toward our car.

"This fellow's going to take me into Cody so I can get a couple gallons of gas," my father said.

The other driver stood near the trunk of his own car with his arms folded across his chest. He was about the same age as my father but he had a big stomach, which, in his tee shirt, dropped down over the front of his bermuda shorts. He wore a tractor cap on his head and he was drinking a beer. The car carried Iowa license plates.

"All right," my mother said.

"If he starts to drink another beer, tell him you'll drive," my grandmother said.

"He's okay," my father said.

"What about us?" my aunt said.

"I should be back in about an hour," my father said. He kissed my mother on the cheek because she still wasn't looking at him. The other driver took one last swallow of his beer, then poured out the last few drops on the ground before throwing the can into the ditch by the shoulder.

My aunt rolled down her window. Her scenarios had obviously become more refined, now visualizing six dead women and one dead boy, death caused by abandonment. "You will come back, won't you?" she called. My father waved, shut the door of the other car, and then was gone; the car went up and over a little rise in the roadway, and we saw the car no longer.

"What do you think he's going to do?" my grandmother said. "Leave us?"

"You never can tell with men," my aunt said.

Inside the car, the temperature immediately began to rise. We all opened our windows. My mother opened the large rear window so Janie and I could stick our feet out the back.

"Mel wouldn't leave us," my mother said.

"I thought like that once," my aunt said, "then I got married. And then I got divorced."

"So you made a mistake," my grandmother said. "Not everybody does."

"You never liked him," my aunt said.

"It just goes to show you," my grandmother said. "Some of us have some sense."

"Stop it now," my mother said. "It's hot enough as it is without you two making it worse. As soon as Mel gets back with the gas, we're going to drive into Yellowstone and see Old Faithful."

"*If* he comes back," Maddy said. She was sixteen at the time and very protective of her mother. "They don't always come back."

"He's gonna come back," I yelled. "Don't be stupid."

"Don't talk like that to your cousin," my mother ordered, and then everyone fell silent.

We had all become conscious of the heat. Flies were buzzing along the roof and the temperature was well into the nineties. My mother was thinking that if my father didn't get back within the next half-hour he'd have hell to pay explaining to Aunt Celia. Aunt Celia, for her part, was feeling torn between wishing my father to come back so the vacation could continue and hoping he'd abandoned us to the coyotes just so everyone would know she'd been correct. My grandmother had fallen asleep. Cousin Maddy had returned to reading a college-prep text on sociology, but her ears were alert to the sound of any more slurs. My mother's cousin's thoughts were not obvious to anyone, except possibly to Janie, who was again reading her O. Henry, this time reading aloud "A Furnished Room." In it, a man searches for his sweetheart, who has run off to the big city. He searches and searches without success. Despondent, he rents a room where, upon lying down to rest, he catches a scent in the air reminding him of his past love. So utterly depressed is he by this fleeting memory that he turns on the gas to kill himself, unaware that in this same room, only a week before, his girlfriend had done exactly the same thing. When Janie finished reading, my mother said, "That was depressing wasn't it?"

"She needs to know what life is like," my aunt said.

"Oh, come on," my mother said.

"And so does his lord and master," my aunt said, tipping her head in my direction.

Actually, what I really needed—and quickly—was a bathroom. Men can hold it, I repeated to myself. But I scrambled out from the back end of the car, pacing back and forth along the roadway with my hands in my pockets.

"What's the matter with you?" my mother said.

"I gotta go kill a tree," I said. Without saying anything more, I hiked away from the car sliding a little in the loose gravel of the shoulder. My father and I went camping, and whenever we went hiking, we rejoiced in the portable nature of men; killing a tree was perfectly acceptable. However, here in northern Wyoming, ten miles due east of Cody, trees were as plentiful as Martians, the only living things being the scrub brush that dotted the sandy, gravely soil. Scrub brush that was maybe a foot and a half in height. I unzipped myself with my back to the car, hoping that the release of pressure on my bladder would alleviate some of the more explosive pressures building up inside of me.

In the car, my mother's cousin spoke for the first time. "You can't judge all men by one bad example," she said.

My aunt was quick to assure her recently bereaved cousin. "You're right, I guess," she sighed.

"Carl was a wonderful man," Maddy said, "even if he did tease me sometimes."

"I liked him," Janie said.

"Of course you did," my mother said. "He was your father."

"No. I really liked him."

Now, outside, my ten-year-old body was demanding relief. So, with one quick look over my shoulder, aware that six pairs of eyes could watch my every activity, I dropped my pants and crouched as close to the dirt as possible, vowing never to touch strawberries again.

"I mean we sometimes had our problems," my mother's cousin was saying to my aunt, "but we always knew that we could work them out."

When I came back to the car, my mother's cousin was just finishing a cry, and my aunt and Maddy were hugging her. My mother's hand was resting on my aunt's shoulder. My grandmother was still asleep and Janie had gone back to her reading.

"What's wrong?" I whispered to Janie when I'd crawled into the back of the station wagon.

She barely looked up from her book. "They were talking about Dad," she said.

"I'm sorry," I said. "I wish he wasn't dead."

She shrugged. "Me neither."

My mother's cousin was still crying a little. If I closed my eyes most of the way while she was pretty much quiet, I could see Carl, and it looked like he was trying to touch her hair. But then she'd start to cry all over again, and he'd disappear. I wanted to tell Janie but she was reading, and as she turned the pages, she was frowning and twisting her hair around one finger. After a while she closed her book and asked me if she could read a story from the Sherlock Holmes. I chose "The Case of the Speckled Band" because I knew it the best, and when she was finished she shivered and said, "I hate snakes."

"They're not so bad," I said. I hadn't been able to tell anyone about Carl and I was feeling annoyed.

"Not so bad, huh?"

"They're just big worms."

"They don't scare you?"

"No."

"Well, speaking of worms," she said, "we all saw you down there when you were going to the bathroom."

"You did?"

"We could've," she said, "but we didn't. We had more important things to do than to watch you."

She pinched my face.

"O. Henry," she added.

"I had nightmares for two nights," I said, "after I read that story. And sometimes I think I see your father."

"Me too," she said, "and sometimes I think I'm crazy."

My father came back with two gallons of gas, an hour after he'd gone.

He kidded my aunt for thinking that he'd abandon us. The man from Iowa had taken him to a gas station in Cody. Then my father had had to wait for twenty minutes until a tow truck could bring him back with gas. Now he was pouring most of the two gallons into the tank, saving a little to pour down the carburetor.

"Gotta prime the old pump, just a bit," my father said.

I held the air filter while my father put the last of the gas into the car.

"So did you keep the harem entertained?" he said.

"Sort of," I said.

In the car everyone had composed themselves: my aunt had apologized to my mother, my grandmother had apologized to my aunt, and my mother's cousin had apologized to everyone for being so teary and emotional. It was high time she was over the weepies, she said. So when my father came back, riding high in the cab of the tow truck, he had found the women chattering happily and Maddy and Janie reading. I couldn't see Carl anymore.

"Sorry to leave you with all these squaws," my father was saying now. He took the air filter out of my hands and tightened the wing nut holding it to the engine. "When we get to Yellowstone we'll do some hiking, and maybe tonight I'll teach you how to play poker for pennies. You can't play Crazy Eights and Old Maid for the rest of your life, you know."

The
Girl
on the
Highway

────────────────
███████████

The sun was setting when Anderson turned back
toward the highway, a corkscrew on-ramp that brought him face
to face with the dying winter sun, and then there was a girl, standing on the shoulder, holding a small boy, and the sun seemed to
explode behind her. Orange flames leaped from the dark outline of
her head, her shoulders. She was on fire.

The car swerved, and he brought it sliding to a stop almost to
the lip of the embankment, ten feet from the edge of an accident.

He rolled down his window.

"Are you all right?" he called.

She walked toward the window. "Everything's perfect," she

said. "This is a wonderful highway." She bit her lip as she peered into the interior of his old car, measuring, it seemed, himself and his own standards of decency and cleanliness. Now that she was out of the direct line of the sun, he could see that he was speaking to a sixteen-year-old girl who was wearing an army parka over white linen pants and black high heels. With the hood pulled over her head, the overlarge coat seemed to swallow her as well as the boy, who looked to be about two years old.

Anderson, who was not in the habit of picking up hitchhikers, whatever their description, felt as though he were speaking a language absolutely foreign to his tongue. "You're welcome to a ride," he said, "but I'm heading to Phoenix. I'll be turning east in a few miles. Maybe you want to go to LA or San Diego?"

"Phoenix will be perfect."

"I don't have a car seat," he said, looking at the boy.

"Do you think we should wait?" She looked to the east, to the approaching darkness with its promise of cold and wind, and almost smiled, and Anderson could not tell if she meant the question seriously or not. Her feet chattered on the gravel in their high heels, and she wrapped the parka about herself and the boy even tighter.

For several minutes no other car had appeared on either horizon. Rows of cotton spread in every direction.

"Well, get in," he said.

She settled in with the boy on her lap, then carefully buckled the seat belt over both of them.

"There," she said, "all safe and snug." She looked at him, again with her lips curving into that almost-but-not-quite smile, then patted him on his knee. "We're ready when you are."

For a moment, with her hair on fire, she had looked like a saint or a martyr or an artist's rendering of the angelic: self-possessed even in the midst of pain and suffering. And even after she was away from the focused blaze of the sun, Anderson still could not shake the image that she had made, even when he saw her in a green army parka with the boy on her lap, humming a tune he dimly recognized as being popular years ago.

"I said we're ready." Her fingers touched his knee, and only then did Anderson become aware he'd been staring at the glow he still saw about her head.

"Yes," he said. "I'm ready too."

He accelerated onto the highway, and the Mustang's interior filled with orange. He would not have been surprised if he had begun to hear voices.

"Stacy," the boy said, "I want drink."

The girl shushed him. "Maybe in a little while. We just now got a ride."

The boy began to squirm in her lap and against the belt that pressed against his legs.

"Jakey," she said. Her voice, rather dreamy before, suddenly became stern: "We all have to live with our discomforts."

Anderson, however, was running away from his discomforts. Or so it seemed to Anderson's wife. There was no reason in the world why he needed to visit his mother and stepfather just now, not so soon after his accident. How could he think of leaving? He was holding himself together like a cracked plate. And yet here he was one hundred miles south of home, ready to cross the mountains and travel through the desert in a car that he'd owned since he was seventeen, but which now ran only when it felt like it.

This is how he happened to be traveling: an associate pastor of a large suburban church, he had climbed onto the sanctuary roof to fix a loose strand of Christmas lights that spelled the word *NOEL*, and he had fallen off. Why he had done this—he hated heights and was notoriously inept with any sort of repair—he would never know; there was no rational reason why he *had* to climb the roof. And yet he remembered ascending the ladder with a sense of mission that seemed preordained and inspired.

A church member from the neighborhood found him an hour later, the back of his head nearly buried in the mulch around the agapanthus. The evidence suggested an accident, and yet, all too often in the early, sweaty hours of morning, Anderson caught himself dreaming of swan dives with a frequency he found depressing as well as frightening. As if he had taken the gospel of Luke literally—"*On their hands they will bear thee up*"—and in the test *he* had been found wanting, not worth the energy of rescue.

He had sustained a concussion of titanic proportions; he had missed breaking his neck by a stroke of luck. What he saw while he was unconscious was a hint of miracles—colors never before defined and the promise of voices to be heard, secrets to be spoken, mysteries to be revealed. At one point in his unconscious travels, he saw Jesus, and he expected to receive apocalyptic messages. But the encounter was disappointing. Dressed in an impeccably cut tuxedo, the Son of God was the center of some sort of reception, and when Anderson attempted to engage Him in conversation, Jesus only looked through him—a terrible snub—as if to confirm his worst suspicions: that he had no being with which to be.

When he woke, his first sight was that of an EMT bending over him in the ambulance, attaching some sort of gizmo to his chest. His most vivid memory was of the thickets of hair luxuriating within the man's nostrils, little planters filled with shrubs. Hardly a vision likely to inspire.

And just then he could have used some dramatic inspiration. In charge of youth ministries, Anderson was expected to perform miracles with bitter adolescents and salvage those grade school children already failed by their parents' deficiencies. He had never felt that youth work was his special talent; it was merely a stepping-stone to a senior pastorate elsewhere. He played the guitar badly, and his personality lacked the charisma and high energy of other successful youth ministers. He could summon up little sympathy for his affluent young charges and their troubles, heightened as they were by imagination and leisure and their romantic longing for grief. And on Wednesday evenings—youth group night—his wife Rebecca visibly shuddered each time she saw a new haircut enter their living room. He knew that she often confided to her friends that she would not have said yes had she truly known the lot of a pastor's wife.

Following his accident, the session voted to hire a youth intern to lighten Anderson's load, a gesture as generous as it was threatening. Who knew how long the youth pastor would hold up? What had he been doing on that roof? In the second it had taken for him to fall, he had become suspect.

When Jack Hopkins was selected, Anderson mentally began to pack his bags. Jack, a star running back in his high school days, had cheerfully dropped out of college after three semesters and his sixth shoulder separation in two seasons. He kept his hair long and his earring bright, he shaved twice a week to maintain a veneer of whiskers, and he'd been in trouble almost every other week when he himself had been in high school. His conversion had been as cliché-ridden as it was dramatic, and the junior high and high school kids loved him. He was one of their own.

Anderson could feel himself plummeting all over again. How could he compete? Who would bear him up? And when would he be substantial enough that even Jesus might see him?

Sweet Lou's rose out of nothing. "A goddamn oasis in the goddamn desert" read one sign a quarter-mile west of the exit. Anderson, who had been yawning and rubbing his eyes for some time, swerved onto the off-ramp, then bounced across the access road without looking for cross-traffic. It suddenly seemed very important to get to Sweet Lou's, order some coffee, move about in a space illuminated by the blue light of fluorescents, slide into a vinyl booth with a paper napkin dispenser on a Formica tabletop. To walk and stretch. Look at the pies in the display case, listen to the local gossip.

From the parking lot, the diner looked like a box of light.

"I need some coffee," he said to the girl. "You want a hamburg or something? Maybe Jake would eat a piece of apple pie."

"We're fine." She cradled the sleeping boy's head against her chest and neck, brushing the hair from the back of his head away from her mouth. "But we'll come in."

"Okay," he said. "Good. It'll be fun."

He locked the Mustang and checked both doors.

Sweet Lou's was all glass in front with booths exactly as Anderson had pictured. A lunch counter with stools ran across the length of the back. Anderson and Stacy and the boy were the only customers, except for a trucker in a corner booth with his cap over his eyes. His legs were up on the vinyl seat, his back against the window.

They settled themselves into a booth, and a thin man with a purple nose and a stained apron brought a towel to wipe the already clean table.

"You're traveling," he said. "I can tell."

"Yes, sir," Anderson said, "we are."

"Nobody had to tell me, you understand. Practically everyone I see is traveling. Plus, you have a youngster with you. Ain't nobody out here in this gracious-be-damned place under the age of fifty-seven."

"You must be Sweet Lou," Anderson said. "I'll bet you've seen a little bit of everything."

The man dipped his head as if he were embarrassed to be privy to so much human experience. "I guess so." He wiped his hands on his apron. "It's nothing so much."

Anderson ordered coffee, and the girl, after a moment's hesitation, did likewise.

With the boy still sleeping in her lap, Stacy worked her arms out of the parka, and for the first time, Anderson saw the silk blouse, the color of Pentecost. There were four gold bracelets on her right wrist that jangled when she moved her arm.

"What?" she said.

"Nothing."

Her right hand pulled thick blond hair away from her face.

"My wife says that I've developed a bad habit of staring."

For a moment, he caught that orange glow again, as if her face were now reflecting the flames of her blouse.

"I'm sorry."

She shrugged; she seemed accustomed to stares; stares were nothing.

He continued, determined to ask: "On the highway, you were standing, and the sun was behind you. For a moment, I thought you were . . ."

She was looking at him now, and he stopped, the words tasting like gravel in his mouth. How could he tell her that he had stopped only because he thought she had something to tell him?

"I was what?"

"I don't know," he said. "Not exactly."

"Did I remind you of someone?"

"I almost ran off the road."

"Yes," she said. "I saw that part."

The boy began to stir. His hand grabbed wildly for her chin. "No," he whimpered. "No, no, no, no, no."

"There, there," she said. She took her bracelets off, offering them to him.

"Lots of people tell me I look like someone else." She said this without vanity of any sort. In fact, she seemed somewhat despondent to be considered so lacking in identity. "But," she said, "I never am."

"Stacy," the boy said. "Stacy."

Sweet Lou held the coffee pot out over the table. "More?"

"Yes," Anderson said, "I'm almost awake again, but not quite." The girl nodded also. "Yes."

A weight shifted in his own mind. "I have to make a phone call. Excuse me," he said to the girl. "Excuse me," he said, as he squeezed past Sweet Lou and the thin man's coffee pot. "Excuse me, pardon me."

He left them sitting in the orange booth. She drank her cup of coffee and looked at the black windows as if she were dreaming. Jake seemed content for now to pour the salt and pepper into mounds contained by the bracelets.

The phone hung to the side of the lunch counter on a wall from which the paint had peeled in ribbons. Messages were abundant. Bertie wrote that any stud in the desert could fuck Darla Richardson if he wanted. An anonymous author declared all marines to be wimpy suckdicks. There were more. Anderson's head whirled. He dialed his own number collect, and when the operator asked for his name, for one frightening, unbearable second he couldn't tell her, as if he had cracked finally and completely, an irreparable break.

When Rebecca answered, his worry, now a day-old problem, seemed to unknot itself.

"I'll take the call," she was saying to the operator. Then, "Mark, what? Where are you? Is everything okay?"

"I'm fine."

"Where are you?"

"Tehachapi, I think," he said. "Maybe Mojave or Lone Pine." Above the counter someone had taped a banner that read *Sweet Lou's — best goddamn pie in the desert.* "I guess I don't know. I just stopped, that's all."

"Oh, Mark."

The concern echoing in her voice was a blue noise.

"I'm fine, Bec, really. I just got off the freeway for a second. For coffee."

He decided not to say anything about Stacy or Jake.

"Do you know what time it is?" she was saying. "It's after midnight. I thought you were the highway patrol telling me you were dead or dying somewhere because you'd fallen asleep and rolled down a hill."

She paused dramatically, and in the background Anderson could hear the theme music for Johnny Carson. "You're killing *me*," Rebecca said at last.

"I'm sorry. I just thought of you all of a sudden, I wanted to hear your voice, and I didn't think of the time. But I'm fine, I'm really fine, everything's going great," he said, "everything's going *perfectly*."

"You're sure? I don't have to worry?"

"Not at all."

"People have been calling all day. They didn't see you at services this morning, so naturally they all want to know how Pastor Mark is doing. 'Is he feeling more himself?' they say. They're like buzzards circling, ready to pick the carcass clean. I have a hard time knowing what to tell them."

"Tell them to mind their own goddamn business," Anderson said.

There was silence on the other end, then a wave of oceanlike static.

"No," he said, "I guess you can't say that."

"I can't, and I won't. But you knew that. Oh, Mark, why are you doing this?"

Anderson knew that despite her own statements of cynicism, she was at the point of tears. He was the lock on that particular Pandora's box, and she would live in torment if he were to allow the lid to fly open.

At their booth, Stacy was now looking toward him. Everything about the girl was noncommittal. She was waiting, but she had no expectations. She would not be surprised if he walked out of the diner without looking in her direction. She would not be surprised if he sprouted wings and flew away, becoming a small dark spot in the sky. She was that composed.

Rebecca put on another voice. Anderson could practically see her straighten her shoulders, stiffen her lips: "Call me when you get to your parents' house, promise?"

She was being so brave. The brave wife of the demented pastor. The effort to be civil, nearly made him nauseated.

"Yes, of course. The moment I get there."

"Or if you have trouble with that wreck of yours and you're going to be late."

"I'll call. And Rebecca?"

"Yes?"

"I'm sorry for everything."

The diner swam in front of his eyes with the force of this untruth, and when he hung up the phone, he did so with an odd sense of dislocation—that he'd been talking to his mother while traveling with his wife.

The headlights cut out a cave in the desert darkness. Anderson began to feel confined by the constraints of steering wheel, gas pedal, seat belt. He opened the window to frigid air. He tried the radio, but the only stations he could find gushed fundamentalist preachers or mariachi music.

"Can you say to yourself honestly," one of the preachers had said, "can you honestly say, 'I love Jee-sus'?"

"No," Anderson muttered, turning the radio off. "How about 'I am pissed off at Jee-sus'? Maybe, 'I'm tired of being used in the name of all-holy Jee-sus.'" He tried to imitate the sounds he'd heard, so that Jesus sounded like Cheez Whiz with ambition.

The girl shifted in her seat, reminding him that he was not alone.

"It's okay," he said, watching her watch her door. "I'm a minister."

The worst indignity was the tacit assumption by everyone— the church session, his wife, the youth group—that the fall had knocked a screw loose. True, he could not begin to explain the blue of the sky from the sanctuary roof, nor could he describe the sensation of falling as the ground rose up to meet him. Such things were beyond his power of utterance. Even less could he explain how off-center everything had since become. He had lost his capacity for charity and forbearance, refusing to suffer bores and boors and fools, of which in his congregation there were not just a few.

In two weeks he had managed to insult every group in church. He congratulated the choir for their performance in the Christmas cantata by complimenting their bravery in the face of such obvious limitations. He thanked the host of the Annual Young Marrieds Dinner for providing so much food—it was good to know that Christians could have a vice they could call their own.

When the church's unofficial matriarch, Lavinia Albright, confided to him her concern over the stray dogs and cats whose *ghastly* future the city was currently debating, he had responded without any internal check. "They ought to grind them up for fertilizer," he said, "and dump them in your roses." She had looked at him in horror before edging toward the coffee urn. As if it might provide her with protection from whatever contagion he would be likely to spread.

With his own wife, he had been even more ill-spirited. He had sent her sobbing to the bedroom when he told her that she was beginning to look like a whale—that not only did he notice the twenty-five pounds she'd gained since their wedding, but he'd noticed where the weight had gone.

"Lardass," he had hissed on one occasion, "Mistress Broad Beam."

He could not stand himself either.

And with the exception of Rebecca—who believed that only she could save him, regardless the abuse he heaped upon her—no one would beg him to stay.

"He's not mine, you know." Stacy nodded to the boy sleeping once again in her lap. "Jake. He's not mine, but you probably knew that."

"I thought you were a little young." A confused thought struggled to take shape in his mind. "Whose is he? We're not . . . I mean, you're not kidnapping him are you?"

"No." He glimpsed her frown in the green dashboard lights. "I wouldn't call it that."

"What would you call it?"

"A rescue."

"You're running away. And kidnapping someone's child. Sweet Jesus, I'm an idiot." He could feel his equilibrium begin to slip. "Goddamn it," he had practically begun to cry with frustration. "I fall off a roof, and now I can't think anything through."

She was shaking her head so violently that he could feel her denial in the sway of the car.

"I told you, it's a rescue."

He pulled to the side of the interstate. They had crossed the Arizona line an hour before. His crimes grew and grew. A truck and trailer roared past them, the backwash rattling the windows. Idling, the engine shuddered, the sound thready and tentative. There was every chance in the world it would die and not start again, and that would make the night complete.

He switched on the dome light. Her face, so serene earlier in the evening, now looked pinched and wan. Anger creased her pale forehead.

"I can't help you kidnap him. Or rescue him. Not without a lot more explanation."

She stared straight ahead. The boy twitched, pursued by some phantasm of dream. Wind blew dust across the highway.

"His mother doesn't deserve to have children."

"Why?"

"Because she'll turn him into a fool." She faced him. Her cheeks were wet, her eyes glistened. "Please drive. Just drive."

He pulled into his parents' driveway at six that morning, and his mother was standing on the porch with her arms crossed, her hands underneath her elbows, as if she'd been waiting half the night. Stars still littered the sky in a mindlessly cheerful array. The day's first cigarette, the end glowing like a poker, extended from her lips. At the bump of the car into the driveway, Stacy and Jake shifted into different positions in the backseat. At Kingman, Anderson had suggested they change, thinking it might be easier for them to sleep. He had also thought it might be easier for him to fall into that hoped-for road trance; he wouldn't think if there weren't the human presence in the front of the car with him. His mother stared at him from her position near the front door.

"Ma," he said. His voice sounded unnaturally loud in the dark early-morning air. "How are you?"

"Rebecca told me you were coming." She did not sound particularly pleased by the news or its fulfillment. "She's worried. She thinks you're off the beam."

"Maybe I am."

"Your behavior has been completely unacceptable."

"I can't disagree."

He suddenly realized that they were facing one another and speaking to one another from twenty yards apart, as if they were going to pull out pistols. "Ma," he said, moving to hug her.

His mother went up on tiptoe, peering through the windows of his car, trying to look into the back. "There's someone in there."

He stopped, looked back. Stacy's head rose above the front seat. "Oh."

"What else have you done?"

"They were hitchhiking, and it was getting dark."

"They?"

"There's a little boy," he admitted. "Jake."

"Mackie," his mother said, for the first time with some hint of tenderness in her voice, "what am I going to do with you?"

He shrugged. The hours on the highway seemed to have accelerated into this one moment, and he sagged with exhaustion. "The general awake?"

"He's stirring. You can talk to him after breakfast. After a little nap." She looked at him critically. "You look terrible."

The girl had maneuvered herself out of the car and was standing in the driveway.

"Ma," he yawned, "Stacy. Stacy, my mom."

Stacy pulled her hair behind her ears, then put out her right hand, the four gold bracelets jangling. Jake began to cry. His screams and sobs echoed throughout the street of neat tract homes.

"Stacy, Stacy, Stacy," the boy wailed.

"Mom," she said, "I've heard so much about you."

Anderson's stepfather, General Harrison Bourdet (USAF, ret.), rose at six-thirty each morning to do fifteen minutes of push-ups and sit-ups and thirty minutes of roadwork. He showered and shaved, and by seven-thirty he would be sitting down to breakfast. He believed in regimen as the most sensible prevention for uncertainties.

Anderson caught only a glimpse of him from the kitchen as he left the house in his grey sweatpants and T-shirt, a pair of yellow earphones indenting his gray crew cut, and by the time he returned, Anderson was fast asleep on the den couch. His mother, who had shown a degree of tact surprising to her son, had, without question or innuendo, ushered Stacy and Jake into the guest bedroom.

His sleep was riddled with fantastic dreams. There was of course the swan dive, but his repertoire seemed to have grown, for there were now also half gainers, a three-and-a-half with a twist, a simple jackknife. The environment was different as well; instead of the brown shingles and green foliage, he seemed to be diving against a background of flocked wallpaper, the medallions large and garishly colored. Jesus stood to one side, shaking His head. "Where the body is, there the vultures will gather," the Son of God said. He was wearing John Travolta's suit from *Saturday Night Fever* and snapping his fingers.

Anderson woke with a start, the sweat running down his sides, the back of his neck and hair dripping.

The general swiveled around in his desk chair. "Well?"

"Good morning, General," he mumbled. He squinted at a clock that read one-fifteen. "Or good afternoon."

"What the hell is the matter with you, boy?" The bristles of his stepfather's gray hair seemed to rise, signal of an imminent explosion. "Rebecca is ready to have you committed."

"I don't know. My head. I don't know."

"You know that your wife's called here seven times in the

last twelve hours while you're riding around with jailbait? You know that?"

He shook his head. "I didn't know she'd called."

His mother stood in the doorway and silently motioned for him to follow. At the end of the hallway, she pointed through the guest-room door. Stacy and Jake were curled in one corner of the queen-size bed. Both of them slept with their mouths slightly open.

"He's her brother," she whispered, "her half brother. They're exhausted, poor kids. Hitchhiking for three days, always afraid someone would turn them in. They aren't used to that sort of thing. They can stay as long as they like. In the meantime, you," she turned on him a savage look, "you need to go and find some real problems."

He stumbled back to the den.

"Here." The general threw him a faded pair of sweats and the pair of yellow earphones. "Quit thinking so much. You're not so goddamn important."

The general folded his arms over his chest, looking like a sultan whose gifts damn well better be taken, and Anderson, unbuttoning his shirt, slowly began to change.

Shades
of the
Prison-house

Strays

_____

After Scot is killed, Frank takes Connie, Scot's girlfriend, to the funeral, thinking it might be a way to score points. He hoses down his old mustard-colored Corolla, dumps the ashtrays, even repairs the four rips in the passenger seat. The morning of the funeral he gets a haircut, then buys a new shirt and tie in solid, dark colors. Scot had been a good friend, his best friend since grade school, but after all, dead is dead.

For her part, Connie has been acting a little glazed about the whole situation. She and Scot had never been real serious, but now, now that Scot's dead, she's been elevated: everyone expects her to act like the mourning widow in weeds, and life is supposed to come to some screeching, smoking-rubber halt, and that might be even more intimidating than the fact that Scot is indeed now dead and not just off somewhere on some fool backpacking trip. Which is the sort of thing Scot could do—like the evening he announced that he was going to walk to Mt. Hood and then hitchhike back, and that he was going to accomplish all this in the space of twenty-four hours. Fifty miles walking and fifty of thumbing rides. Jerry and Frank just laughed and said they'd talk to him later, like when he got to Sandy and tired of the whole thing. But they didn't hear anything, and then there he was, pulling up to the curb in the back of some farmer's pickup truck, asleep. The farmer went to the back, woke him up, then helped him down to the ground. His boots were off and his feet were bleeding, but he'd gone to the mountain and back, and he'd done it in a day.

But that doesn't mean Frank can't take Connie to the funeral. They both have to go anyway, the girlfriend and the roommate.

At the mortuary, the undertaker motions them to the waiting room. Connie looks right at home. She's practically been living here for the last three days, ever since the accident, and Frank imagines she knows every bit of the funeral business by this time; she could give guided tours of the place.

Scot's parents are already there and waiting, and they're ready to pounce. "Connie," Scot's dad says, "Connie." "Frank," Scot's mom says, "dear Frank." They shake hands, they hug, they say one another's names about a dozen times; then they stand looking at one another and shifting their weight from one foot to the next.

"Glad you could make it, kids," Sam Coldine says. He tries to make himself sound like the good dad complete with barbecue apron and beers in the reefer, no matter how indifferent he is toward Connie and Frank. Their respective parents are mediocre nonentities, and their prospects are even less promising; they're just two strays that Scot picked up.

"Wouldn't have missed it," Frank says. For that he gets a nudge in the ribs from Connie, a gesture he doesn't mind in the slightest.

Scot's old man is the hale and hearty type—white shoes, white belt, and curling gray sideburns. He's big enough that when he wears a tie there's no proof to his ever having had a neck. He has a glad hand and a booming—"ain't we having fun, yet?"—voice. He looks like the stereotype of a used-car salesman and acts the part, when in fact he's the largest manufacturer of optical lenses west of the Mississippi. A success. Someone who knows. Frank has never figured things out. He once went camping with Scot and Sam at Scot's request, and the three of them were drinking from a bottle of Jack Daniels, quietly getting drunk together. While it was happening, he could almost believe that he was on a level—equal, connected with Scot's assumption that the world was orchestrated for one's consumption and enjoyment. In the daylight, however, the connection was broken; he was again just a satellite orbiting around the Coldine planet of energetic enthusiasms, forbidden by the law of social gravity ever to land.

He would like to think that he was too smart to get greedy, to let himself hope for some sort of sign that he was regarded as something other than a parasite, but he knows now that he has *always* carried this buried wish: that Scot's dad would put his arm around his shoulders, tell him that he, Frank, was indeed one of the good guys. He also knows that he has failed somehow, in some desperate too-eager way—that with Scot gone, he can forget about the Coldine door swinging open ever again. The thought makes him want to slash Sam's tires.

Scot's mom, on the other hand, is one of those timid types, a mouse with dead brown hair who has been folding her husband's underwear for the last thirty years and still pretends he's some kind of demigod. She's Mrs. Loman with a lucky husband and never a doubt to test her loyalty. So Frank is not a little surprised when she puts her hand on his arm and says, "I blame him, you know." By this time there are plenty of other prostrate mourners in the room and Sam can spread himself out, deflect his own grief by treating his son's funeral as a summer cocktail party, mingling, playing the room, acting the good host. "No," Frank says, "I didn't know."

"Him and his motorcycles."

"It wasn't anybody's fault, Mrs. Coldine, except the drunk in the truck. If he'd been driving Sam's Caddy, it wouldn't have made a damn bit of difference."

When you are coming up the on-ramp to the interstate and get hit by a cement truck that is coming down in violation of all the driving laws known to man, a Sherman tank is maybe your only possible protection. What does it matter what you're driving when afterward the only question is how much twisted metal they'll have to pull apart in order to find what's left?

"If you want me to go after that son-of-a-bitch cement head, just let me know."

"Frankie, Frankie," she says. She makes his name sound like tsk-tsk, as if she is speaking to her other, more troublesome son. "He just had a light about him, don't you think?"

"You just let me know. I'd kill him." He is only jabbering, of course, killing the direction of Scot's mother's thoughts, unwilling as he is to start debating Scot's luminosity. But the words seem to be sufficient. He would like to be able to say something like, 'I'm sure Sam's going to miss him in the office,' something of the sort of thing that Jerry—Eddie Haskell in another life—knows how to get away with because he can say it with all sincerity while not believing a word of it. It's just not in Frank's vocabulary. If he tries, it will come out an insult, so he sticks with threats of violence, which seem like safer social territory. As it is, Mrs. Coldine pats him on the arm, then moves away to greet others of her family—more timid, sad-eyed mice.

The room is filling now, knots and clusters of sober-suited men and women, friends of Mr. and Mrs. Coldine's, all of them looking at their watches and darting quick looks at the door, wondering when the whole shebang is going to get under way. At the fringe of one of these groups, Connie sits on a metal folding chair, her knees together, her feet apart. She seems to be studying the heel of one shoe.

He grabs her hand. "Come on."

"I can't." She waves her free hand to indicate the room. "I should stay."

"They don't care. All they want is out of here. Besides, we can find out what chapel we'll be in."

She rises reluctantly, a tall girl in a borrowed, too-short black dress, who collects stares and ready-made disapproval from the dress-for-success-ers. The mortician is nowhere to be found, so they stand on the front steps, watching more of Sam's business acquaintances go trooping inside.

Outside, the air is golden and hot, perfect weather for a picnic or a softball game, a trip to the beach or a bike ride, a mockery of their purpose. Frank and Connie hold hands and create a nice little picture of the two friends comforting each other in their time of grief.

"It's such a sad and sorrowful day," she says in a voice she must have borrowed from the sixth grade, a voice used when confronting adults.

"It won't take long. Then it'll be over," Frank says.

He watches as the sides of her nose begin to quiver, and she begins to comb her fingers back through her hair. "Shit," she says. "I'm not going to cry."

He puts his arm around her shoulders, but she pushes him away.

"I'm okay. I don't want to cry. It's just when you say something stupid like that, stupid and mean, then I feel like I ought to cry, to make up for what you said."

"I just can't help thinking that once Scot's in the ground, it's over. All these dickheads will go back to their offices and wish they hadn't wasted the morning."

"Don't." She sits down on the steps, folding herself into a jack-knife of beaten reserve. "You just want to see me cry, don't you?"

"Yes." All of a sudden he wants to see her face collapse in a flood. That 'sad and sorrowful day' business has gotten to him. The feeling that this entire business has been scripted for them without consultation. He hasn't felt anything about Scot's death except guilt. He doesn't feel even the quiver of a tear. *My best friend is dead.* It doesn't work. He feels pissed off and horny when he looks at Connie. But Scot? Nothing. He finds himself humming some meaningless fragment and wondering when the rush will come. In the meantime there's Connie, who's got all the symptoms, and he wishes suddenly that he'd never seen this girl before. "Cry till your eyes fall out."

"You're such a shit." She starts to get up, and he can visualize quite a scene starting—the grieving girl widow running to the ladies' room in the funeral home, her mascara streaked into stars around her eyes; the shithead roommate getting a closed powder-room door in the puss. But before things can get too out of hand, Jerry and Tabitha arrive, Jerry pulling his father's Corvette into the space reserved for the hearse. "Is this the party?" Jerry says.

"You got it," Frank says. "This is it."

"Scot's dead, you know." Connie's lower lip is trembling, and her fingers are again raking her hair. "Scot's dead and all you dumb fucks can say is, 'Where's the party?'"

Jerry slaps her face lightly, a glancing, almost caressing type of slap. Just a touch. But Connie's face goes slack all the same, all the little muscles around her cheeks turning rubbery and soft.

"Don't try to hog it all, Connie," Frank says as softly as he can. You can push them and push them, and then, just when they can't take any more, if you're nice, they'll fall all over themselves with gratitude. It's cold, but that's how it is: Scot dies, Frank starts campaigning for Connie. Besides, he has seen her face turn to mush and he can't be angry at her for his own failing. He can't feel a goddamn thing. And he's tried. "You're not the only one who's trying to figure it out."

Connie crumples back to the steps, her head between her knees. "I hate him," she says. And now . . . now it hits *him* like a slap to his own face, but it is a different blow from the one he's been expecting. He remembers Scot, the morning after he first brought Connie to the duplex; he remembers him sitting at the kitchen table, his face smudged and blurred by his night's exertion, laughing about the little slut who was still sleeping in his bed, the little slut who snored like a truck. Frank remembers the Scot who could say the word *slut* and make it a term of near-endearment. He remembers thinking that Scot needed him, needed Frank, if for no other reason than that he needed the audience, that Scot needed Frank and the girl in the other room, who turned out to be Connie; he needed someone to whom he could condescend. Now, Connie has continued to say, "I hate him, I hate him, I hate him," but whether she means Jerry or Frank or Scot, it is impossible to say.

———————

Ultimately, Frank has to admit that Connie holds her end up well. After that little episode outside on the steps, she pulls the strings of her composure together, and no one hears any more high notes of manufactured grief. She holds his arm, going in and out of the church. After the funeral, they drive to the cemetery, and at the grave site, she rests her head on his shoulder and closes her eyes. They listen to more mumbo jumbo, then wait to see the coffin go down. But, evidently, they don't do that anymore. Frank thinks it would be nice to throw a clump of dirt on top of Scot; it would put a little finality on the day. As it is, they leave with the casket still resting in the shade of the awning, as if everyone has left before the party is over. Frank half expects Connie to face around backward in the car so she can watch the grave site as they drive away, turn herself into self-righteous salt. But she does no such thing. There's nothing to see anyway, just the casket and the awning and the community of the tombstones, and who knows what happens after dark? Even so, it doesn't stop him, as much as he tries not to, from looking in the rearview mirror; it doesn't stop him from waiting for some sort of *National Enquirer*–style miracle—"Best Friend Rises from Dead to Mock the Ravishment of Girlfriend"—something so out of this world that all of his doubts about the value of his own life are confirmed. As if by fucking Connie, Scot has now raised the ante beyond his reach. Nor does it stop Frank from whispering to himself, so low that Connie can't hear: *Ass. You're such an ass.*

Just because his best friend in all the world has just died doesn't mean Frank gets to take a day off from work. He would like to go off somewhere and get drunk or try his luck with Connie, but no way. He works at Widmer's in the mall next to the freeway, and although he broached the subject of time off to his crew chief, he knew it was a lost cause right from the start. He goes in at six in the evening, three hours before closing, and along with the rest of the janitors begins cleaning the executive offices up on the second floor. Then, at nine o'clock, when the customers have been chased out, they move out onto the floor and try to repair the damage that another day of consumerism hath wrought. At two o'clock in the morning, the doors are unlocked, the alarms momentarily turned off, and they are free to go, but there is always a security guard standing by the door, checking for suspicious bulges. It is not a place to inspire trust.

Tonight, Frank is in no mood for it. He sits in the executive can and smokes sixteen cigarettes down to the filters while he is supposed to be cleaning the office suite belonging to Mr. Donatelli,

Jerry's old man, who happens to be the vice-president of marketing and who also happens to be the one responsible for getting Frank this shitty job. Jerry also has an office upstairs, and Frank has been meditating for the last forty-five minutes on the sabotage that will occur tonight in honor of Scot. In his lunch bucket he has included—besides the usual bologna and cheese, potato chips, and forbidden bottle of beer—a nice, gray piece of three-day-old, unrefrigerated bass. The offices all have floor vents for the air conditioning, and Jerry's office has a vent right underneath his desk. It is a perfect coup, made even more so by the knowledge that Jerry would never rat, not even with dead-fish breath permeating his office air. It's a small rebellion but better than none at all.

Five minutes later he's replacing the vent cover when Lou Chabala, the crew chief, orders him down to the basement to break up cardboard in the compactor. Lou sniffs the air tentatively, but Frank is as bland and unfathomable as an angel.

Downstairs, Frank finds that Lou has teamed him up with Headcase Harry. Harry is a fifty-eight-year-old fruitcake from the VA on a life-experience furlough. It is the sort of program that looks good for Widmer's even though the VA pays them to babysit Harry for eight hours a day, and Widmer's gets a little work out of him besides. Harry is carefully slicing up cardboard boxes with a razor, then just as carefully placing them in the open jaw of the compactor. When the bin is full, he punches the red start button and waits outside the compactor room until the noise has subsided. Frank bides his time. When he sees that Harry has wandered over to the Coke machine, Frank slips into the compactor room, locks the start button into place, and when the jaw opens wide, slips a full box of fluorescent tubes into the open maw. Frank slips out, Harry wanders back inside. Suddenly, hellzapoppin in the compactor: sparks, lights, sizzles, dying electrical gasps. It sounds a little like gunfire from a distance. Harry comes tearing out, arms and legs clawing the air, his face ashen, his eyes bulging. His screams are those of a raped, homeless cat. Frank begins to laugh, but the humor cuts itself off before the ha-ha can make the freeway interchange between his throat and mouth. A dead fish in Jerry's office is one thing. This only has the makings of depression. Part of adulthood, Frank decides, is knowing the appropriate targets for revenge.

He makes it home, whipping his poor, gasping Corolla into the driveway at two-thirty in the morning. The August heat has settled like a buzzard in the trees, and even the air pouring through the car windows do not come close to alleviating the rank smell of vegetable summer. It is hard to picture Scot as now part of the soil's corruption and decay. Despite the late hour, lights are still on in the back half of the duplex, his own habitation. The front half, occupied by a retired couple named Cloud, is as dark as a tomb. Cars are double-parked up and down the street. Before he can get his key into the lock, the door flies open and Jerry pulls him into a party.

Even though Jerry is educated, college and culture and all that crap, he still lives with his parents and uses Frank's place whenever he wants to party or quick-bang Tabitha. Scot gave him a key. Now, there must be thirty people in the twelve-by-fourteen living room and eight-by-ten kitchen. Connie is not among them. Before he can say whoa, Frank finds a beer in his hand. And while he wants to ask what's going on, there is no silence in which to place the words. Instead, he squeezes through the sweating throng, down the hallway, and, slipping through the thinnest dark crack of the doorway, into Scot's room. The window is shut tight, and the air in Frank's nose smells like the second-floor fish. Connie is stretched out on the bed, face down. She is still wearing Tabitha's black dress, and the skirt has worked its way up to her hips. The reverberations from the outer rooms drum through the shut door. This figure on the bed is the epitome of absolute wretchedness. Unconscious, she can break his heart; a photograph of her now, in this position, could drive him to suicide. He is about to touch her when Connie rolls over, pushing her hair away. "I took Valiums, Frankie," she says, "and I feel ever so much better. I feel like I've been gift-boxed in cotton."

"Good. That's good."

"I never knew."

"What?"

"I never knew it felt so good." She sits up, hugs him around the legs. "I don't do drugs," she says in all seriousness, "you can't high when you're fly."

"That's right."

He pulls her arms from his legs, then settles her head back among the pillows. Like an idiot, orphaned child, she plays with her fingers in front of her face.

"Frankie?"

"What?"

"Scot. He didn't like me all that much."

Frank fights back the smile that is spreading across his face and the wave of gratitude he feels washing in from his stomach.

"Sure he liked you."

"No," she sighs, "It's a lot more complicated than that."

"Go to sleep," he says.

Just then, Tabitha bursts into the room, crying, "What's going on in here, you two?" Then, waggling one finger: "Ah, ah, ah!"

She is a silly girl, and Frank has, on more than one occasion, wished he could break her neck. What Jerry finds in her, other than a humping partner, he can't understand. Tonight her hair is the color of bricks. She speaks in whispers and shrieks and lisps. A little-girl pout hangs like a cigarette from her lower lip.

"Get out," Frank says. "Now."

"Touchy, touchy."

He begins to push her toward the door.

"Hey," Tabitha says, "what's the big idea?"

"Out."

"We're all friends here, right?"

"Out."

Frank grabs her around the waist and throws her across his hip, much as he would a particularly obnoxious child.

"Out," he yells to the crowded living room, while the babbling Tabitha says, "He means it, I think he really means it."

Jerry—red-faced, angry at being interrupted in his pursuit of a seventeen-year-old brunette with cantaloupes for tits who is already halfway out of her sweater—Jerry begins to go British, with an accent full of starch and offended propriety: "What is the meaning of this?" *I say*, Frank thinks, and after setting Tabitha into the trash can filled with ice and beer, he rips the needle across one full side of Jesus and the Mary Chain and the noise quacks and dies.

"Really," Jerry says, "that's really quite unnecessary."

"Party's over," Frank says.

Later, Frank watches Connie. In her drugged slumber, she snores like a storm drain, her mouth sagging open, a glob of spit zigzagging its way down her chin.

When he sits on the side of the bed, his weight sends the headboard thudding into the wall, the sound and movement promoting its own idea. "I'm sorry, really," he tells the unconscious girl, uncomfortably aware as he does so of how tarnished his chivalry is. "I'm sorry. What can I say?"

"You didn't get a helluva lot of sleep, did you?"

"I'm sorry," Frank says. "I got them out as soon as I could."

"I'm not talking about the party."

It is seven o'clock the next morning, and Joe Cloud is lying on his back underneath his '67 Rambler Cross-Country station wagon. Frank can see only Joe's black dress shoes, his white socks that look like remnants from a Goodwill sale, and the bottoms of his green khaki uniform pants. Just because he has emphysema and he can barely breathe, the Transit Company has forced Joe to retire from his position as a driver. So now, the Rambler gets its oil changed every four hundred and fifty miles while Joe and the Mrs. try to live on disability. The last few times Frank has been inside their half of the duplex, he has found Amway brochures littering the coffee table and the sofa.

"They're fuck-ups," Joe says. Looking up: "You too"; then, after another moment's consideration, "Maybe just half a fuck-up."

"Well, I don't think they'll be back for a while. And I'm sorry about the other."

"Connie's okay."

"Yeah."

"But those others." Joe lights a cigarette and struggles to a sitting position on the rollaway. "Those others are fuck-ups. Scot too. The last conversation I had with Scot was about his goddamn bed and his goddamn headboard. 'Put it in the middle of the goddamn room,' I told him. Fuck-ups."

"I know it, but I've known them for as long as I can remember."

He can't remember not knowing them, nor can he remember not being envious. Because even if they are fuck-ups, their asses are always covered and their feathers are always dry. From their money and their education, they know all the secrets; they know the way to the offices, all the things that Frank is afraid he'll never know. He'll always be a janitor in some store with lousy stuff. Fuck it. Fuck them. Year after year, hoping that something, some secret, would rub off. How did he get so stuck?

Joe leans his head back against the ice-blue skin of the Rambler. "When you gonna trade me cars?" he asks, the opener to a conversation they've had about a million times.

"I'd be stealing from you."

Joe wants to trade his mint-condition, impeccably maintained Rambler for Frank's mustard-colored ruin. Joe is bored by retirement.

"You'd be getting a sweet deal."

"I know it. That's why I can't figure it."

"Straight-six engine with overdrive, never gets above twenty-eight hundred rpm. You baby it on the freeway, she gets twenty-five miles to the gallon. New tires last month."

"I'll think about it."

"I'm just changing the oil now."

It's a process as mysterious to Frank as inherited income. Joe once tried to show him on the Corolla. Frank drained the oil, replaced the filter, funneled in the new four quarts of oil. The one thing he forgot to do was replace the drain plug. Joe came out of the front half of the duplex just in time to see the spreading brown puddle underneath the mustard-colored car. He said, "Hirohito's Revenge," and turned on one black dress-shoe heel. Since that time, Frank has not once changed the oil, checked the tires, or opened the radiator; he has taken a vow never to touch the innards of any automobile ever again, and he is waiting for the moment when the engine seizes, so he can kiss this testimony of his gross incompetence good-bye. Good-bye forever with dignity. Although by all rights he belongs on the fuck-up list as well, Frank understands that, in the strangest sort of way, his disintegrating car and his conscious refusal to do anything about it may be the two reasons Joe has for respecting him.

Three weeks later: Frank wakes, encrusted from the waist down in the dried sea rime of sex. Connie is lying on her side, breathing through her mouth, snoring with pharmacological abandon. She has discovered that she really and truly likes the Valiums, and he can no longer tell if her nightly dose is medicinal or recreational or simply, given all circumstances—Scot's death, his own need— the last, best escape. Frank can't sleep because of the heat: the windows are open but not a lick of air breathes through the screens. He also can't sleep because of Connie, who, besides making her shit-faced racket, also takes up more than her fair share of the bed. She's slept here for the past two-and-a-half weeks, and Frank wonders if, between the novelty of unaccustomed sex and Connie's vibrating palate, he will ever sleep undisturbed again.

Scot's folks came three days after the funeral and hauled his furniture away—the bed, the headboard, the dresser, the kitchen table, the sofas, the TV, all the pots and pans, and the vacuum cleaner, which Frank wasn't about to use anyway. They even took all the clothes hangers. They asked him if he wanted to buy anything before they set up the yard sale. They'd make Frank a special deal, they said. It made no sense, neither as purge nor greed. They are crazy, he can see that now, their grief manifesting itself in this war between their obsessive thrift and their insatiable appetite for the comforts of money. He will probably never figure out why Scot lived here, lived in this junky hole. Other than slumming, he can't figure it. To believe that his own personality could be so compelling would be dreaming.

Sam couldn't take the closet, so Connie's jeans and her T-shirts and her shoes lie in a heap in one corner of the closet in Scot's empty room while she sleeps in Frank's room on top of Frank. He would like to think that they are sleeping together for reasons of passion, but the absence of available beds is probably closer to the truth. He has a mattress but not much else; when he gets up now, he's walking through the litter and leftovers of the Coldine Transfer and Resale Company, out the screen door to the patio, there to watch the hot stars.

Actually, there is a third, simpler reason for his failure to sleep—time. It is only twelve-thirty. Tonight is the third week of cohabitation, but only the second week of sleep at such an early hour. In other words, this is the fourteenth day since he's been fired, and his body is still having a hard time getting used to the idea. Two weeks ago, he mounted the backstairs at Widmer's—the servants' entrance—in the presence of a familiar aroma. He opened his locker to find his fish, his aging friend, going grayer and greener by the minute. In its mouth was a folded, spindled, and mutilated payroll check marked "Final Compensation," a door key, and a note from Jerry containing suggestions for the demise of said bass. The suggestions were neither pretty nor possible nor, given his long-standing acquaintance with Jerry, predictable. The unpredictable is sucking him down a drain that he is not at all happy about.

And maybe a fourth cause of sleeplessness is also rearing its ugly head: Connie. The idea of Connie. *Be careful what you wish for*, he thinks. She's turning herself into a zombie, walling off her pain behind a dam of Valium, even as he struggles to feel anything. A great match. Maybe Mr. Coldine had it right: "You two kids look good together," he said, as he left with the last of Scot's stuff. "Everything will work out, you'll see."

Frank sees both sides of his meaning. Charity might say that Frank and Connie can be good for one another, that even in the midst of tragedy, there is an order and orchestration in the events. His own sense of what Sam means is this: he and Connie are just more of Scot's leftovers, more Coldine junk, not the sort of people for whom Providence exists. They don't have either the money or the position, and if his own son had to die in order to dump them, so be it. Frank can see it, too, in the indifferent stars that stare down at his patio night after night, stars that, in the eyes of Jerry and Scot and their kind—fuck-ups or not—form constellations and relationships and connections, but that in his eye hang separately, hundreds of thousands of cold miles away from one another. Orion, the Dipper—nothing but dot-to-dot pictures for adult children wishing to find order where there is, in fact, none. No connections. That's the thing with Connie and him. They're both strays. Both of them. And when you get right down to it, down to the bottom line and the fine print, where the rubber meets the road and the cement truck meets the bike, Scot and one bed and this one refuge for the abandoned are the only attachments they've got.

Mid-Clair

For weeks now, Grimshaw's wife has started each morning by consuming a pot of coffee by herself, memorizing the insults printed in the Living section of the morning newspaper, and repeating them to her husband, with Grimshaw as the butt of the joke.

"Is this normal? Can this be good for her?" he asked Clair's therapist.

The therapist, an older woman with varnished nails and a hideous suit of peach tweed, did not answer one way or another. "I told her to let go. She's too afraid of looking foolish, she regulates herself too much."

"Holy Christ."

"If your brains were in a bee, you'd fly backward," Clair reads. "You're cross-threaded between your ears."

Her laughter, when she reads the paper, is as harsh and artificial as a tinfoil Christmas tree, and when she recites her insults, she does so with the delivery of a schoolgirl reciting scripture on the second Sunday in June, a white presentation Bible on the line.

She wears a blue terry-cloth bathrobe and bunny slippers despite the heat of a seventy-degree morning. She claims that Grimshaw has, in the past, taken advantage of her while she slept, so now she refuses to wear anything revealing, much less to undress in front of him. Rather than be relegated to the guest bedroom, Grimshaw has taken to sleeping in the garage in the reclining front seat of his Buick, and he wakes up smelling of transmission fluid and the pine-scented air freshener hanging from the volume knob of the radio. Several mornings, their daughter Sophie has opened the Buick's door and shaken him awake on her way to school. She knows about her father's sleeping arrangement and goes out of her way to check the garage before she meets her bus. Whether she considers it unusual or aberrant for her father to sleep in his car while her normally oblivious mother has of late become host to sudden lightning strikes of rage, she does not let on.

"Good morning, Daddy," she says, kissing him on the cheek. "I'll be home after band practice." A freshman in high school, she lifts her flute case for his inspection, validating her claim.

"Have a good day, sweetheart."

He rubs the stubble on his chin with one hand while gripping the steering wheel with the other. Educated within an inch of his life, he is not unaware of the incongruity: that the three of them maintain this veneer of the familial even as he folds his pajamas to put them back in the glove compartment; that to kiss his daughter good morning he has fallen into the habit of turning the key in the ignition so the electric window will work; that there is some strange comfort in sleeping with the lawn mower, the electric hedge trimmer, and the other eager garden tools of summer.

Inside the house, Clair waits for him.

"You're walking around dead and don't know enough to lie down," she says.

"You'd think there'd be some sort of medication," Grimshaw

said to Clair's mother when, concerned about her daughter's welfare, the older woman came for a visit.

His mother-in-law looked at him through eyes untroubled by the gloom of thought. "A pitcher of margaritas and a ballgame would brighten your disposition considerably, I think. Never underestimate the power of the national pastime."

"Your lights are on," Clair says, "but nobody's home."

How has this happened? After marrying for sex and the satisfaction of his eye, Grimshaw has finally admitted what he has always known: that Clair—who is a beauty, a one-time pageant hopeful—possesses no great intellectual capacity. It is part of her essential charm. Blond, blue-eyed, and vacant, she is a gorgeous endorsement for stereotypes. Her oblique mind turns global turmoil into problems of diet and existential despair into a dilemma over hair-care products. A Ph.D. in American political history, Grimshaw has suffered his share of social distress in the face of Clair's pronouncements, but he has also been swamped by the desire to protect her from those who might judge her without the benefit of love, and he has been forced to recognize that her perspective on other people—if not events or ideas—often has a certain off-center intuition. He has had his own failures to face as well—the denial of his tenure at a college in Washington, his bankruptcy, following a short stint as a stockbroker, which led to his lowest point as a salesman of new and used cars—and he sometimes wonders whether or not those failures were in some measure his own attempt to demonstrate his understanding of his lovely wife's sense of inadequacy.

You see, he might as well have said, *we're in the same boat; we both have known disappointment*. But then, isn't claiming such extreme empathy just another way of blaming her rather than himself?

Ten years later, he has at last found another teaching job. A junior college in the homely, impoverished heart of California. It is not university teaching, but then it is not selling Audis either. And while he can say with certainty that Fresno is not Seattle, he has not yet found another town that is inferior by comparison, except possibly Bakersfield, which is a little like comparing the two hard-boiled eggs left over from last Easter.

Materially, their fortunes have been restored, at least brought to some point of equilibrium; even so, he can date Clair's dissatisfaction from the time of their move. The changes are radical and easily documented. Once as lethargic and contented as a farm animal, she is now an insomniac with a wild look and puffy skin around her eyes. Normally choosing silence to mask ignorance, she has become as voluble as a radio commentator. Although she used to surprise him with her sudden bouts of sexual energy— especially when company had come to visit, as though an audience in the next room brought out her best performances—she has begun to refuse him with a finality that brooked no discussion. She initiated therapy with Dr. Felder at no one's prompting but her own, and since she started her weekly sessions, he's felt double-teamed. The Buick is not so unwelcome, after all. It is his own. He drives to work in it. His nightclothes are there. He shaves with an electric razor that plugs in to the cigarette lighter. He washes in the utility sink next to the recycling bins. He gets by and begins to think of it as home.

Clair eats a bran muffin with her coffee and says, "Your IQ is two points above plant life. You were born stupid and lately you've had a relapse. You'd buy hair restorer from a bald barber. The chip on your shoulder is from the wood above it. When God passed out brains, you thought He said trains, and you said you'd rather fly."

From his opened office window, the rat-a-tat-tat of drums floats from the football stadium at the high school. Benign machine-gun fire. Marching bands practice year-round, he has discovered, even when there is no game to act as sandwich. A picture of Sophie—high-stepping in gym shorts, her flute held poised, inches from her lips—comes and goes in the space of a drum beat. The late spring air, filled with warmth and sound, rolls through his window, engulfing him in a tide of misery that he is at loss to explain for its particularity.

He has called Dr. Felder for the second time in as many weeks with the same unsatisfactory result.

"I respect the confidentiality that exists between yourself and my wife," he said, "but you have to admit that I'm affected too."

"Of course," the psychologist said, and Grimshaw imagined her leaning back in her chair, tensing the painted nail of her index finger against the equally garish nail of her thumb.

"I can't sleep in my car forever."

"And I can't tell you what you want to know, Dr. Grimshaw. Clair will have to tell you that, but suffice it to say, she does not need you to overreact. And sarcasm will only be counterproductive."

"She insults me every morning."

"Surely you know how damaged she is, how disadvantaged she feels. Her method for balancing the teeter-totter is to insult you. It's not too much of an accommodation for your own healthy ego, now is it?"

What could he say? He could think of nothing then; he can think of nothing now.

Clair rises from the jumble of ungraded papers on his desk. Her opaque blue eyes do not regard him so much as look past him, look through him. "You're so stupid," she recites, "you think the law of relativity will keep cousins from marrying."

Down the hall from his office, there is a class waiting for a lecture on the immigration policies of the 1920s and the case of Sacco and Vanzetti. The students, their postures reflecting a loose-limbed, open-mouthed spectrum of boredom and impatience, will groan audibly when he opens the door, not because they actively dislike him or the class but because they are fulfilling some ancient pledge that—he is certain of it—has been genetically refined in generation after generation. Spring is here, the air is warm, let Sacco and Vanzetti die already. The drummers hammer away, and the brassy notes of trumpets arrive in their own time, jumbled by the wind into the discordant union of distant noise.

Every semester, though, there is a new crop of little birds who keep him intrigued in his classes and in his work—girls fresh from high school and young women fresh from motherhood and divorce—but until this spring he has never before been tempted beyond trivial speculation. For all her faults of logic and intellect, the mere sight of Clair has kept him locked in the grip of virtue. But this semester, in the vacuum created by Clair's anger and withdrawal, there is someone, an advisee, of whose romantic overtures he has, thus far, been able to feign blindness. Divorced twice in four years, Desi Amador has once again returned to school. Other instructors speak of her more as a member of the staff than a student. Since her last failure in marriage, she has developed a passion for presidential campaign trivia, seeing in the eager coupling of America with her politicians a failure of matrimony at least the equal to her own. A redhead with ironic green eyes, she possesses a cache of finely honed cynicism that he recognizes. She could be, he thinks, Clair's opposite. Where Clair was once silent in the face of her own obliviousness, Desi is effusive with analysis and quick to judge. Clair's perfect contours are a contrast to Desi's figure, the lines of which carry hints—a bulge here, a swelling there—of a future slattern. Clair is a habitual taker of showers, morning and night, whereas Desi, who takes a rather negligent attitude toward hygiene, often exudes odors that, to Grimshaw's olfactory sensibility, signify exotic origin. Ordinarily unattracted to women with red hair, Grimshaw has discovered himself lost in the lively skepticism of Desi's eyes and in the promise of conversational give and take. He is also—he would confess it—desperate for love and the approval of another breathing soul.

She is there, in attendance on the day of the lecture on Sacco and Vanzetti, a day in which he feels as though, with her as the lone exception, he is speaking to the walls, and such is the torpor of the rest of his students that he allows himself the kind of evangelical fervor he usually associates with the preaching seen late at night on cable access: "To say that Sacco and Vanzetti were naive martyrs may be a gross oversimplification; their political ideology did, to some degree, compromise their innocence. However, by today's rules of evidence they would have undoubtedly left the courtroom free men. Instead they were executed, political expediency being the primary motive, not unlike the Rosenbergs, whose punishment greatly exceeded the extent of their crime. All of which is to say that national phobias *ought* to induce in those who are educated the greatest caution instead of the greatest reaction. Whether the target is immigrant, anarchist, communist, Jew, African American, Asian American, Native American, Buddhist, Muslim, Baptist, or cultist, we have a duty as citizens to defend those who have been persecuted for their differences from the majority."

And then the clock mercifully signals their freedom and his. His students yawn. They collect their books, and Desi says, "Amen, brother," in good-natured sympathy.

Under the guise of asking advice about baccalaureate and graduate programs, she invites him to coffee at her apartment, an invitation he knows well enough to refuse but does not, carried along by a sense of inevitability that under normal circumstances he would find ludicrous. She lives in one of the dank student hovels that line the perimeter of the college, a squat cinder-block affair that lends even greater squalor to Desi's notion of housekeeping. He obeys her instructions and throws clothes from the couch to the floor in order to have a place to sit—"Anywhere," she says, "throw them anywhere"—and as he does so, he contemplates with wonder the back of this younger woman now filling a teapot with water from the tap in her closet-sized kitchen. The red hair, bound by a rubber band in a bushy braid, traces the line of her spine. A green tank top, the color of which reminds him of those shrewd eyes, allows one wing of a small butterfly tattoo to wave from her right shoulder blade. Her shorts, her bare feet, her olive skin, the thin gold ankle chain— what a difference fifteen fewer years can make! Youth—so at ease in the poverty of the present, in which the imagination of better days is possible. At some point, following the denial of his tenure, he lost that pleasant gift for daydreaming a better, more ideal life. He knew then that his life would follow a predictable, disappointing course, that his past energies of ambition and hopefulness would only be recast into the toil of bill paying and the suppression of dimly remembered dreams.

In such a state, in which the abscesses of self-pity and regret have been reopened, he rushes eagerly to fill the space created by Desi's generous openings, no better than the fatuous boys she has already tried and rejected as husbands. And when they retreat to the dim shadows of her bedroom, he pretends an experienced moral disinterest that exists only in the make-believe of his most idle fantasies. On the unmade bed are more clothes to throw to the floor, and in a brief pause in their exercise of pulling clothes from each other's limbs, she extends to him a packaged condom without a trace of guilt or embarrassment, a meticulous gesture of premeditation for all the disorganization implicit in the rest of her personal history, a badge of how suspect, how carefully monitored, sex in these troubled times has become. Even as they arrange themselves together, his responses to her gifts of flattery and sex sicken him—the too-hearty male laughter, the tone of knowingness that masks nothing, his off-handed assurances to himself about the minimal importance of fidelity. He is passing off this most profound indiscretion with the rationalizations of the habitual offender—"My wife is nuts, we've never been well matched, we're in the process of separating"—explanations that wildly overstate the distance between sanity and unhappiness, between their bedroom and his garage, a distance that causes him, while Desi moves to the rhythm that he is now setting, to remember Clair's latest assessment: "Your brainstorms are drizzle and fog. You're as intellectually impotent as a castrated cortex."

The blinds in Desi's apartment are always banked against the sun, and for a place that is baked by sunshine and heat nine months of the year, it smells curiously mildewed, like a bunker, a tyrant's last refuge underground. Each Monday, Wednesday, and Friday afternoon, after class, they walk across the street like shift workers home from the mill, unlock the dead bolt on Desi's paper-thin front door, then grapple with one another until the dinner hour. Desi lectures and questions, even during sex, as though conscious of a shortage of time.

"Did you know that Lincoln ordered his musicians to play 'Dixie' the first time he visited Richmond?" Desi asks her question while guiding his hands and his face to her breasts. "Some Great Emancipator."

Grimshaw has heard the story before but never during foreplay, and his attentions are prone to wander; at any other time but this, he could justify Lincoln's choice as a symbol, a conciliatory gesture after a long and bloody war. Indeed, this is a continuing problem: this habit Desi has of conversation—generally at the most inopportune moments—that he must either correct or swallow. It makes him too much the teacher with too short a lectern. Who could guess that in this moment he would yearn for Clair with an ache that is as academic as it is visceral?

Desi has also begun to take liberties that Grimshaw finds frightening. Her attitude in class is by turns patronizing toward other students and intimate with him. She has, on at least one occasion, called him honeybunch while contradicting him, and a nervous titter of laughter ran about the room like a wave. She calls the house at odd hours, pretending—when Clair or Sophie answer the phone—to be taking a survey or offering a free gift or simply to have dialed a wrong number. She never hangs up without speaking. In one of the oddities of his house, there are phone jacks in every room, including the garage, and at two o'clock one morning Grimshaw answers the phone next to his workbench, his feet dancing on the cold concrete, Desi's voice breathless in romantic parody: "I didn't wake you, did I, honeybunch?" while a cough echoes in his ear.

"Clair?" he calls. "Clair? Is that you?"

He hears a receiver being placed on its hook, and then Desi's voice again. "Just me and the chickens, sweetheart."

Such incidents are enough to convince him that he is not suited to the life of a philanderer, even if Clair has declared herself unavailable, and following finals—the week of his mother-in-law's visit—he breaks off with Desi while sitting on a pile of her dirty clothes.

"Nothing has changed at home," he says, "but I just can't do this anymore."

He goes on to list the various reasons for his failure to maintain the relationship. He does not spare himself, says the fault lies with his own fear of living in a situation that is morally ambiguous at best; even so, her mouth curls when he says that it's over.

"Well," she says, "at least I didn't marry you."

That night the silent darkness of the garage is broken when the passenger side door opens and the Buick's dome light comes on.

"What?" he fumbles. "What is it?"

His seat is reclining against the bench seat in the back. His head lies against the headrest and the pillow that he has spirited away from his bed, the sheets of which he has not seen in weeks. At first, the light and sound are merely equal parts of a turbulent dream about that first afternoon with Desi and his peroration on Sacco and Vanzetti, especially Vanzetti, whose radical distrust was leavened by a dumb peasant faith in the blindness of justice. The sound of the door opening and closing, the light going on, then off, are portentous of the chairs that wait for the two men. Guilt and not-guilt. Why should he be allowed to sit outside their windowed room?

A hand touches his face. Fingers undo the drawstring of his pajamas. "Bobby."

"What? What is it?"

Clair has come to him naked, like a vision sprung from a dream, and after they have maneuvered from front seat to back seat, he traces her perfect hips and haunches, catches her nipples between his teeth. Her pale stomach has the luminescence of birch trees by moonlight, and he longs to immerse himself in the middle of Clair, his perfect Clair, the flesh of her abdomen, the ridge of her rib cage, the wings of her hips, the abstraction between her thighs. Her presence here seems like compensation, divinely granted, for his decision of this afternoon, and when he kicks open one door that they might have more room, the dome light bathes them in the dull gold of reward.

"No, no, no," Clair moans. "No lights."

"But sweetheart," he says, "Buicks are big cars but not that big."

"Please?"

He closes the door, condemning them to love with bent knees.

"We could go to bed," he says, attempting to keep hope from overwhelming his voice. "We could be comfortable."

"No."

Afterward they curl together in a sweaty, awkward tangle, and she says, "That was lovely."

"Are you through being angry then?"

She considers her answer for a long time. "No. Not yet."

"Can we at least go into the house?"

"No," she says, "you would just want us to sleep together, but you've been very mean to me. And we shouldn't really sleep together—like in the house—until I can tell you everything that I think without you laughing. Ginnie—Dr. Felder—says that I have to remember how angry I am. I can't tell you how much I hate saying my opinions and then listening to somebody laugh, especially when I'm not supposed to hear. That's the worst. I have a lot of good ideas, but no one will ever listen to me, like the idea I have for an attachment to a can opener that will squeeze the lid on a can of tuna fish so the oil won't get on your dress. Mother thinks that I'm silly, but that's a good idea don't you think?"

"Very good," he says, understanding for the first time that Socrates's use of agreement only delayed the perception of pain by the one receiving it. Still, he can't help himself. "I think that's a lovely idea. I'd never thought of it myself. There's probably some real money in that."

"You think so?"

"Of course."

Her observations pour out in a torrent: "I think that certain drivers ought to have training wheels, you know, teenage boys with bad haircuts and old women who need cushions to see over the steering wheel, and I think that lingerie designers should make shoulder straps that don't cut grooves into your shoulders, and if you get a grocery cart with a wheel that wobbles, the store should give you a coupon for something free."

He grunts his assent to each new evidence of her imagination, his voice a chorus for her encouragement.

"I have so many ideas," she says, "that sometimes I have trouble sleeping at night. Not like you. You snore like a storm drain."

"It may have something to do with my present accommodations. Which your mother may find a little bit odd, don't you think, my sleeping in the car?"

"She didn't say anything."

A nagging question comes to him. "When did I ever laugh at you?"

She is about to answer when the phone on the workbench begins to ring. Grimshaw lets it go, hearing in the metallic jangle only a wedge into what he hopes is reconciliation.

"Who could be calling in the middle of the night?"

Clair bites her lips. "It could be an emergency," she says.

"I suppose."

He picks up the receiver just as the phone stops ringing, and he hears Sophie's voice cautiously saying hello on another extension.

"That's all right, sweetheart, I've got it," he says.

Desi—of course it's Desi—says, "The daughter of honeybunch, I presume?"

"I believe you have the wrong number," he says, "and it's very late, too late to be making prank calls."

"Daddy?" Sophie says.

"I have a right to call. Whenever I want."

"Just hang up, sweetheart."

His mother-in-law also comes on the line. "Who is this?"

"What is it, Bobby?" Clair is standing next to him, shivering, holding herself with her arms.

"Just hang up," he says again to his daughter.

"Just hang up," he says to his mother-in-law.

"Wrong number," he mouths to his wife.

"I see how it is. Everything back to normal at the Cleaver household? Moved out of your garage, have you? So much for your fine moral sensibilities."

"I'm hanging up now, Daddy."

"So am I," Clair's mother says.

"Don't go, Ward, I'm not through with—"

He gently places the receiver in its cradle.

"What a strange call," he says to his naked wife. "What a strange, strange call. Everyone on the phone with a wrong number."

"You're so full of hot air," she says. Her voice has returned to that starchy singsong of rebuke as she opens the door to the house; it is clear that Clair intends that she and only she will go through it, but her arm movements indicate that he is still required to play a part. "You're so full of hot air," she repeats.

"How full am I?"

"You're so full of hot air, you get an energy credit every time you open your mouth."

The door remains cracked open. "You're so full of hot air," she says again.

"How full?"

"You're so full of hot air, you need a dirigible license to speak. You're so full of hot air—"

"I'm not playing anymore."

"You're so full of hot air," she insists.

This is supposed to be therapy?

Through the open doorway, he can hear Sophie talking to herself in her bedroom.

"How full am I?"

"You're so full of hot air," she says, closing the door and locking it, insulting him for the first time, he realizes, without a punch line.

By midsummer, Sophie greets her father every morning at the breakfast table. She and her mother eat healthy breakfasts as prescribed by Dr. Felder—dry, coarse-grained breads and tart fruits, the sight of which is enough to make him gag. They read the paper together, sharing the insults in which Grimshaw is only mentioned in the third-person.

"If ignorance is bliss, Daddy must be the world's happiest man," Sophie reads.

"Your father is often lost in thought," Clair says, "because he's a stranger there."

"Daddy should never let his mind wander—" Sophie begins.

He can take no more. "Enough!" he cries. "Enough, enough, enough."

"I have a joke for you, Daddy," Sophie says. "How many historians does it take to change a light bulb?"

"I don't know," he says, "thousands?"

"One maintenance worker to change the bulb, and two scholarly forums—one to give arguments for the old bulb, saying it hadn't really burnt out, and the other to defend the new bulb's right to profit from the sufferings of another. See, Daddy, it's a revisionist joke. I know it's not very funny yet, but I'm working on it."

He nods his head and attempts a smile for her benefit, even as Clair turns her back on them to pour sugar on her own bowl of fruit.

Lately, he has been waking up with nosebleeds, bright red flowers dotting his pajamas. Blood drains down the back of his throat, and he wakes as he tastes the salty, forbidden flavor of himself. His doctor cauterizes the likeliest sites, then throws up his hands.

"Stay out of the heat," he says, "use a humidifier, pinch your nose at the bridge when it starts to gush, pack it with tissue, and apply ice. There's not much more I can do."

The first morning he wobbles into the kitchen, blood draining off his hands and arms.

Clair's mouth drops open. "Bobby, what is it? What's wrong?" She begins to move toward him until she hears her daughter's voice.

"It's okay, Mom. Daddy was finally hit by an idea."

How long will he have to put up with this?

The nosebleeds become just another entry in his log of complaints for his weekly call to Dr. Felder.

"That garage is killing me," he says. "One of these mornings I'll wake up, and there won't be any juice left, just pulp."

The doctor pauses. "What deceptions are you hiding, Dr. Grimshaw? Is this the form that Pinocchio takes in you?"

She does not let him hang up until he has agreed to participate in a group study she is conducting. She has a free hour at four and he must come. He hems and haws, but she is insistent, and in the end he folds. Yet why is it, he wonders, that every personality disorder comes with a Disney character attached?

So this is how he will spend his summer: bleeding in his sleep at night while during the day he talks to a psychologist about how his nosebleeds are symptomatic of his need to declare the truth even as he distorts it. Dr. Felder will take copious notes on this puppet of impulse who hopes someday to be a real boy.

There is one more thing. He receives notice from his dean that a former student, Desirée Amador, has filed sexual harassment charges against him. It is the dean's suggestion that Grimshaw meet with the student and himself to see if a settlement can be reached before the case goes to court. The dean's memo is typed on the school's blue letterhead, and the longer that Grimshaw looks at it, the more suffocating it becomes.

This can only be the last straw, can't it?

He tells Clair that a situation has come up, a legal matter, that they may have to cut their expenses to pay for lawyers.

"We may need to take a break from Dr. Felder," he says.

"Oh, Bobby," she says, "baby." She reaches out for him. "I don't need to see her anymore, but I think maybe you do."

She rubs his temples with her thumbs, and he remembers that the morning after Clair's visit with him in the garage, her mother opened the Buick's door and said, "Maybe you need a chiropractor or shiatsu massage or a trip to Mexico." The older woman's gray hair was flying, and she was clearly worried about him.

"What's the difference," Clair murmurs now, "between your brain and headcheese?"

His anxieties balloon in his stomach, and no answer presents itself. "I don't know," he sighs.

She smiles for the first time in weeks, her expression an equal mixture of joy and cruelty; her voice, though, is triumphant: "And you thought I was dumb."

The Whole Lump

Being the confessions of a lesser known,
albeit also fallen, minister of the gospel

I saw the picture during my illness. The author, staring from the back cover of the dust jacket, smiled crookedly at me through my antibiotic haze. I knew he was dead, and I had seen the picture before, but his visage, immortalized in this way, affected me so strongly that I began to cry; I have officiated at the funerals of strangers, which extracts from me the gestures of professional compassion, and I have eulogized friends and relatives while maintaining my professional reserve, but now I wept in such great shuddering bursts that Elaine, passing through the living room with a load of warm clothes in her arms, enveloped me in an embrace that smelled at the same time of Estée Lauder and Tide.

"There, there," she murmured. "He's just a little sickums," she cooed.

"Daddy needs his rest," she said when Danny—our nine-year-old and a tough little nut—said with a sneer that he had seen me cry. How could he have not seen? My eyes were awash, my nose a faucet, my whole being in direct opposition to the image of Presbyterian decorum and order.

"Stop it," she finally hissed. According to the clock, she had allowed me two full hours of self-indulgence. "Things can't be that bad."

She was right, of course. I had a fever and an infection, brought on by my own doing. But then I wasn't crying from the fever, which was real enough, or from some ambiguous, drug-induced regret, but from the very specific sorrow that, unlike the author on the back cover, my time had not yet been concluded. Providence was merely letting me hang, His severity proving far more gentle in this temporal life than His kindness.

On the other hand, the author had received his just reward immediately after his conversion. A virtual alcoholic, he and his liver had been failing for years. He was a three-pack-a-day smoker, and his medical records indicated heart disease and emphysema. Rumored to be a homosexual, or at the very least sexually ambivalent, he had died before AIDS could catch him in its tidal wave of notoriety. Instead, he had died of pneumonia from a cold caught during a fishing expedition—safe, beyond-recrimination, morally unambiguous pneumonia. After living a life twice as hard and twice as long as he had a right to expect, he had declared himself a sweet Christian, and *bingo*, dead as a housefly under the swing of the cosmic swatter. Who says His forgiveness leads to earthly benefit?

So I wasn't surprised by my own situation. My illness had come quickly enough. One day while I mowed the grass in the backyard, a rosebush (that symbol of love, which for my perversion can only have ironic significance), leaning out beyond its planter to catch the sun, hooked me and held on. The skin on the back of my left hand ripped, and I finished my chores, feeling bloodied and abused.

A day later the tip of my middle finger had swollen to the size of a grape, a lump the size of a walnut had formed in my elbow, and in my armpit I found another growth, this the size of a lemon. I could not sleep on my left side because of these sudden strange fruits, and two nights later at three-thirty in the morning I woke up, my pajamas soaked in a night sweat. I was suffering the heat and hallucination of a high fever, and facing my wife who slept beatifically, I prayed for death in the presence of her gentle snore.

I knew why this was happening to me, and her name was Diana Wales. A temporary replacement for Mrs. Brondiglio (our blue-haired office harpy, whose hemorrhoid surgery kept her from her secretarial duties for a blissful eight weeks), she was . . . and here I wish that you might hear my long, expiring sigh . . . beautiful. Her short hair was blond and light and fine, inviting a hand to touch the exposed back of her neck. Her body was of a type that has been out of style since the early nineteen sixties and the death of Marilyn Monroe; as I watched her move (and oh, how I watched her—surely there was no more devoted General Halftrack, no more oblivious Miss Buxley), I caught her in those secret little stumbles, those momentary acts of awkward gracelessness that voluptuous women are prone to, as if the body, through no fault of its own, with too much sexuality to guard, loses the capacity to coordinate itself. For two weeks we conducted a good-natured working relationship that bordered on flirtation at lunchtimes, and I succeeded in convincing myself that developing a friendship with an attractive, unmarried woman was an easily passed test of fidelity, not an invitation to evil. No Swaggart in Presbyterian drag was I! I knew her faults and accepted them. She was not a brilliant conversationalist; her mind was good but easily distracted by tangents, diverting her away from the highways of dialogue and into the alleys of word association. At times her youth betrayed her; confiding in me her dreams of becoming an operatic diva or a model or a clinical psychologist, she spoke with that breathless self-absorption that only a woman in her early twenties can manufacture. Seeing these flaws only served to reinforce my belief that I was firmly on the other side of that invisible line, that demarcation of maturity that separates the ranting evangelist from the theologically sound. I had mastered that banal demon of the daydreaming promiscuous self; I could be friendly but dispassionate with an attractive woman.

As it turned out, I was merely the victim of self-deception. On her last Friday afternoon, the last, sweet breath of spring before the return of grim Mrs. Brondiglio and her foam-rubber doughnut, Diana invited me to her apartment for an iced tea. She wanted to celebrate, she said, the start of her vacation; she was leaving the next afternoon on a cruise of the Mexican coast. And it took no more than thirty seconds in a more intimate milieu before (choose one):

a) we laughed, admitting to each other our confusion over how we should behave,
b) we were, in a four-handed frenzy, ripping each other's clothes, or
c) uninvited, and without provocation on her part, I was fumbling with the straps of her sundress, responding mechanically to language only half-heard—*Acapulco, sunbathing, lotion.*

The correct answer is *c.*

Of course.

In the sunlight from an open window, her shoulders sparkled. I think I wanted to eat them.

"What do you think you're doing?"

I didn't know.

Until that moment I had been acting like a somnambulist, aware of my dreams, unaware of my own participation. Her voice was an alarm, but I was not yet awake. I brushed those shoulders, easing toward the neck.

"I love you," I said.

The words jumped from my mouth, circled the room once, and then, like some falling angel, plummeted to the floor at my feet, a smoking heap of good intentions rendered flightless by stronger desire.

"No," she said, "don't even think about it."

"Really," I said. "Really."

"You, too," she said. "Well, you're the last one I would have suspected. I guess I shouldn't be surprised.

"You're married, too," she said. "You seedy little man."

We were standing in her kitchen. Our glasses sat on the tiled counter. Sunlight from the window above the sink pierced the tea in each glass and exploded into its elemental parts. She readjusted her straps.

"I'll tell you what I tell all of them. I'll tell you what I want. To enjoy a man's company. Is that so much?"

She grabbed my tie, yanking it up so the knot was pressed in, way up, underneath my Adam's apple, digging into the flesh of my neck. I felt my face turn red; I heard the sound of my blood stopping. "I don't want lovers. I can get lovers."

"I surrey," I croaked.

From a drawer she pulled a pair of silver scissors, and finally, I was awake.

"No," I said. "Pliss."

And then, all that was left of my tie was the knot, so tightly pulled that half an hour later I was begging—in half a voice—for a service station attendant to cut me free.

"What the hell," he kept saying.

"Don't ask," I said when the noose was gone, "I can't even begin to explain it."

But later, when Elaine asked what had happened to my tie, I told her that I had thrown it away, having dragged it through a bowl of gazpacho at lunch time, an explanation as unsatisfying to her as it was to me. For we had both seen the bruises on my neck.

A day later I was mowing the lawn.

I had never before allowed myself, much less initiated, an opportunity to jeopardize our marriage, and now some long-dormant seed of medieval flagellantism germinated inside me along with the infection. Could there be, I reasoned, some longing for a fundamentalist's hair shirt that I had never known before? Could I so desperately love my guilt the way one's tongue loves to pester a loose tooth? I refused to see a doctor, although our congregation includes more than its share of physicians. I drove to church each morning, one hand on the steering wheel, the other wiping my forehead with a bath towel. Each time I passed a truck bearing flammable liquids, I composed a prayer for conflagration.

For amazingly enough, rather than despising the absent Diana, hating her as the source of my rejection and humiliation, I found that those moments in her kitchen had only scratched the mosquito bite of an obsession: I saw her everywhere; her car populated every space on every road; her scent lived on in the air conditioner. Was there a crueler joke—to rise from my study in response to that olfactory memory only to find in the outer office a pinched and squirming Mrs. Brondiglio? My hand reached for the telephone at least ten times a day: I could call the ship; I could talk to her; I could make her understand. I had to restrain myself from entering a travel agency and demanding a ticket for a cruise already half-completed. I was the victim of irrational urges, and no matter how well I argued, my desires ran counter to rational choice. I found no comfort in *The Book of Order*. I only hoped that my death—by immolation or sudden tumor—would be merciful and swift and that I would never have to confront Elaine's silent stare, or even worse, a session of congregational forgiveness.

Finally, decisions were made for me. Against my objections, Elaine bundled me into the car one night and drove me to the emergency room. I was too weak to argue. My fever was 104. I had been sweating so steadily that even her side of the bed was clammy, and this, I think, was the final straw.

The young resident who examined me seemed to have just come from his junior prom. His eyes, magnified by his glasses, were omniscient and condemning. I felt that he was waiting for my first false move.

"I don't know what's the matter with him," Elaine was saying. "He's been sick and sweating for a week, and he won't do anything about it."

The resident said nothing, and for that I silently thanked him.

I mutely showed him my finger, my elbow, my armpit—my buried treasures.

"Ah," he said. "We've been someplace dirty." He held my swollen finger, examining the scab across the back of my hand.

He wrote out a prescription with a preoccupied and satisfied air. When Elaine left to sign insurance forms at the cashier's window, I asked him, "Am I going to die?"

He snorted unprofessionally. "Hardly." I suppose he thought it ridiculous for an otherwise healthy man to ask such a question. "Just a little staph infection is all."

And so I was returned safely home, totally unsatisfied by penance so easily dismissed.

I fell asleep on the couch, which Elaine had made up for me, only to dream hot and feverish dreams of my frosty goddess, in which she begged my forgiveness and demanded my atrocities. When I awoke, I found that I had sweated through my pajamas, robe, bedclothes, and halfway through the cushions of the sofa. I changed my pajamas, changed the sheets and blankets, and then, while Elaine readied the children for school, I tried to read. Only to find myself hooked by the picture of the author who had died so correctly. And then I began to cry, the Prodigal's elder brother.

When my two hours were up, I shut up. The children had boarded their respective buses. Elaine curled her hair, reapplied her make-up, adjusted her dress, and announced that she needed to do some shopping, run a few errands.

"Will you be okay?"

"Of course," I said, "I don't know what my problem is."

"Your medication, maybe."

"Maybe," I said.

I stood at the living room window and waved to her as she backed slowly out of the driveway. I pretended that she was Diana. In the kitchen was the vial of antibiotic capsules. In the spare bathroom I found Elaine's stash of codeine tablets, kept hidden for when her period is especially uncomfortable. I counted the contents of both containers—thirty-eight capsules, twenty-two tablets—then took them all. I am not a very good pill taker, and it took me half an hour and two very large glasses of orange juice. When it was done, I lay down on my freshly made couch and drifted off.

I suppose that the nature of sleep has always confused me. Is it merely a dropping away of consciousness? A shadow within the mind that comes and goes with the passage of the sun? Or is it, as Paul of Tarsus claims, a physical metaphor for death, that event we all must endure? Is waking a daily resurrection?

As the drugs sped into my system, I was conscious of little else save the sound of the stereo from across the street. Our neighbor, a sixty-eight-year-old widow, had been a vocalist for an orchestra during the forties, and some mornings, when she is terribly depressed, she plays record after record and sings along while wearing an ancient evening gown. On this particular morning, I heard Linda Ronstadt and Vivian Nussbaum singing "I Got a Crush on You" as a duet, the music drifting across the street on the wings of a lazy breeze while I waited for the codeine to drop me beneath the sofa cushions. The air was sweet. I tried to keep my eyes open, but the darkness intruded from the edges, finally capturing the center, of my field of vision.

All the day and nighttime/hear me sigh . . .

I was dropping with the speed of a runaway elevator in a mine shaft. I waited for the explosion that would occur when I reached bottom, bursting through the earth's surface, into God's mysterious core. But the moment never came. Instead a bump, a screech, a grinding of pulleys, and the elevator began to rise again, not steadily, but rise it did, jerking and swaying and shuddering, and finally I was at the surface, and daylight came flooding back along with the nausea of that bumpy ride.

I was vomiting in the back of an ambulance. Its siren wailed as we bounced through intersections and slalomed through stalled traffic. I was curled in the fetal position on my left side, and expulsions were splashing against my knees, breakers against the pilings of a pier.

"You stupid." I could hear Elaine, from somewhere very far away. "Stupid, stupid, stupid. How could you do this to me?"

An ambulance attendant with butched hair and a face like a slab of uncooked pork pounded me on the back.

"Don't you worry, honey." She spoke sweetly to Elaine, and I imagined them holding hands, commiserating with each other over the injuries inflicted by men. "If you still want him, he'll be available."

"Come on, jerkface," she said, her tone toward me not nearly so sweet, "you got bills to pay. You owe us, you owe us. Don't stop now."

I didn't.

And in the tinted glass of the ambulance, I saw my own reflection. My mouth was ringed with the orange remains of digestion, but my lips smiled crookedly at the angel who touched my back.

The Sisters

My Aunt Scilla is a generous, noble, and spirited woman, but when she speaks of her neighbors, the Langoria sisters, she loses command of her usual graciousness. After one particular visit, one that sounded like imprisonment by manners, insinuation, and guilt, she said, "If I ever get that way, for godsake, put a bomb up my ass."

At the age of eighty-one, my aunt is obviously no longer young, and she, too, has learned the usefulness of age when she feels it necessary to make demands. The Langoria sisters, however, are even older, and they wield their age like a whip, even on Scilla, who—strong though she might be—is hardly a match for their hoary insistence upon the rights and privileges of the truly ancient.

I do not see the sisters often, only once a year—on the occasion of my annual Thanksgiving visit to see Scilla, with whom I once lived for fifty-two months forty-two years ago. I have come every year, ever since my Uncle Evan's death in a traffic accident some ten years ago. He drove underneath the trailer of a stopped semi while doing seventy-five miles an hour on the Fremont Bridge, and the reporting officer said that while it was impossible to say for sure, it had some of the characteristics of a suicide. A remarkably photogenic wreck—twisted steel in designs worthy of Giacometti—pictures of the accident were spread across the *Oregonian* like moral icons for the young. My uncle, it was reported, was a recovering alcoholic, one who had been involved in treatment and maintenance programs for the past twenty years, and yet the intimation was clear—that the accident had been the result of a momentary moral failure, a lapse of will that proved to be terminal: a fresh six-pack was recovered from the floor of the car.

In fact, he had been on his way to see the doctor, with whom he kept a standard monthly appointment. His blood-alcohol level was negligible, and the cans had not been opened; they were only part of a grocery list that included balogna, shaving cream, and pimiento loaf. The six-pack was for Scilla, but who could believe it? The caption on the front-page photograph read "Tragedy on the Fremont," illustrated by my uncle's car, the roof of which had been torn from its body—its windshield turned into diamonds—by the back edge of the trailer. The photograph was later picked up by MADD and used as a warning poster for high school graduations. The poster and its implications grieved my aunt terribly and seemed to place a permanent blight upon the twenty years of my uncle's sobriety. The accompanying story also led one to assume that the driver had been decapitated, his body left to flop like a stem without its flower, and in this case the assumption was correct.

It occurred the day before Thanksgiving, and so this time of year my aunt suffers. My wife and three daughters have been remarkably accommodating: Charlotte folds my shirts and packs my bags; Grace, my oldest daughter, supplies me with books to read on the airplane both coming and going; and all four of them escort me to the airport, where they will lose husband and father for the Thanksgiving weekend without a word of reproof or bitterness. We celebrate Thanksgiving together the next week, but I suspect that their tolerance has other sources, that each year, as they've grown older and more mature, my four women are secretly glad to see me walk down the jetway corridor. Without a male presence they can speak uninhibitedly about boyfriends and sex, college life and sex, money and sex. Sex and sex. My daughters are not promiscuous—of that one can never be entirely certain, I know—but they enjoy a frank conversation, Charlotte tells me, just as much as Thoreau enjoyed a walk in the woods. With the youngest, Lena, home the day before from her first quarter of college, Paula a semester away from law school, and Grace a CPA and a rising associate in an established firm, my children were no longer estranged by the pangs of adolescence and the differences of age. They now drink and talk, and when I return, I see the spoor of empties in the recycling bin—the remains of their week. Our daughters tell her all their love stories, and in the spirit of equity my wife must tell her own—all of which are compromising, I'm sure—because for a week following my absence, my daughters lift their eyebrows at me in a look that is pure innuendo. They go to church together on Thanksgiving Sunday, having imbibed the Protestant sacrament of confession. But my imagination tells me that while I'm gone the time passes at our house in the humid atmosphere of a locker room no less ribald than a barracks full of marines.

This past year, I left the morning before Thanksgiving. Charlotte kissed me more fiercely than I expected. Grace handed me my travel bag and books while Paula and Lena exchanged looks that as much as said, *Thirty more seconds and the old man is history.*

Oh, ho, ho, ho, I thought. They are getting ready for quite some week. Charlotte will have her hands full. "Be good," I said, breathing the words into Charlotte's ear while she gave me one last hug good-bye. "God be with you."

"And also with you," Charlotte said, and her cheeks flushed as if we'd spoken of matters improper, immoral, and obscene.

Somehow our voices sounded unnatural; regardless of the fact that our Episcopalian custom has made us more than familiar with such responses, we are not usually—or easily—given to such statements of piety without some shade of irony.

It was an odd farewell.

Scilla met me at the airport despite my objections. The previous week I had told her over the phone that it wasn't necessary; I'd rent a car. I would welcome seeing Portland again alone. But when the plane landed, an early-season ice storm was just beginning, and I wondered about my ability to drive in such weather. Twenty years ago I had lived here, and during one winter, I slid into road-side ditches four times. So much for experience. I decided to take a cab, spend thirty dollars on the fare, and risk sharing my first moments in this beautiful city of rivers and bridges with a possibly talkative stranger. But as I walked into the warmth of the terminal, there was Scilla, seated in one of the uncomfortable chairs next to the gate, waiting with her purse in her lap.

"There you are," she said, rising. "I was beginning to wonder how long I'd have to sit there."

"You shouldn't have come out," I said, "not in such terrible weather. I was planning to take a cab."

"Nonsense. Cabs are for women who wear bedroom slippers while grocery shopping."

"I'm wondering," I said, looking out the tall windows, "what chance we'll have getting up your hill."

Aunt Scilla cuffed my cheek lightly, as if I were once again her eight-year-old nephew and she my impatient and unwilling guardian.

"We'll drive right to my doorstep, we'll get the fireplace going for heat, and then we'll drink brandy to get warm." She tilted her head back to look at me, and the white halo of her hair seemed to expand. "Don't be surprised when I say I told you so."

But our journey was not to be so simple. Scilla's car, the LTD purchased after Evan's death, started on the first try, but the ice was already making the pavement in the parking lot slippery, and I nearly slid us into the retaining wall. I had told Scilla that I didn't have much faith in my skills on ice.

"Nonsense," she had said, "just do what I tell you."

And now she said, "Don't slide so much."

"I'm doing my best."

We crept toward the gates and the exit booths at the edge of the parking lot. Ice had formed on the roof and overhang of each booth, and every time the cashiers reached out for a driver's ticket and money, a gust of steam came out with them. The defroster in the LTD sounded like a blender, but even so, the side windows looked fractured; when I rolled down the window to pass my ticket to the woman in the booth, the weather stripping squealed.

"Silver thaw," the woman in the booth said. "Hell of a holiday greeting. Drive carefully now."

She seemed at the moment a genuine messenger of goodwill and her imperative a blessing for our safety, a wish that hovered like a held breath for forty-five minutes as we crept onto the freeway leading to the downtown interchange with Interstate 5 and the trip across the Willamette on the Markham Bridge. The Markham is two levels, and for the traveler headed south as we were, the bottom level is dark and claustrophobic, reminiscent of the sort of structures that fall during earthquakes and crush with a sort of Thornton Wilder determinism the unlucky souls trapped upon them. And yet we weathered the freeways and the Markham, as well as their unfortunate reminder of Uncle Evan, only to slide into the ditch near the off-ramp that led to Scilla's neighborhood and home. We slid to the right with no more control than a bottle cap and landed with a strangely silent collision, and then another quiet crash as a full-size pickup followed our trail.

"Not only are you a bad driver," my aunt said to me in that instant before we were hit, "you're contagious."

We were trapped for an hour before the wreckers could clear the other vehicle away. Our passenger side was wedged against a grassy embankment now turning white with ice, and my side looked into the passenger-side window of the pickup, dented from other such encounters. The driver rolled down the window. We were so close we could have touched noses.

"You want to climb through?" he asked pointing to the tunnel of our two windows.

My aunt looked at him as if he were loony.

"We'll wait, thank you," she said, speaking over me.

"Suit yourself," he said. "I'll go fetch the mounties."

While we waited, Scilla told me her latest story about the Langorias. The rain fell and froze, and we huddled in our overcoats while we sat canted at twenty degrees.

It seemed that Cara Langoria, the younger of the sisters, had fallen while coming down the main stairs of their old house. She broke her hip and landed at the bottom of the stairwell in a tossed salad of housedress and rolled stockings. Cara is a large woman, just over one hundred and eighty pounds, more than twice as heavy as her sister, so when Felicia came home two hours later, her only recourse was to call 911 and let her sister lie. They passed the time by singing "Just a Closer Walk with Thee" and rounds of "*Frère Jacques*" and "Row, Row, Row Your Boat." Their multitude of cats swirled around them and sang along.

"That was a brave thing to do," Scilla said, "on the floor like that, Cara in as much pain as she was. I can just imagine them singing—off-key and barely audible—counting the seconds until the ambulance arrived. I yelled at Felicia later that she didn't call. I could have at least sat with them and sung alto. Lent a little volume on the chorus.

"But now all they do is call. Scilla do this, Scilla do that. I could spend every one of my remaining days and nights running errands for those two. They'll outlive me from their wheelchairs and hospital beds out of spite that I didn't go to the veterinarian's for their cats' thyroid and bowel medication yesterday.

"Last week they had an electric bench installed in the stairwell. Everyone in the neighborhood has had to try it—up and down, up and down—even the paperboy. The way Felicia talks, they should have installed two, so they could bet on the races."

As Scilla talked, her face took on an expression that was foreign to all my recollections. Her eyes, normally blue and unclouded, were now veiled, and a trace of bitterness could be found dwelling at the corners of her still-attractive mouth. I would not have expected it of her, for bitterness is a cautionary word between us. She would not yield to it while Evan drank, during the days following Evan's death, nor after my mother, her sister, ran away, and left me—literally as well as figuratively—on her doorstep. "You cannot give asylum to anger," she told me once in the first month of my mother's absence. "Blow it up, then go on. There's no sense in poisoning the happiness of a new day." She is often guilty of mixing her metaphors without mercy, but her point was not lost on me, even at the age of eight. I could choose to hate my mother and lose my life, or save my life by forgiving and forgetting the injuries of the past. And so, when my mother finally did return for me four years later, I had not lost her entirely to resentment. I could kiss her cheek and go on. Scilla was responsible for that, so I worried now to see it creeping into her face. What did it matter how fast two old women went up and down their electrically powered stair-chair? Certainly Scilla understood how to limit their incessant demands.

"They're old women," I said. "Let them have their fun."

She did not say another word.

Two hours later we were deposited at Scilla's house by a wrecker with studded tires, the driver of which charged us one hundred and fifty dollars for the privilege of movement. When he picked up the LTD, the right front wheel fell off and bounced like something out of a cartoon.

"People oughtn't to drive on ice that don't know how," he said.

"I couldn't agree more," Scilla said. As soon as she could get the house unlocked, she went into her bedroom, slamming the door as punctuation. We still hadn't spoken to each other, only to the driver of the wrecker. I opened my wallet. Did he, by chance, take credit cards? He did not. I counted out all the money I had on hand, ending with the change in my pocket. One hundred thirty-seven dollars and twenty-three cents.

"Good enough," he said. "No reason to make you beg. You've got enough troubles."

"Thank you," I said. "Thank you very much."

Even after the wrecker backed out of her steep driveway, Scilla did not come out of her room. I stood in the back hallway and stared at her closed door, waiting for some sort of sign of common sense and reasonableness before deciding, at long last, that there is nothing to be done about closed doors.

I raided Scilla's ancient refrigerator and, while drinking three quick Weinhards in succession, felt as though I had found, despite our seven-hundred-mile separation, some common thread with Charlotte and our daughters. While drinking the first bottle, I called home, only to hear Charlotte on our answering machine.

"Yes," I said to her recorded voice, "I'm here; I slid Scilla's car into a ditch during an ice storm. There were no injuries or fatalities."

On the second beer, I said, "It was minor really. The accident with Scilla's car. Just bodywork, a broken spindle, and ego. Not to worry, but now Scilla won't speak to me, all because I said something in defense of the Langorias. They have an electric bench for their stairs, and Scilla is outraged."

And on the third call and third beer, I said, speaking with an accent that I've always associated with voyeurs and lingerie-fetishists: "*Ma chérie*, what I wouldn't give to have you here, hey ba-bee."

After the third call, I could think of nothing else to say; my theatrical powers are easily exhausted, and with each call the sound of Charlotte's voice on the answering machine seemed more grating.

The beer was ice-cold and tasted grainy, and the smell brought back my own college days and fraternity trips to the brewery's tasting room on Burnside, where the smell of hops was as potent as nerve gas. I drank the last three, sipping them slowly this time, savoring the beer's corporeal nature more than the taste, remembering less about fraternity brothers and more about the tenderness of a girl named Polly the year I was a sophomore, the year in which my truant mother died.

A hostess in the tasting room, she was not particularly attractive or gifted, but she was enormously endowed and therefore a target of postadolescent scrutiny and heartlessness. We went out for weeks. After her long days of promoting free beer and professional cheerfulness, she would fall asleep during movies. She hated foreign food of all kinds, and discussion of art, politics, or religion bored her. Her lower lip sagged a fraction of an inch lower on the right side, and her long, mournful face often reminded me of that image that the word *horsewoman* suggests. And yet I could not give her up, even in those weeks when the steam in the back window of my car was only smoke without fire. I was so anxious to witness her disrobing that when she did finally and reluctantly yield herself, I was overcome: I whistled. And when she blushed, the flush started first at her cheeks, dropped down along her throat, and extended in wings along her collarbone and the flat valley of her sternum. I began to weep, I was so weakened. But having obtained satisfaction of my own curiosity, my interest just as quickly cooled, and three weeks later, with a cruelty I could not have thought myself capable of, I broke off with her. And then my mother died.

Even now I cannot be entirely certain that there was no cause-and-effect relationship between the two events—crime and punishment—although the punishment was directly borne by another. She died of a heart attack in the Benson Hotel. The man in whose name the room was registered claimed not to have been present, but his statement was greeted with a great deal of skepticism, and the hotel shortly thereafter announced a shake-up of its security staff. My mother's funeral was conducted with as little notice as possible, yet even so, there were reporters and curiosity seekers, because news of her death and its circumstances had made the front page, just as Evan's would twenty years later. In the side room reserved for family, my grandparents sat like stones while Scilla merely seemed crushed. For my own part, I had no idea what to feel until I saw Polly walk by my mother's casket, and then I only felt despicable. When Evan saw her, he leaned over to me and whispered, "Look at them knockers," not knowing the degree to which I'd already seen them. Outside, in a thin rain, she stood in a black overcoat, waiting for me.

"I'm sorry, James," she breathed, so quietly that her words did not even qualify as a whisper. "Do you need anything?"

Oh, why had Scilla chosen to be obstinate and resentful? And why had she left a six-pack unattended, the trigger—on an empty stomach—of memory, a reminder of shame? I wish that I could say I declined Polly's offer graciously, but I did not. Following the funeral and grave-site service, I went back to Polly's apartment and did not leave for the next ten weeks. I dropped all my classes, stayed in bed until two, and waited each evening for Polly's return from the brewery, her black, belted overcoat carrying the smell of hops and fermentation. She had told me that she felt she understood my mother, understood something of her heartache and desires; she told me that, from what she'd read in the newspaper accounts, she felt some sort of kindredness with my mother, which was much more than I could have possibly said.

After the ten weeks, I began to feel as though there was a limit to the amount of penance one could do. I again became restless and bored, left without a note, and reenrolled in school, refusing all offers to go for free beer.

And now, Scilla's beer was gone. Due to Evan's legacy, she buys one six-pack and only one in honor of my visit. But suffering the weight of such bad conscience, I could not possibly stop drinking. Scilla's door was still shut, her car was unusable, so speaking to her closed door, I told her that I was going for a walk to the market at the bottom of her hill. They took credit cards, I said. I heard the aggravated sound of her breathing, so I knew that she hadn't died.

The air outside was cold and wet, a clammy twenty degrees. Everything was sheeted in silent ice, and if I'd had a sled or skates I could have saved myself some falls. As it was, I spent much of my trip downhill on my nether side, and weakened by beer and remorse, I let myself slide and roll.

At the market, I bought a suitcase of beer, then struggled mightily to climb the hill back to Scilla's. If there had been spectators to my effort, I'm sure they would have found me a pitiful sight—down on all fours, grasping shrubs and small trees with one hand, my suitcase of beer with the other. If Evan's accident had been used by a temperance organization to illustrate the consequences of a moral lapse, then I—scrambling up this slippery and allegorical slope, an ape with his cardboard suitcase—could have been its poster child.

At Scilla's, I drank and called home, and when the beer began to taste too much like food, I broke into Scilla's brandy. I called at midnight, one o'clock, two, three, and four, and it became absolutely important that I call at the exact stroke of each hour. I kept no exact record of alcoholic intake. Each call was answered by Charlotte's recorded voice, whose diction and syntax annoyed me more with each successive hearing. What could it mean that my wife and adult daughters were not answering the phone at four o'clock in the morning? I left no messages except at two o'clock, when a long, wet belch seemed to erupt from my very soul. At some point I became convinced that—like Nebuchadnezzar and his cattle—alcohol and bad behavior had turned me into a dog, and that only by baying at the moon could I vent my despair. Some trick or dream of memory had me barking and rolling in the frozen grass of my aunt's backyard, but the image was wild and unclear. Sometime after four, I passed out among the beer cans and the empty brandy bottle, dreaming of my family, especially Lena, who is an emotional replica of Polly, a dreamy child with lackluster grades from a third-rate college, and I slept restlessly until six when I was awakened by a well-placed foot in my stomach.

"Happy Thanksgiving," Scilla said, using the toe of one shoe like a spade among my ribs. "Nephew, favorite nephew, it's time to celebrate."

Grief takes on many shapes, many masks, none of which is predictable or untroubled. We are punished by tragedy, and we dish out our troubles to others. We dream, and we weep, and then we suffer the guilt of happiness. And years later we meet again—unchanged and immutable—the sadness of our youth. I woke on Thanksgiving morning, weeping for the loss of my mother, who had not merely died but—even worse—had left me, and for Polly, whom I had betrayed in the same way, grief begetting itself again and again. I wept as well for Scilla, the woman who had mothered me though she had no children of her own, whose sensibilities I had somehow so thoughtlessly offended. But most of all I wept for my daughters in general and Lena in particular, whose future, I felt, had somehow been compromised by my mother's genetics and the sins of her father.

But Scilla assured me that, as far as she was concerned, I was being a ninny, that all was forgiven in time. A night's sleep without whiplash was all that was necessary. She further assured me that the day's agenda was full as well as impossible to modify. I would have to pull myself together. We would first have a full breakfast, after which we would stuff the turkey, followed by a visit to the Langorias, of whom I was so inordinately fond. Didn't that sound like fun? I nodded, though the room kept turning and tilting and my head seemed about to float away.

But as it turned out, Scilla did not go with me to see the sisters after all. Pleading headache and stiffness—brought on, no doubt, by the accident—she sent me out the backdoor with a pecan pie, a jar of cranberry preserve, and a bottle of blackberry wine.

My aunt's neighborhood is old, but it has aged gracefully in fir trees and new exterior paint and so far has resisted the excesses of new money and gentrification. Realtors call her block charming when, truth be told, it is simply holding its own. The houses conform to no architectural style, but they are all large and wood-framed, and the oldest among them still feature three floors, impossibly small bathrooms with gravity-fed toilets, servants' quarters, and coal cellars. The backyards are tiny, the side yards an illusion. There are no fences, and the only demarcation of one yard from another is the alley that, bisecting the block, winds its way from side street to side street. In short, the place is far from up-to-date, and to look from my aunt's back porch is to look at what was a gentler, more pastoral time. The sounds of dairy herds drift upward from the block's collective memory, and by closing one's eyes against the light, one feels the alley again become the thoroughfare of neighborhood commerce, where iceman and vegetable peddler and rag collector ply their respective trades.

Transported by such visions, my equilibrium none too solid, I picked my way carefully down the back steps, which still wore patches of recalcitrant ice, stepped over the low picket fence of my aunt's rose garden, and crossed the alley to the Langorias' backdoor. In my weariness, the journey seemed nearly insurmountable.

Felicia received me. She is tiny, and her dimensions are of the nineteenth century. Four foot nine and seventy-nine pounds, she was attired in a dress topped by a lace collar, her legs cloaked in black stockings, and she wore her hair in the severe bun of the spinster schoolteacher, an image that—in her case—is as accurate as it is stereotypical.

"Come in, James, come in. Cara and I were just talking about you."

She took the gifts from my hands and set them atop a cluttered counter in the kitchen. Four cats began to orbit our legs.

"Nothing wrong with Priscilla, I hope," she said. She guided me to a parlor draped in dusty velvet and gold brocade, and she indicated an armchair, occupied by a disdainful tom, upon which I might sit.

"No," I said, "nothing awful, but we did have a little accident on the ice yesterday, and she's not feeling quite up to par. She sent her love and hoped I'd do as a substitute."

"Oh, my yes. You tell her we hope she feels better, won't you? She has been so good about running small errands for us ever since Cara's little fall. Frieda Bilsten told us that she saw a tow truck in your driveway yesterday, so we had our suspicions, didn't we, Cara *mia*?"

Cara Langoria had rolled into the parlor on noiseless tires. "Yes, Freida gave us the report, but now it's confirmed." She wheeled herself to face me: "Frieda is not always reliable, you know." She touched one temple with a shaky finger. "She makes up things."

"Ah."

"There is nothing that disturbs us more than rumors based solely on air."

"I can see that, but it looks as though you keep a sharp eye and ear out."

"We do like to keep abreast," Felicia said. She had brought in a silver tray with dusty liqueur glasses filled with something amber. Brandy, I guessed.

"Cheers, James," Felicia said, offering the tray.

"Yes, thank you. Cheers."

The two old women knocked back their drinks with a speed that dazzled me, while I sipped like a puritan looking over his shoulder. My stomach rolled in disbelief, then resigned itself to this newest violation.

"Drink up, Jimmy," Felicia said. "A little snootful never hurt a man with willpower."

"Your Uncle Evan, for instance," Cara said. "What a darling man, but what a tragedy. My Walter admired him so."

Her late husband, Walter, whose oil portrait loomed at the top of the stairs, had growled and glowered for seventy years before succumbing to bleeding ulcers, and if he had spoken two words to Evan in their entire lifetimes, I would have been surprised. But I declined to take issue.

"Evan overcame a huge obstacle," I said, choosing to agree with what I could. "He stopped drinking when no one thought twice about drunks."

"Of course, dear." Felicia leaned forward and patted my arm with one of her dry, papery hands.

"Felicia, he hasn't yet tried the stairs," Cara blurted. "You have to try our new toy, James, really. We've so fallen in love with technology. I think my little accident may have been a blessing in disguise."

"I've heard you've gone electric."

"My, yes. We're thinking of buying a computer and a microwave and a coffee pot with a timer."

Felicia gave me precise instructions. The control was a simple lever, but the sisters flew their bench like the Concorde.

Seated with my back to the stairs, I rose in reverse. The sensation was slow and, given my hangover, not unremarkable; in fact, I was reminded of those Sunday school pictures showing Christ's ascension.

The bench arrived at the second floor landing with a lurch, and then I started down again to earth. I was followed in both directions by an orange tabby who seemed to be part shepherd.

"Do try it again," Cara said from her wheelchair.

And so I did. Up. At the top of the stairs, I looked to my left and saw the portrait of Walter, whose eyes looked distrustful of such frivolous modernity. Then down.

"Isn't that the most fun?" Cara said. "Whenever I get bored now, I simply pop onto the stairs."

"It is ever so much better than television nowadays," Felicia added.

From there they launched into a two-hour recitation of various ailments: Cara's mending hip, Felicia's arthritis, the cats' various and sundry health problems, from abscesses that didn't heal to glands that would not secrete to bowels that would not move—all of which, Scilla claimed, was evidence that they were being loved to death, that cats had been designed to be neighborhood looters and bandits rather than pampered houseguests. As the sisters talked, acting as chorus for each other, they drank more brandy and turned girlish and silly and looked stricken when I refused more for myself.

"Don't push him, Felicia," Cara said. "Actually, we heard you last night, didn't we dear, about three o'clock in the morning. You were howling."

"Three o'clock," Felicia confirmed. "Howling. And when I peeked out my bedroom window, I thought you might be having some sort of fit."

"Howling?" I said.

"Yes. Something about the inconstancy of women and the boorishness of men."

"And we were merely curious as to whether or not you'd inherited the family troubles."

"Family troubles."

"Yes, dear," Felicia said, "you know—drink. And immoral behavior. Your Uncle Evan was no blood of yours, but your mother, now there was a girl. She put it away until she no longer knew the front door from the closet."

Cara chimed in: "My Walter said that he had all the respect in the world for Mary Jane Detweiler even if she was a lush and mother to a bastard son—it's a term of accuracy rather than offense, James—but he hated to see her giving herself away so freely. Financially and morally."

I sat dully, my elbows resting like lead weights on the horsehair-covered arms of the chair. They were not offering new information, but it was not something that I wished to hear from others.

"Your mother," Cara said, "worked for my Walter at his Sellwood office for three months—he was trying to be helpful to Evan and Priscilla—but my goodness there was trouble. She had enormous difficulties. One day she was gone for three hours during lunch, and when she came back she began to walk on the desks while unbuttoning her blouse, and so Walter just had to let her go. He had no choice, you see, and then four days later she died. Somehow she'd gotten Walter's chief auditor into that hotel room with her, and you can believe that there were some scenes about that at three different homes. You know there was. I was terribly unfair to Walter at the time."

I rose unsteadily to my feet. "Thank you for the brandy and the chat." I smiled as sweetly as I could. "And please kindly please go to hell." And then I added lamely, no better words offering themselves just then, "Please."

Felicia covered her mouth, but she rose from her chair to show me to the door.

"We mean you no harm, James, really; we just have nothing better to do. Cara misses Walter terribly, the old dinosaur. And I'm just an old woman who . . . I'm just an old woman. You tell Prissy to stop on by when she feels better."

We live in impossible times, in which velocity seems to count for more than permanence. Those in the public eye—our politicians and our evangelists, as well as our other entertainers—experience censure and rehabilitation with a speed that defies our comprehension. Our economies are made to balance and totter on the basis of tenuous credit; our legislators give dispensation to the wealthy in the stubborn assertion that charity begins with one's own while the rest of us move restlessly from place to place, hoping that one town, one job, one dwelling place will announce itself as home. Even as our rush to movement leads us farther and farther from happiness and rest.

I flew home that Monday. A taxi picked me up at Scilla's house and deposited me at the airport under the lidded eye of a dull, late-autumn sun. The ice had disappeared, and as the plane banked, I could make out the seven city bridges, each as different in design as the sides of the city they connect.

I took another taxi home through patches of fog and shattering sunlight. Charlotte would be at work, Grace would have returned home, Paula to her apartment. Lena, I assumed, would be visiting friends. I did not bother to call for a ride.

I had finally spoken to Charlotte the day before. On impulse she and the girls had driven to the coast after dropping me off at the airport; they had no idea I would be worried. The messages on the answering machine had sent them all into great hysterics, she said, and Paula thought I did a great imitation of a Dumb Guy. They had stayed in Pacific Grove and shopped for collectibles and wandered through art galleries in Carmel. My fears had been groundless, the product of a nightmare fed by beer and brandy and a guilty conscience. Charlotte told me that something differ-ent had been in the air for all four of them. Lena seemed particu-larly affected, preoccupied and moody, no doubt the residue of her indifferent performance at school. They drank sparingly— wine with dinner only—and instead of blue stories, Grace an-nounced her engagement to a dentist from Madera, and that any revelations concerning their physical union would come only after divorce. Charlotte said that Grace had blushed, difficult for a young woman raised in an era of license and indulgence, but that rather than pressing her, Paula and Lena had followed her lead, had discussed wedding plans and honeymoon plans, had acted as sisters ought in anticipation of another one's joy.

"That's nice," I had said, " 'the marriage of true minds,' and all that."

"You won't say that," she had said, "when you find out how much this is all going to cost. Dentists don't come cheap."

And so I came home. I paid the driver, and then, rather than going inside to an empty house, I took a walk around our block. The air was cool and clear. The last of the morning fog had burned away, dissipated by the sun and a slight northwest breeze, and I marveled at the white caps of the Sierra against the deep blue of the sky. I am not often home at noon on a weekday. No one is, for during the week ours is a neighborhood of empty houses. Hus-bands and wives both work, the children who still live at home are in school, and the streets are quiet, but the aroma of dryer sheets still pervades the air, as if to imply that the essence of do-mesticity, even that which is arranged at four in the morning, is still valid.

As I write this, the bills for Grace's wedding have already begun to come in—deposits for a reception hall, the caterer, her dress. By June, I will not recognize myself. I will look into the mirror and see only Spencer Tracy or some other cliché of the man who gives away a girl as if she could be both chattel and jewelry. The lamp burns bright above my desk. I am imagining ways to pay for Grace, then Paula, then Lena, and I remember what Scilla told me as I carved the turkey I would not be able to eat.

"You were born in a bad time," she said, "and your mother had no interest or intention in motherhood. But I don't blame her. There were times with Evan when I wished that I could walk out the door, sign on with a circus, and play Godiva. You were a sweet boy, Jimmy, so lost, but you were just one more reason why I couldn't do that. I couldn't join the circus, be unfaithful or irresponsible. Your mother never worried, and I both hated and loved her. Then she died *in flagrante delicto*, whereas I've had a long, secure life that will end with me tottering around this house like a third Langoria. You tell me who made the right choice."

I remember also that the day I came home from Scilla's, I first took my walk, and then I went into the darkness of my house, expecting it to be empty, only to find Lena lying on top of her bed. She was staring at the ceiling, and water trembled in her eyes.

"Sweetheart," I said, putting down my bag, her anguish tearing at me, "what can I do?"

"It's nothing, Daddy," she sobbed. "Nothing you'd understand."

Hints
of His
Mortality

___

I. STEAM

Years later Ferguson would remember—as the disabled 727 in which he was trapped as a passenger sank into the twilight of morning clouds—how his first wife had disappeared or died (he never knew which) in the fog of the Central Valley of California. They had been married a year. Helen had kissed him good-bye on a Friday morning following a Thursday-night argument, saying that she would return in three days after visiting her mother in Los Angeles. From their apartment over the dry cleaner's, he watched as she backed the Volkswagen out of the parking lot. She waved, giving him a mock salute, forgiving him or dismissing him, he couldn't be sure. Twelve hours later her mother called. *Wasn't Helen going to come after all?* The police were notified, a missing person's report was filed, but her disappearance remained a mystery. Her car was never found alongside Highway 99, nor was her body admitted to any hospital in the state. No unidentified victims of accident or amnesia were reported during that weekend. One investigator insinuated that Helen might have wanted to disappear. Unwilling to admit the possibility, Ferguson waved the idea away as quickly as it had mingled with the smoke of the officer's cigarette. But a month later, having recognized that her return was not probable, that her disappearance would in all likelihood remain a mystery, Ferguson drove the route that Helen would have taken, drove down 99, with its tidemarks of agricultural flotsam, drove into the fog bank that threatened to swallow him in Stockton and continued unabated through Modesto, Merced, Madera, Fresno, Tulare, and Bakersfield, only lifting when he had begun the ascent through the Grapevine, drove until he had found an empty spot at a water turnout, where he could stop the car and look back like Lot's wife at the bowl of mist he had driven through. *Forgiven or dismissed?* Only then could he accept the fact that she was gone. Vanished. He assumed the worst. In front of him the tule fog—in the company of unwelcome emotions—hovered, reminding him that the first time he had seen her, she had appeared to him as something of a mirage, an image out of steam.

His father shot himself during the fall semester of Ferguson's junior year of college, and the estate provided certain bitter revelations. A romantic, Ferguson *père* had gambled every last scrap on a California cotton field, site of what the developer's brochure called New Town, a dreamer's utopian community of fresh air, clean streets, and happy children. That the cotton field was still just that, that the developer faced a shopping list of indictments for fraud and illegal use of the mails, that in order to settle the last of her husband's debts and to provide a small income for herself Ferguson's grieving mother was forced to liquidate the holdings of the trust left by her own father—it all seemed to possess the inevitability of Greek drama. A crueler joke, perhaps, was his father's farewell note, which read in part, "engendered by love, prompted by memories of a world known but never seen, it was a kind risk."

. Kind or not, Ferguson was broke, deprived by his foolish father's love, and his only recourse in the middle of that awful semester was a financial aid advisor who directed him to a dishwashing job in the basement cafeteria of Holman Hall. On his first evening of work, he had descended the concrete steps with resignation. While he couldn't claim to be political, he couldn't fail to spot the irony of his own self-pity. Outside he had walked along the perimeter of a rather chaotic war protest. The beneficence of a high draft number (328) and the bad luck of having a romantic for a father had conspired together, and he now found himself neither in Vietnam nor protesting it but guiltily following a conveyor belt stacked with a trail of lasagna-encrusted plates to the bowels of a dormitory kitchen. There in a haze of moisture, a woman, with the aid of a pair of wooden tongs, was yanking a tray of plates out of the steaming dishwasher. Her back was to him, a sweat-soaked Grateful Dead T-shirt, the outline of her brassiere showing whitely through. A braid of frizzy, copper-colored hair slipped to one side of her neck, around which a black rubber apron was tied.

"I'm here," he had yelled above the thunderstorm of the dishwasher, a stainless steel cylinder with a sliding door that seemed more spaceship than appliance, "I'm here about the job."

She turned, frowning. Her eyes, blue agates, seemed unnaturally bright.

"What job?" she said. Her black rubber gloves slashed through the mist. "I don't need anyone."

"I'm a hardship," he said, speaking quickly and at a pitch higher than the *boom, boom, whoosh* of the dishwasher.

She viewed him critically. "I'm sure you are."

"My father died."

She shrugged. "I'm sorry."

He stood, staring at her eyes, which seemed to have been clarified by the steam, staring at her nose, a slight midwestern bump misaligning it, its imperfection also its beauty. Couldn't she see that this job wasn't of his own choice?

"Financial aid sent you?" she sighed. He nodded. "Here." She stripped off the gloves and handed them over. Ferguson put them on, feeling as though he were wearing another's skin. "We'll see how it goes."

Later, when the conveyor had ground to a stop and the plates and the glasses and the institutional silverware had been returned to their respective slots and Helen had untied the rubber apron, they left the comfort of the steamy basement together, entering into the forgotten memory of the world and an evening of clear, indifferent stars. In one corner of the common a bonfire burned, marking the conclusion of the war demonstration. An effigy of the president was burning, only the nose and two fingers of one hand visible through the flames. A flag was incinerated. Cheers erupted as sparks rose.

"Fucking hypocrites, most of them," Helen said when she saw the protesters, her vehemence surprising him more than the profanity.

"I would have been a part of it if I wasn't up to my elbows in other people's food," Ferguson said, aware as he did so, that his voice had somehow ascended into his nose.

"Of course you would have. Poor baby has to wash out mama's dishes." Her hands were on her hips as she stared across the common. "Five years from now you can drive your daddy's Cadillac, excuse me, mommy's Caddy, and tell yourself that you did your part—you marched, you sang, you wrote letters, you were a part of IT, you were on the right side, the decent side, you got to rebel—and you had a terrific party besides."

"You want the war to go on?" he asked, annoyed not only by the continuing defection of his voice but by her knowingness, her certainty, her cynicism about his own best motives.

"The war stinks, but you can't hate its smell, then light some incense to cover your own."

"You'd just do nothing."

"You have no idea. Listen, hardship," the wind had shifted directions and smoke from the fire drifted between them, "I'll see you tomorrow at six. Unless, of course, you decide to become a revolutionary in the meantime."

It was not the last time she would act as his conscience, but having a conscience, whether one's own or embodied in someone else, wasn't necessarily such a bad thing, now was it? Helen was quick to judge, easy to anger, and sensitive to the faintest trace of self-interest. That she was so often right in her judgments of others' motives might have been due in part to the close scrutiny she'd given her own. At the age of sixteen, she'd rejected her father, president of an electronics firm specializing in defense applications; more importantly, she'd repudiated his money. Her mother, although already divorced from Helen's father, upbraided her daughter for throwing away the thousands of dollars she could have expected in continuing support and the possible millions in inheritance that one day might have been hers. In 1970, Helen's father's company sold $14 million of equipment to the American military, and Helen's father moved to the Hollywood hills to a facsimile of a Roman villa. Helen's mother owned her own mansion, financed by the divorce settlement. Helen lived in a studio apartment above a dry cleaner's and stamped her father's letters *Return to Sender*.

It was to this apartment that Ferguson came with Helen eight weeks after his own father's death. The room was filled with books; many of the titles he recognized as ones he was supposed to have read. Helen had read them, debating their ideas in silent conversations between herself and the images of the authors she'd created from the pages of the texts. Her interest in him confused him still. They sat on the floor, a gallon of wine between them, and talked, Helen instructing and criticizing, Ferguson listening. She seemed to need her own lectures, and if listening helped—even though his attention was directed not to the shape of her words but to the shape of her lips—what of it? She spoke of moral imperatives, personal integrity, and uncompromised interests, topics that few can tolerate, especially if one listens. He tried to listen only to the tone of her monologues rather than their substance, enjoying his intimacy with her passions more than her thoughts.

"I don't even open the envelopes," she said. "I'll live here until I die before I take his money. If I open an envelope and see a check, there's too much temptation. I'm his daughter, not his accomplice. I don't have to stink because he does. There's a better world than that inside me."

Later, because they had just come from the dishroom, they showered together before they made love. Even so, Ferguson couldn't help thinking afterward, as he wedged himself between the wall and Helen's inert form, listening to her slight, open-mouthed snore, his nose buried in her wet, coarse hair, he couldn't help sensing, somewhat repelled, that no amount of scrubbing, bristle-brush or moral, would ever remove from the two of them the odor and confusion of other people's food.

And now, as the 727 pitched forward, it seemed analogous to his own life. It seemed as though he'd been living in anticipation of this moment for years, the slow rise to the top of the roller coaster's tracks, the climb, the struggle, knowing that achieving the summit would also mean the screaming descent, the wild ride, fear and pleasure indivisible, each necessary to define the other. Ferguson sat with his seat belt buckled, his wallet opened to the picture of Charlotte, his second wife, able to think only of Helen, his first. Remembering those late nights, when they had been the only ones in the dishroom, when they had worked naked in the steam, when her unreachable idealism became sentimental fantasy: "Two woodland creatures," Helen had breathed, running one finger along his glazed hip, "at play in the original world; one noble faun, one perfect nymph."

"We've been notified of a minor problem."

The pilot's voice, an intrusion, had intended comfort but in Ferguson had induced only remorse: *I'm so sorry*, he had thought, *I was wrong, I was always wrong. My poor, dear Helen.*

The ventilation system shut off, and the air became stuffy, used up. In the smoking section, a woman began to moan. If only her conscience had been strong enough to serve both of them, he wouldn't be here now. An irrational thought. Through the claustrophobic windows, he saw clouds reaching up to touch the wings. Gravity pulled at his stomach. A flight attendant made her way to the back of the plane, checking seat belts and tray tables, pulling herself along by the seat backs, the pitch of the floor as steep as stairs. Suddenly a rending. Ferguson watched, disbelieving, as the skin of the roof peeled back, the cavernous sky sucking out purses and magazines and overnight bags. The attendant fell to her knees, grabbing Ferguson's legs and the legs of his seat. His wallet flew from his hands. The stars were pouring through the tear in the roof, swirling in chaotic order, dancing among the luggage compartments.

The pilot announced that they were not to worry. *Just a routine emergency-type landing.* Routine?

The attendant's fingernails were digging into the meat of Ferguson's calves; her face was pressed against the floor, her skirt snapping against her legs like a flag while she intoned the same prayer over and over, "Oh God, oh God, oh God." Ferguson touched her hair. Then they were in the clouds, and there were clouds inside scudding down the aisle; the plane angled another degree toward the vertical, and recognizing that a thirty-eight-year-old man without a conscience of his own was not likely ever to own one, he gave himself up for lost.

Which was the same realization he'd had that morning standing at the turnout on Highway 99. A certain resignation to the state of his own soul. A certain disgust. For what he couldn't control, as he stood looking back at the fog, were the alternating currents of horror and joy that Helen's disappearance had caused to well up within him. If you had been standing there at that turnout, a tourist, say, driving an overheating station wagon, you might have seen him and wondered, wondered at the flickering of emotional responses that Ferguson himself could feel, like birds' wings playing around the corners of his eyes, nose, and mouth. If you had seen him there, and if you were the compassionate sort of person who was not afraid to involve yourself in another's affairs, you might have touched him on the shoulder, asked if he were all right, so extraordinarily, visibly torn was he by the depth of despair he felt over her absence as well as the gorgeous, liberating relief, the freedom he likewise felt, and then the guilt, the guilt, the guilt . . . of feeling so good when everything was so, well, wasn't it supposed to be tragic?

Without a conscience, who could tell?

Conscience, as he stared into the opaque mist below, seemed to be the tune from a forgotten song. Known once intuitively, but elusive now and forever, it recedes farther and farther the more the mind probes. Helen had known about that, of course. The night of their argument, before they had begun to yell, before Helen had begun to methodically break the juice glasses in the sink, he had found her sitting cross-legged on the floor, an open book in her lap, her mouth settling into a frown at the sound of his entrance. She closed the book, then said, "It's all just words, isn't it?"

"I guess so." Her admission frightened him.

"I used to think that the words were little cracks, and I could see through the cracks and see something really good. Really right.

"I don't think that now."

"They're the same words," he said.

"The same words," she agreed. "But things," she said, looking at him, he realized, as the violator of her perfect peace, "things are different."

So now, after he had failed—although he'd tried, he'd really tried—to find her, he lifted his hands over the valley in benediction and gave it, gave her, his blessing, that she could have loved him so much to leave without a nagging trace.

After all, Helen's father had begged him to take the money. That was the way he always told it. Her old man, bereft by his daughter's refusal of him, saw in Ferguson an ally. If he could not reach her, then through her husband he could satisfy his parental obligations. He worked out an arrangement with Ferguson, sending him a check each month, which Ferguson then deposited into a brokerage account, some of which, Ferguson was sure, wound up returning as stock in Helen's father's company. Tainted capital multiplying itself as it served its maker. He never asked specific questions while the account climbed, and it soared until 1972, the year Helen found the broker's statement on the kitchen table. A foolish thing to do, leaving the thing lying around like that, so foolish that he often wondered whether or not he secretly meant for her to see it, to infuriate her, to drive her away.

So he was going to die, his mind filled with self-recrimination, his eyes faced with the judgment of clouds.

The pilot, surely a maniac or an imbecile, announced—enthusiastically, Ferguson thought—"We're not having a real good day here, folks. A little trouble seems to have come up with the landing gear, so we'll ask you all to get prepared as we ease her on in."

Ease? This hunk of disintegrating metal?

The plane leveled, loose objects settled back to the floor, and the attendant rose shakily to her knees. "I'm *so* sorry," she said to Ferguson, holding in her hand a rectangular piece of his pant leg.

Murky lights shone through the clouds, through the fog, and Ferguson allowed himself a glimmer of hope in this connection with life lived safely on the ground. A cold wind roared through the roof, and the plane shuddered. The engines whined in another key. Evidently an airport was below; he could dimly see the haloes of streetlamps, the movement of cars, the outlines of houses, the darkness of canals.

Automatically, he began mumbling, "Mary, Mother of God," though he had not been a communicant since college. The young man in the window seat bit his lip until it bled; the banker across the aisle held his head with his hands as if he were afraid it might float away.

Then, lights and poles, cars and streets, all too quickly rushing up from the ground. The fog would cushion them, Ferguson thought; it would bear them up. But when they hit the runway, it was a sliding crash, with sparks flying from wingtip and engine. The control tower skipped across the window, the terminal—they were never going to stop. There were pieces of metal and jet engine strewn behind them like a trail; next would come baggage and passengers and crew until the trail unraveled and there was nothing left. Ferguson put his head between his knees. He could see the runway through the floor. Helen would have known what to do; his only impulse was to puke. Smoke surrounded them all. He was vaguely aware that he as well as everyone else was screaming. Windows broke. The seat ahead of him buckled, he heard his own legs snap like uncooked spaghetti, then the window was filled with trees—they must have slid into an orchard—and an attendant—*his attendant?*—was announcing the need for a prompt, orderly departure, the taint of fright in her voice acting as contagion in everyone else.

"I can't move," he muttered. "My legs. I'm stuck." He worked his seat belt. Broken. Stuck twice. The young man near the window climbed out over him. "Could you give me—?" he began. "Help," he said. "Could someone give me a hand?" Amazingly, no one else seemed to be injured; no one else seemed to be experiencing the slightest difficulty in making the mad dash for the exits and the ramps. "Someone?"

Where was the crew? His attendant? The pilot with his false cheer?

Surely they knew he was in trouble.

"Help," he said again. "Help," this time more softly than before, under the impression that his life, his existence, hung on a fragile, precariously balanced scale.

The overhead lights blinked once, then off for good. Red lights—from an ambulance, perhaps?—flickered along the broken seat backs; shadows danced across the movie screen of this, his broken metal cave.

"Helen?" he breathed. "Help me."

Trapped, he sat still, watching her shadow braid illusory hair, listening to the sound of unknown liquids dripping in the dark.

———

One Sunday morning, not long after they were married, Ferguson was complaining about their lack of money, bitterly reviewing the old list of grievances against his father; Helen told him that if all he wanted to do was to get rich he should talk to *her* father, but that if he ever did, she'd be long gone. "It's a simple choice," she said. She left him sitting morosely, pondering her books, her bed, her seed of an idea now his. She was in the shower, and steam drifted along the ceiling. Framed by the shower curtain, she moved translucently, a creature alien to himself. The curtain fell away from his hand. She was standing under the nozzle, her face to the water, her closed eyes an illustration of absolutes. Light from the frosted window above the toilet irradiated her wet, copper-colored hair. As he stepped into the shower fully clothed, holding her from behind, whispering his already corrupted assurances, he knew that this moment might never be duplicated: he might never again be so transported by the elements of water and light and steam; she might never be so clothed in these clouds of glory.

II. WINGS OF HEAVEN

When she was in her dotage, Aunt Mary Brown Cartwright fell victim to a series of wasting fevers, from which she began to see visions, and her dreams bordered upon the prophetic. Her family, those nieces and nephews still alive as well as their children, became increasingly alarmed when, in her waking moments, she failed to recognize them, seeing at various times the angels Gabriel and Michael and at others the demons Beelzebub and Lilith. It was, after all, a jarring experience to visit one's favorite aunt and, upon pushing open her infirmary room door, flowers in hand, to be addressed as a creature of the netherworld and consigned to everlasting flames in the name of Jesus Christ. What may have been most disturbing, however, was that in her periods of extreme dislocation, even when blasting the most heinous of demons, her demeanor was calm and serene; it was in her lucid moments that she grew fretful and restive, as if she had been cut adrift on an uncertain sea, doubtful of ever reaching land again.

So, before Ferguson accompanied his wife from their home in Palo Alto to Aunt Mary Brown's retirement center in the Central Valley of California, Charlotte had warned him of what he would see. He was not entirely unprepared. Still, it was a shock to see this once-vibrant woman, a woman whom he'd met three times before—once at their wedding, once at his oldest son's baptism, and the last time at his wife's Uncle Farley's funeral—it was a shock to see her so wasted by fever ... and fervor. There could not have been seventy-eight pounds left to her. The pillows supported her head; her body, however, appeared to float above the bed. Her skin was transparent. One blue-green vein, delicately tracing the hollow of her temple, seemed more decorative than anatomical. She was otherworldly. This good woman, who had served family and faith for seventy-plus years, looked as though she were nearing a point of translation—as if she were dematerializing into one of the invisible beings she so clearly saw just to the left of the wall-mounted television set, the garish images of tawdry soap operas, in her eyes, pale by comparison with the heavenly throngs peopling the airspace of her universe.

As they entered Aunt Mary Brown's room, Charlotte set her packages down—the occasion of their visit happened to coincide with Aunt Mary Brown's birthday—and then left the room again, announcing over one shoulder her intention of "finding that little shit of a head nurse." Ferguson was alone, watching the translucent skin of her cheeks and forehead, the rise and fall of Aunt Mary Brown's slight chest, the barely noticeable disturbance of blanket and sheet. Unnerved by his proximity to this woman who was so obviously a part of other worlds and glad that she was separated from him by her slumber, he sat in the one chair at the foot of the hospital bed, thinking that he would be happy to leave this flat, dusty town, happy to go home, alone, away from his wife and her dying relatives.

Together he and Charlotte had driven down the peninsula, through the coastal mountains, and three-quarters of the way across the San Joaquin Valley to this ugly, ramshackle series of expiring one-story stucco buildings inside which an old woman was noticeably disappearing. Outside the window, ancient men and women sat in wheelchairs dozing in a gray courtyard landscaped in cactus. Tomorrow morning he would leave, flying back to his own poor choice of a life. He would fly back only, he vowed, at Charlotte's express request. In the meantime, he had eighteen hours of dull regret to kill.

If he were cornered, Ferguson would have confessed himself to be an honorable man, happy in his life—his marriage, his family, his career. But he was not without misgivings or fear of exposure. If self-respect could be defined as an awareness of one's flaws and the refusal to allow either self-excuse or excessive guilt to accumulate in one's life, then, Ferguson decided, his honor was easily enough established. His own catalogue of character deficits was simple: a lethargic temperament during moments of crisis, a tendency to incite gossip among his co-workers, and, worst of all, the rather unfortunate habit of copulating with secretaries, receptionists, baby-sitters, retail clerks, nurses, etc. Any female economically and intellectually inferior was fair game. No Lothario exactly, he had discovered the method for his own brand of seduction—the fact that women liked to hear him confess these flaws of character; they liked to think that they could heal him in some way, that they could convince him that he wasn't really so lost, that they could help him find some peace within himself. And following such confessions—*mea culpa*—he found himself in more than one compromised position, wondering how he could have come to such a pass: these twisted sheets, this rank taste—not only in his mouth but even in his throat, his nose, his eyes—of mortality.

An unfortunate habit, of course, but one that he had lived with and accommodated. He was old enough now, however, for it to be frightening rather than exciting. And yet as he thought of leaving this hospital room in which a spectral wraith delayed her death, he found himself thinking not of his crimes against Charlotte, nor of those committed against his first wife, Helen, but of those misdemeanors certain to be realized with Magda, the twenty-five-year-old actress/typist/palm reader whose taste he had most recently savored. He needed to leave this place, needed to leave Charlotte, with her sprayed helmet of hair covering a mind bereft of imagination or soul, her clothes with creases sharp enough to cut passion; but he also needed to end what had become a tedious affair with Magda, who wore caftans and wooden beads in some vague, misunderstood tribute to the 1960s, who plainly hated to wash, whose odor during lovemaking often reminded Ferguson of the dirty towel bin in a high school boys' locker room.

He had met her at his son's school carnival. Her hair was pulled back in a scarf, and she was dressed in her habitual, he realized later, gypsy style, a fashion she preferred because it required no underwear. She held his right hand, lightly tracing the lines with one blood-red press-on nail, and he had known—at the moment when she pronounced his love life to be one of indifference and confirmed what he already knew—that she would invite him home with her. He had known even before their first thrashing together that her body—her odor, the mole on the back of her right knee, the wild thicket of her pubic hair, which spread upward to her belly—would fascinate him even as it repelled him, and that her exoticism, like her dirty second-story apartment, would begin to bore him five minutes after he first thrilled to it. He had known all this for some time, but where was he to go after Magda?

So absorbed was he in the memory of her peculiarly fetid taste, now two hundred miles distant, that he failed to notice when Aunt Mary Brown's strangely clear blue eyes first opened.

"Hello," he said, struggling to surface. "You're awake."

She said nothing, staring, as if seeing everything for the first time. Her hands fussed atop the blanket.

"Charlotte went to speak with the nurse." He was aware as he spoke that, in order to be heard clearly, his voice had become loud, prissy, with elaborately precise elocution, as if he were speaking to a foreigner, but he could find no way around it. "She should be back presently."

Her eyes, blank as a movie extraterrestrial's, consumed every-thing—the room, her bed, himself—and saw nothing.

"Can I get you anything?" he asked.

The woman continued to look at him. Not precisely at him but near him, as if there were something other than himself occupy-ing similar space. Spooky. For a moment he imagined that he too saw something, some disturbance in the air above the foot of her bed. The watery light from the courtyard window projected shad-ows at once alive yet indistinct.

"Can I get you anything?" he asked again. Just for something to say, some sound to keep that space filled.

A change seemed to fall about her features. She raised her head from the pillow, her eyes narrowed into focus, her hands reached for the steel railing on either side of the bed. Her mouth sagged.

A blob of spit escaped from one corner, an unintelligible sigh from the other. Where had Charlotte gone? A cloud seemed momentarily to intrude between his eyes and hers.

Curious and, in that moment, glimpsing the depths of his own guilt, desperate for accusation and confession, believing as he did that his crimes must be evident to any who cared to look, believing even more firmly in the revelations from strangers, he asked: "What? What are you trying to tell me?"

Aunt Mary Brown's head rocked back onto her gray pillow, exposing the valley of her old woman's throat caught between the tired cords of her neck. Jesus, he thought, don't die now.

But the old woman, with no sense of drama or irony, had only fallen asleep, her cracked lips crossed by a look that he could only regard as sly.

Ferguson met Charlotte a year after Helen disappeared. He had taken to driving along Highway 99, looking for absolution. He had fought with Helen the night before, and he could not be sure that upon leaving—driving, she said, to her mother's house—that she had yet forgiven him. He could also not be sure, to this day some twenty years later, whether he was sorry that she had gone, that she had disappeared somewhere along this highway to nowhere, that she was for all intents and purposes dead, and that his own financial statement had benefited hugely from that fact. If there were justice at all, he sometimes liked to reflect, he had received whatever punishment was his due for his behavior toward Helen by meeting Charlotte.

He had driven from Berkeley to Fresno, driving numbly without seeing anything of the road or the country except what was necessary—the taillights of the semi in front of him, the turn signal of the Volkswagen in the next lane. For a year he had experienced the regret of a man unable to celebrate separation from his wife because she hadn't simply left, she had disappeared; and on top of that, he was afraid that she'd been right for leaving in the first place and that his own material and emotional gains were, because they had come at her expense, forever tainted and therefore unendurable.

In a hotel bar that night, he'd noticed a group of three women having drinks in one of the red leather booths. Two of the women, blond and bouncy and full of self-absorbed laughter, sat across from the third, a straight-lipped brunette in a plum-colored suit, who drank beer from a bottle and tapped cigarette ash into her empties. When the blondes left in tandem to go to the Ladies, Ferguson slid into the seat across from Charlotte. She was an accountant, she said, when he asked. Her father was a retired air force colonel, now a farmer of peaches and grapes. Her mother did charity work for the children of migrant laborers. Her father, she said, was a good, strong man, and her mother was only good. Ferguson thought that he had seen her smirk as she spoke of them.

What he couldn't know, of course—as he sat across from her in the anonymity of that red leather booth—was that what he'd presumed to be an intelligent skepticism was in reality a simple absence of imagination. The only other time he saw those straight lips change, they curled (into something like Aunt Mary Brown's sly smile) when he told her about Helen, sparing her none of the details, condemning himself as a moral bankrupt, his integrity lost, his honor forfeit. It was the first time he had used this routine with a woman—indeed he hadn't recognized it as the opening salvo to seduction until afterward, not realizing until much, much later, either, that she hadn't even understood the apparent intent of his story, much less the uncertain motive: a betrayal confessed, an act of penance and contrition. She only heard him relate the details of a pragmatic business decision and the reaction of an over-emotional wife. He had thought at that moment that such a woman might be just the answer to his most pressing need, someone who looked reality in the face and did not expect anything except that which was on the surface, that which could be seen and counted and measured, someone in whom a teasing spirit could not pander.

So it was that Charlotte drove him to the airport at six-thirty the following morning. Ferguson felt as though he were strangling. A bank of lead-gray autumn clouds dropped a faint drizzle.

The roadway glistened, the moisture standing on top of a season's worth of oil. They drove through fruit orchards, cotton fields, and vineyards, all recently harvested. Field workers in green slickers were pruning the fruit trees. Smoke hovered as rain floated to the earth. They drove through this dull country, and suddenly a swarm of black wings, like the black bows on a funeral wreath—the only way he could describe the objects—surrounded them, falling and fluttering in the heavy air, turning end over end and spinning the way certain seedpods do. He had heard stories of dogs and cats or slaughtered sides of beef falling from open cargo-bay doors, and he looked—didn't this sort of thing happen all the time?—craning his neck for an upward view of the sky, but there seemed to be no airplane, no rational explanation, visible or aural. The wings, inexplicable, swirled against the windshield, then slipped to the side, flying upward again in the sudden wake of the automobile. If he had been given to such sentiments he would have said that the sight made his heart jump. Indeed, his eyes felt enlarged in their scope, as if they now saw a deeper fact. If he could somehow know how this other life, these heralds of other worlds, could fall and fall and spin—if he could somehow enter into their inarticulate exaltation—he might be able to know his own, his better self.

"My God," he breathed, "what do you think—"

"Raisin trays," Charlotte, the farmer's daughter, said.

"What?"

The wings turned and turned as they fell.

"Paper raisin trays. The grapes are set out on butcher paper between the rows. The sun dries them, then after they're taken up, the trays are burned." Charlotte flicked the wipers into action, a movement that physically hurt Ferguson and smeared several of the black objects against the glass.

The mystery, little enough, was explained; the problem was solved, and, as usual, he'd made too much out of nothing. When he looked now, he wondered how he could have failed to see them for what they were—burned scraps of paper. She was obviously right. He had simply gotten carried away. Why, then, did he feel so lost? He watched the charred wisps swirling in the updrafts, and then, as if a direct result of Charlotte's explanation, he saw a fire burning in the middle of an open field and a Mexican in khakis throwing crumpled streams of butcher paper—and with them the wings of heaven—into the center of the flames.

Not unlike the day before: a doctor, a lawyer, and a minister had each come to visit Aunt Mary Brown Cartwright, and if Ferguson had not been there to see it, he would have considered it the opening line of a badly told poker-night joke. The doctor had come, a perfunctory gesture, on his every-other-day visit. He appeared tired and not a little bit cross, and when he spoke to them he looked over the top of his glasses. These things, he said, standing beside Aunt Mary Brown's bed as he took her pulse, sometimes go on for months. The family—Charlotte, her parents, a younger cousin—nodded without rebuke. The lawyer, a fat man nearly as ancient as Aunt Mary Brown herself, came with papers to deliver and a copy of Aunt Mary Brown's power of attorney for Charlotte's father. He patted Charlotte on one knee and cast a rueful look at the hospital bed, as if measuring its length and width. Dandruff fell from his ears in a cheery imitation of snow. I think we're all covered, he said to Charlotte's father. Now all we have to do is wait. Yes, Charlotte's father said, that's all that's left, isn't there? The minister came in last of all, a youngish Episcopalian wearing, for no discernible reason, a clerical collar underneath a green golf cardigan. He held Aunt Mary Brown's hand and then, seeing the straight-lipped looks on the family's faces, replaced it next to her side. She was a good woman, he said. His lips trembled from something other than grief. Yes, Charlotte's mother said, an exceptional woman, but these past two months she's not been herself at all. Last week she called me the whore of Babylon. It is so hard to see, the minister said, someone you love brought to this point. That's for sure, Charlotte's cousin said, that's for sure. She had a good life, Charlotte's father said. Without question, the minister said, an exemplary life, a pillar of the church and her community. They each stared at her, watching the sheet struggle to rise, then fall. Ferguson waited, hoping to see once again that disturbance in the air, hoping to see those invisible wings. Would you like me to pray? the minister asked. If you want, Charlotte said. Go ahead.

The air above Aunt Mary Brown's bed was absolutely still. Ferguson wanted to scream.

At the end of the jetway, his plane loomed, a black silhouette in the rain-threatened dawn; heaven's lumbering, mechanical messenger, it bulked on the runway, dour in purpose, irrevocable by nature. It suddenly seemed that the poles of his life had become awful in their clarity: to remain earthbound in this dusty valley was to cling to Charlotte; to reach Palo Alto was to confront Magda and his own need for something new, something young and dirty. But to board—*nagging thought*—to become airborne was somehow to risk meeting Helen and her appalling idealism.

He paused for one moment, suddenly hesitant. Charlotte was waiting, watching him from the rack of Mutual of Omaha machines. He raised his hand, drawing her eyes. "I'll come back for you on Friday," he called to her. He had intended to say, "I love you." Even so, while the line behind him began to bottleneck between the blue cords, his tone and expression, he imagined, were that of a man demanding the answer to a proposal. But from her distance, Charlotte could hear only the surface of the words, not their intended depth. "Have a good trip," she said pleasantly. She held her purse in both hands. Her good winter coat, her navy dress underneath—both held their uniform press. Ferguson had to suppress a sudden desire to vault the blue cords, tackle his wife, and violate the military concision of her life and imagination.

Distrusting his impulse and believing finally that such things are best left as dreams, he did nothing. He walked into the tunnel of the jetway, fighting an unexpected congestion of claustrophobia. A smiling flight attendant ushered him to his place athwart the wings. He cinched his seat belt uncomfortably tight and closed his eyes, fearing what he might otherwise see, vowing not to open them again until he was home.

Small fires danced behind his eyes. An odd music of invitation filled his ears. He was dimly aware of hands—hands touching his face, hands pulling at his broken seat belt, hands fluttering like moths in the red-stained darkness.

Helen?

They were carrying him then, holding him beneath his armpits, telling him to walk when *goddammit* didn't they know, those sadists, that his legs were brittle, broken sticks? It seemed such a long, such an uphill climb, this blind stumble through the wreckage of turbulence and impact. And all the while fire was licking at the corners of his eyes, the light flickering blood red, the danger of which these sadist-angels were obviously stupid and unaware.

"Stop it," he tried to say. "You're killing me."

And then they were out, moving in the foggy fall morning, a morning unremarkable except for seventy-seven people, all with their respective burdens of conscience and guilt and fear, seventy-seven people who had fallen from a sky so murky and gray as to be nothing.

Ferguson's father had never claimed to be anything other than a failure. His own father, owner and founder of a company that built prefabricated housing, had tried to teach his son the intricacies of business and finance, two-by-fours and brackets, but proved spectacularly unsuccessful. Not for lack of trying. Ferguson remembered being eight years old and waking up into darkness, startled by his father's shadowy form above him, his father's voice whispering, "I'm sorry I have to do this." This occurring just before his father tried to leave his mother and him, going, he said, somewhere, anywhere . . . away. Ferguson never entirely understood the mechanism by which his grandfather compelled his father to stay. Only one dim memory remained: his grandfather and father sitting together in the kitchen of his grandparents' house, his grandfather silver-haired and profane, his father broken, sitting before his own father, his hands pressed between his knees, his head nodding slowly, reluctantly, as obedient as Ferguson himself. His grandfather punctuated his sentences with plumes of acrid cigar smoke while his father ducked his head yet lower and water rose in his eyes. And Ferguson had known, with the clarity of instinct, that he might never love his father more than at that moment. That rather than hating this adult child for his weakness of will, he was obligated to understand his father's deficiency of moral fiber as a prescient gaze into his own future.

And then too, he also understood, his certainty inarticulate yet profound, that the ploy his grandfather had used—condemning his father to failure, into this posture of abject servitude and responsibility—was himself.

They carried him through a wasteland of wreckage. The jagged, torn metal of the aircraft, the earth smoldering and charred. Suitcases, their contents strewn in all directions, littered the orchard of Scotch pines in a parody of Christmas cheer. The air itself seemed to have become smoke. Two men in stiff, buff-colored crash coats, their arms locked beneath him, laboriously ran with their raving burden, not looking at him, relegating his moans for the losses of his life to that realm of nonsense common to all victims of tragedy and anguish and horror.

Following the shot, Ferguson was the first to find his father. At two in the frost of a fall morning, aware of the cloud of gunpowder blown about by the night winds, he and his mother stumbled in pajamas and bare feet into the backyard, screaming his father's name, knowing already the outcome of their search. By the stone bench underneath the barren apple trees, Ferguson saw the crumpled form. He waved his mother away then, feeling as though he had become a character scripted by others, rolled his father over. By moonlight, his father's eyes appeared startled, puzzled by the violence of this latest decision, this last disappearance. It had seemed to Ferguson a horrible exit from one life for the sake of entry to another, and he could only imagine the despair that had driven his father from prefabricated housing to New Town, from wealth to ruin, as if his choice, under the delusion of the ideal and immortal, had been one of escape by destruction.

A door had been opened, a threshold crossed. He awoke in a room so white as to be stripped of recognizable features. A rough institutional sheet lay across his chest. He was clothed in a hospital gown, his legs elevated, wired to pulleys above the bed, his wrists shackled by IV tubes and a paper bracelet. His fingers, probing his head, found bandages, a caricature of injury. A nurse with red hair and white uniform entered, stacking some towels on the vacant second bed. "You're awake," she announced as though he needed the news confirmed. She paused, reviewing his records with a skeptical frown, and Ferguson watched, heartsick, when she turned, revealing the single, coarse braid of copper-colored hair.

"How about a little light?" She moved to open his curtains, pivot the blinds.

"I'd prefer not." He stopped her just short of allowing this invasion of golden fire, knowing now that Charlotte would come soon with flowers and stock assurances, that Magda would call, excited to know someone so nearly dead. That everyone would announce how lucky he was to be alive, and only he would know that it was no real cause for celebration.

Epilogue

What am I to say about two brothers whose wives have argued, who are thus forced by their immediate loyalties not to speak to each other? Or the surgeon—in love with the deftness of his hands and the choreography of his fingers amid the vital slime of human life—who has sadly set his scalpel aside, his passion imperiled by muscular degeneration? Or the woman who refuses to act on her own desires because she is attracted to a married man, one who represents moral integrity and uprightness of heart? What can I say but repeat the usual clichés: that life is indeed a garden of pain, that men and women are born for trouble and heartache, and that the lyricism of experience is nothing but a chimera of our most fraudulent desires?

That the world which seems to lie before us like a land so various, so beautiful, so new, etc., etc., is in reality a smoking landfill, one that exacts its own price for the dumping of a load?

Why bother, why bother saying anything at all?

Let us say, instead, that one hot June morning, the dew even at five-thirty already burned away, Len Farrington returns from his daily run sweaty and happy, illuminated by the sunrise and pleased by his own virtue to find his brother, with whom he has not spoken in a year and a half, sitting on the bench to his front porch.

"Frog," his brother says, using a nickname he hasn't heard since his childhood, "how you can sweat like that, I'll never know."

His older brother, Max, pudgy and uncomfortably Episcopalian in his short-sleeved black shirt and white collar, is the very image and picture of grief. His forehead is creased by anxiety, his eyes are clouded with preoccupation. Ever since he and Max stopped talking out of deference to Sylvia and Patrice, Len has known intuitively that Max's life is nothing he would trade for. He knows that he and Sylvia are miserable, their lives circumscribed by her cycle of antidepressant and sleeping pills. He knows that Max harbors resentment toward his parishioners, with their savage and selfish complaints, their dull needs, springing as they do from their twin tragedies of loneliness and dread. He once envied Max his sense of calling; he does so no longer.

"Sweat's a blessing," he says now, using his brother's language. He chooses to ignore the recent history that hangs between them. Instead, he focuses with pride upon the bright front of his white house, the gleam of newly painted black shutters. "After a run, I've drained all the poisons out of my soul as well as my flesh," he says. And then he adds, "No offense."

His brother visibly winces at the word "soul," as if Len does not possess the qualifications for its utterance. *Fuck him*, Len thinks. Fuck him and his black shirts of depression, his white collar of propriety. It is an anger that suffuses his whole body with radiant heat, an emotion he rarely permits and never expresses. He cannot know that Max only winces whenever the language of his trade reminds him of his own shortcomings. He cannot know that even now Max is thinking that he—Leonard Farrington, independent insurance agent representing all lines of life, home, and auto, the Frog Man of their childhood now thirty years in the past, so named for his refusal to touch their slimy green bodies, his general refusal to dirty himself—that he would have made the better priest.

"Maybe I shouldn't be here," Max says, looking to the pale, flat sky, his round face gone gray in dawn's twilight. "But I've needed to tell someone."

"Tell who what?"

It is here that Max buries his head with its few pale threads of sandy-colored hair in his hands, groaning from that well of human despair located just below the diaphragm, "I'm in love." This last syllable of misery still hangs in the rising heat of the morning when Patrice, as if on cue, steps outside onto the porch for the morning paper.

"Love," she sniffs, her eyes still smudged by last night's mascara, "the most highly overrated thing on God's green earth." She pulls her flowered housecoat more tightly around herself, picks up the paper, and snaps free the rubber band with a whack that echoes along the quiet street like pistol fire. She steps inside the house again, leaving in her wake nothing, not a word, not a greeting, not a single acknowledgment for this brother-in-law she would rather not see.

"Maybe I shouldn't be here," Max says again. "Maybe I shouldn't have come. It was a bad idea. A bad idea from the start."

"No, no, Maxie. You're here. After all this time. And you're in . . ." He can hardly think of the language for it. "You're forty-three years old."

"And in love. Again. Fat and stupid and terminal with love."

"And married. Still."

"Yes. Well."

"Well? And Sylvia?"

"I'm not in love with Sylvia."

He says this with such utter seriousness, such Episcopalian gravity, and yet with such obvious adolescent misery commingled with joy that Lennie can't help himself. He laughs. If Max knew how pitiful he looked, how pleased with himself, he would be mortified. This is not the first time that Maxie, resonant with

Episcopalian rectitude, has listened to the dictates of his hormones rather than the doctrine of his church. He has, after all, known his share of organists and secretaries, the bored and the lonely. But now, this affair of his heart has left him so miserable and so moved, so emotionally elevated, that on his walk over this morning he was nearly driven to his knees by the sight of a young woman riding in the bed of a pickup truck; in the glossy heft of her auburn hair he could see, he is sure, all the promises of eternal life. In matters of yearning, in short, he has the emotional stability of a fourteen-year-old girl.

"So," Len finally says, "who is it?"

"No one," Max says. "No one you know. A woman named Virginia."

"You want to come in?" Len asks.

Max shakes his head. Patrice and Sylvia, although unseen, are present nonetheless. A failed counseling partnership has left the sisters-in-law, registered marriage-family therapists, embittered and angry, their anger extending to the respective families. They were client-poor but asset-rich. Office furniture decorates both houses. Three feet from Len's front door, a cherry-wood rolltop stands accusingly. A couch, upholstered in industrial-grade fabric, faces Max's fireplace. It exudes the false cheer and real pain of waiting rooms.

"No," he says, "I better not."

"Come on." Len pulls his brother's arm. "Patrice won't mind. Have some breakfast."

"No." Max's face brightens for a moment. "Let me buy you breakfast." He names the coffee shop on the corner. "A brother can buy his brother breakfast, right?"

Doubtful now, Len checks his black runner's watch. "I've got an eight-thirty meeting." He checks the watch again. "Oh hell, I'll cancel the meeting. But I've got to shower."

"I'll get us a table. Eggs sunny-side up, hash browns, rye toast?"

Len shakes his head. His brother has named his breakfast of the past, as if it had come from a time capsule. "Oatmeal. Half a grapefruit."

"That's not a—"

Len raises a hand before Max can go further. "My cholesterol's at 215, my blood pressure's a little high, and I'm eight pounds over my goal weight. I'm forty-one years old, and I'm trying not to fall apart. You get to do the funerals, but I have to write the checks."

"Okay, oatmeal. Half a grapefruit. How about some prune juice? Maybe some Geritol? A Maalox and Metamucil shake? A hair shirt to every fifth unhappy customer."

"Get out of here. I'll meet you." He steps through the doorway into darkness. "Go on, Maxie, I'll meet you."

After the door closes, Max waits for just a minute on the front porch. The sky is cloudless, the dome of the world shaded from black to azure to aquamarine. Bands of pink and red outline the mountains in the east. By noon it will be nearly white, a furnace. This is not an easy land in which to live, he thinks. Their family moved to central California when he was five, and he has not yet come to an accommodation. It does not lend itself easily to either liturgy or reflection. The routines of habit are not appreciated, and thought—under such merciless glare—is nearly impossible. Sex, however, is a banquet. And the sky a metaphor for judgment. So, to the coffee shop he walks, wearing sunglasses against the promises of the dawn and murmuring, "We do not presume to come to this thy Table, O merciful Lord," in defiance.

Patrice stands in front of their bathroom mirror, outlining her lips. She wears one towel like a turban, another as a wrap. The thought strikes Len that the probability of his standing his brother up could be measured in the thickness of terry cloth and gym shorts. But when he turns the tap for his shower, Patrice also turns: "Do you mind not doing that while I'm here?" she asks. "It's steamy enough as it is."

So he goes to the shower built in to one corner of the garage and curses the cold cement under his feet. The water begins hot, then peters out to lukewarm while he is midshampoo. Patrice, he thinks, wiping soap from his eyes. Goddammit. Goddammit to hell. Ever since the collapse of their office and her estrangement from Sylvia, Patrice has been a different person. She took a state job, issuing counseling and prenatal care information to teenagers who look at her with bemused and barely tolerant expressions. She hates them. They remind her too clearly of how fine the line is between success and failure. Patrice now speaks of retirement as her career objective; her résumé is a ticket to old age. And as the cold water drains from his legs, Len once again feels a surge of anger that his money, the sweat from his brow, must be used to pay loans for a business that no longer exists. He has an urge to chop the rolltop desk into kindling.

She is dressing when, irked and shivering, Len enters their bedroom. From behind he can discern only the barest outline of the woman he married seventeen years ago. He imagines that he hears his son and daughter begin to stir. They are the children that he and Patrice never bothered to conceive except as jokes, images of misfortune they've avoided. When the toilet clogs, they blame it on the second child they never had. Would real children have made life worse than this? he wonders. Have they been telling a joke on themselves?

His life could be worse, an honest-to-god nightmare, but he can't at the moment imagine how. His work is routine; his material needs are met. His neighbors are kind and, in a pinch, when they observe true need, generous. Although abstracted and unsatisfied, his wife says that she loves him. But there are those unpredictable moments, when a voice breathes the word *Tahiti* into his ear, when he imagines himself as Gauguin. How ludicrous when, in truth, he looks forward to the next appearance of the Victoria's Secret catalogue. Why, he wonders for the umpteenth time, does his brother the priest seem to understand matters of sex, of having what one wants, better than himself? Why has he been chosen as the virtuous one? He cannot imagine the next thirty years except as a gradually steeper descent. Could anything be worse than the dull ache of killing time in this world?

In such a mood, he watches as Patrice packs her brassiere.

"Don't watch," she says. "It ain't pretty."

She shrugs herself into a blouse, steps into a jumper, choosing clothes as cover for her multitude of sins.

"So how is Max?" she begins again. "And how is the poor bastard's wife?"

By chance Max meets a parishioner in the parking lot of Gaylord's. Dr. Klinefelter has been retired for seven years, ever since he diagnosed himself as suffering from multiple sclerosis. The disease has worked quickly. He walks now with twin canes in a jerking, spasmodic, hitch-hop gait. His hands resemble talons; his mouth twitches between words. Dr. Klinefelter has attended St. James's, Max's parish, for thirty years—long before Max was on the scene—and Max measures his Sundays by Klinefelter's lurchings, as if the condition of the older man's debility were a barometer of his own unrest. He counts the doctor's illness as one complaint that is entirely verifiable, distinguishing him in this regard from the dozens of complaints that are intangible—either emotional or purely imagined for the sake of having something, anything at all, to say.

"Don't eat the hash." The doctor grunts as he settles himself into the booth by the door. An old joke—they first met when Max had food poisoning. "Try the waffle," the doctor advises. "Safer."

"The waffle it is."

The doctor places his hand on Max's arm. "I have a riddle for you, Father. How can Paul consider the law to be an agent of death when it is by the law that sin is made known and the grace of God is made both necessary and manifest? Is the law then not an agent of life by virtue of its role as the causation of grace?"

Max smiles. "You're more argument than I can handle."

He knows that Klinefelter will be unsatisfied without an answer, but Max has no intention of exegeting Paul's thesis in his letter to the Romans. Max gently refuses the doctor's offer to share his booth. Klinefelter is widowed and childless, lonely as well as crippled. Any other morning, Max would be glad to eat breakfast with him. His mind is as sharp as any scalpel, and he is a devoted, albeit untrained, student of theology. But any other morning is not the occasion of a reunion with one's brother, especially when that reunion is occasioned by one's latest announcement of infidelity and a continuing absence of principle.

"You be good, Father Farrington," the doctor says, "or I'll open you up."

He makes a slicing motion with his shaking right hand.

"Goodness," Max says, fully aware of all the attendant ironies, "is a vocational risk."

His conscience buried for months, Max has not allowed himself to think about the ramifications for himself or for Sylvia; he is still thinking only of his desire rather than its consequence.

Max goes to the bathroom to wash his hands. Pilate could do no more. In the one stall, another man is on his knees. He is throwing up in great, shuddering heaves.

"Are you all right?" Max calls. "Is there something I can do?"

"No, no," the other man sings out—cheerfully, Max thinks—before another surge hits him. "I need to get to work anyway."

Leaving this non sequitur unexplained, the other man rises and throws the bolt on the stall door. He holds the metal frame as if to steady himself. Flecks of vomit dot his shirt, his sport coat looks slept in, and the whites of his eyes have turned muddy as swamp water. He exudes the odor of alcoholic decay.

"You're okay?" Max asks. As a member of clergy and as one who feels his own personal compromises keenly, he takes this human responsibility to be an absolute. The parable of the Good Samaritan was successfully drilled into him as a child, that to be one more ordained failure is too much to consider or bear.

"Tip-top," the other man says. "Absolutely."

He aims himself for the sinks, and Max moves out of his way.

"If you're sure," Max says.

"Of course. Absolutely. Sorry you had to witness that." He buries his head in the sink and opens the valve wide. Spray jets everywhere.

"It's quite all right," Max hears himself say.

This courtly graciousness has become a little strange, and he edges out of the bathroom, flagging down a girl in an apron before he sinks into his own booth. Sabrina is printed on her name-tag. He gives his brother's meager order as well as his own, then stops the girl with one hand on her arm. "Do you know that man?" He tilts his head toward the bathroom door, from which the other man has just now emerged, his hair sticking up in several wet, unruly spikes.

The girl wrinkles her nose. "Yeah, he's one of ours." Her face darkens. "Pathetic," she says. "You expect better of people. You wanna take him home? Reform him? It's okay by me."

"I just wondered."

He sits down to wait for Len. His brother has surprised him. While he knows there is no love lost between Sylvia and Patrice, he expected greater shock from Lennie, his puritan brother. Moral outrage. Judgment. Castigation.

As if to answer this question, the sun frees itself fully from the rim of mountains to the east, and its full potency pours through the plate glass windows next to the booths. The harsh light has the force of a fist, and Max turns his head away. So this is the answer, this stark exposure. The bank of windows has become all glare, and Sabrina busies herself, lowering blinds, pivoting louvres. Before she can arrive at his window, however, Max has turned back to the fire, opening his eyes, thinking, *Give me your worst, go ahead*, knowing full well that the worst has not even begun to occur.

As it happens, Len is not the first to meet Max. Virginia has beaten him to it. She is desperate with virtue. She called his home only to hear Sylvia's sleep-thick, pill-disfigured voice; she disguised her own, hoping to sound like an elderly church member, but Sylvia evidently doesn't care that a woman might be calling for Max. She doesn't know where her husband is, he could be anywhere, she says, and it is obvious that she only wants this bothersome caller to go away. Virginia called St. James's and listened to a recorded message announcing the times of worship. But then she called his brother's number, the number just above Max's in the phone book, a long shot at best she knew, but there it was: Patrice, much more cheerful, more accommodating than Sylvia, told her about Gaylord's.

So when Len enters the coffee shop, he first sees Max and Max's worried look, and then when Max stands—a polite gesture that he doesn't, at first, understand—he sees the glossy dark hair in the seat opposite Max's.

"Lennie," Max says, looking at the other tables, glad that there are not too many others besides Klinefelter to observe this moment: an older woman with a grandson, both eating pancakes; two men at the counter, drinking coffee and smoking cigarettes;

the drunk from the bathroom, his hands tentatively raising a glass of water to his lips. Max nervously shifts from foot to foot, hands restlessly jingling his change in his standard, diocese-issue pants. "I'd like you to meet Virginia. Virginia, my brother, Lennie Farrington."

Her eyes are red, and Lennie is struck by these twin facts: first, that this woman is so young, and second, that his brother could mean so much to so beautiful and so young a woman as to be the cause of her tears and unhappiness.

In fact, she has just told Max that this will never work. They were fools ever to think it would. In the first place, she has realized that she loves him *because* he's a minister; she's attracted to men, she knows this now, who represent stability and order, the sanctity and meaning of human life.

"Don't you see," she said, "if I get any further involved with you, I'll start being the *cause* of evil in the world?" When she said this, her nostrils quivered as if she were about to cry, and it was all Max could do not to leap across the table and tackle her, force her down onto the vinyl seat, his coffee shop Leda. To tell her in the language of sex that she had it all wrong—he was neither stable nor pure. She couldn't begin to corrupt him. But would saying that undo the attraction all the more certainly? He could feel a headache begin its bloom behind his eyelids.

"And truthfully," she added, "I think I just may be nutty about the uniform. You know, the vestments, all that brocade. The Eucharist at Passiontide." And here she did begin to cry.

Which was when Lennie entered, to shake her warm hand, to marvel at this young woman's presence, to feel the pulse beating steadily at her wrist, to wonder all over again what she could possibly see in this fat, confused older brother of his who once again is the perfect picture of misery caused—Len can see it now—by the pure pain of loss. He feels sorry for Max. He can't help it. Even as he's glad that such a messy situation might be so easily resolved.

They are each given a moment of reprieve when Sabrina comes with their orders. Virginia sniffles, says she must go. Max says, "No, wait." And to his brother, he says: "We met at the movie theater, did I tell you that? At *The Fisher King*?"

"No," Lennie says, "I hadn't heard that."

"Isn't that right?" Max says to Virginia.

"I have to go."

Sabrina has placed Lennie's breakfast in front of Max; Max's plate has landed in front of Lennie—scrambled eggs, sausage links, hash browns, a biscuit and gravy. Intent on the byplay in front of him, he puts a sausage in this mouth without thinking and is in the act of swallowing when the taste of pork grease hits him. When he tries to spit it out, it happens: he chokes. This piece of pork makes the roller-coaster ride over the top of his dumb, half-asleep glottis and wedges itself into his airway like a cork—*thunk*—the sound of suction audible in his own ears.

"No, please," Max is saying. "Stay a little longer. We need to talk."

"No." She's crying again, dabbing at her eyes with a paper napkin.

"I'll call you, then."

"Please don't."

"I need you. I haven't talked to my brother for years, but here we are—I had to tell him about you. You're good for me."

His mention of Lennie reminds them that this is a scene with an audience, but when they look at him, everything changes, everything else is forgotten. His face is red, nearly bursting. Soft, squeaking noises come from his wide-open mouth. His hands are at his throat. This has come as such a surprise that Lennie has had no chance to panic or thrash around. His body is rigid with confusion and puzzlement. In front of him are Max and his maybe/maybe-not girlfriend, and their faces begin to twist and run; he cannot get a fix on color or shape.

"Doctor Klinefelter!" Max is screaming from somewhere far off. "My brother! Look!"

The doctor rises slowly to his feet, pushes himself forward on his canes. "Heimlich," the old man says. "Do the Heimlich."

Max dimly remembers descriptions from television and magazines. He pulls his brother to his feet, his fists underneath Lennie's breastbone. His efforts are spasms of anxiety. Lennie squeaks, his face the color of wine. Max feels tears of failure falling onto his brother's shoulders. He has wasted his own life on riddles and tootsies, tootsies and riddles, and by the queerest sense of divine fairness, it is his brother who is going to die.

Doctor Klinefelter fumbles in his large pockets, extracts a silver penknife. "Hold him good," he says, pulling the stiff blade free.

It is the one thing Lennie sees, the bright bead of light from the silver blade as it erratically moves toward the hollow of his throat, that blocked conduit of life-giving air.

He does not review his life, nor does he think with fond regret of Patrice. He does not ask forgiveness for his often-uncharitable spirit. He only has room in his consciousness for the bright silver blade and the bright pinpoint of light that burns his eyes.

"Hold him now," the doctor says.

"Oh God, oh God," Max says, then yells to Virginia: "Call 911."

But then Lennie feels his legs go out from him. Has his brother dropped him? If he could just get some air, he will cry for this, he knows it. For his pain. For the unfairness. That Maxie the minister, his oversexed, irresponsible older brother, is the one who will get to live. And now other arms are around his ribs.

Max has not dropped Lennie. The drunk from the bathroom has shouldered the doctor and his knife aside and pushed Max into Virginia's lap. He takes a large, sour breath and jerks so hard that Lennie's ribs crack. The sausage flies across the room in a weightless arc, a lazy pop fly through a clear summer's day.

Lennie comes to in the sour draft of his rescuer. As his eyes clear, he believes that God looks like Christopher Lloyd, that he has died only to be revived into an odor of piss and rotten shellfish. Max is holding one of Lennie's hands in both of his own and crying. "Oh, dear sweet Jesus," he says over and over again, the strangest sort of mantra for this most professional of Episcopalians. "Oh, dear sweet Jesus, it was all my fault."

"Let him have his air," Doctor Klinefelter says, his tone critical of the stranger, who, although ignorant and unwitting, has succeeded where sobriety and knowledge failed.

The man from the bathroom stall stands. The color drains from his face, he looks about to faint, but he edges backward, surrendering himself into the waiting lap of an empty booth, and the critical moment passes.

Others now cluster quietly around their little group. Sabrina has come with water. The Vietnamese short-order cook flaps his apron, working a breeze.

Virginia quietly leaves. She touches Max's shoulder with two fingers, leaving him with her blessing, although at this moment she is forgotten. He will, she knows, think of her later. But by then, she will seem only like a remembered hurt, a pain from the past.

For now though, Max cries. Lennie breathes. Breathing, for the moment, is sufficient.

The front door opens, admitting a gust of sunlight and a large, startled trucker. All these people on the floor, he must think, what is he walking into here? The door closes. Cut off, the light burns everyone's eyes for long moments after it no longer exists.

"The frog man," Lennie croaks, patting his brother's arm, "the frog man lives."

Grace caroms around the room with the velocity of hockey pucks.

What am I to say to such things? That this is a small story after all? I suppose it is; I can't call it otherwise, even with its few moments of danger and risk. It would not even make a credible subplot for an hour-long courtroom drama. Two brothers, their wives, the young idealistic love interest, the aging doctor, the purple, bloated face of the virtuous victim. The improbable savior, a drunken *deus ex machina*. How can we believe it? What *am* I to say?

That on that early June morning I had just sat down at a booth in Gaylord's coffee shop, unsteadily holding a water glass to my lips when a man began to choke? That I had most recently knelt down, my head inside a toilet bowl, vomit burning my esophagus? That my week's odyssey had begun when my wife and daughter and son packed our station wagon with the barest essentials, saying enough is too much, before driving west into the harsh central California sun? That I had begun to believe that if our birth is but a sleep and a forgetting, then the dreams of this life are nightmares only?

I could say that, I suppose. But then, I could just as easily claim that I am Lennie or Max, or Doctor Klinefelter or Virginia, for that matter. That these multiple lives are merely fractions of one life. I could say that in the moment when I fell backward into the booth at Gaylord's—my vision blurred by strange clarity, by the fluttering of some ethereal curtain—that I saw in those figures before me my own life revealed, my own apocalypse, an uncovering, a lifting of a veil. I could say that. Absolutely . . .

Yet why not say what happened? That and merely that.

That in those dark hours before our early dawns, I would wake to hear the sounds of our house: my wife, her back to me, muttering in her sleep, confused even in her slumber over what was to be done with me—with my rages, my silences, my criticisms, my depressions, my sarcasm, my self-loathing; my daughter turning over, restless in the rush of change even now overtaking her; my son crying out against the terrors of the darkness. I would wake to the distress of these sounds, stripped of any capacity for compassion, overwhelmed only by the realization that I could no longer remember the slightly fetid taste of a particular girl's skin. A Gypsy girl with orange hair who made her living by vandalizing parking meters and duping unwary tourists. A girl so exotic to me now that she might as well have been a native of some South Pacific island. One who made me believe at the age of nineteen that the future was indeed limitless, that no wrong choice could not be undone.

Some days before they left, my daughter asked me what it would take, since I was so obviously miserable, for God to forgive me. She is twelve, theologically precocious, with a penchant for Socratic irony. The lines above the bridge of her nose are clear signs of her resentment toward me. Arguing with her is a debate with the Grand Inquisitor; I was lost without speaking a word. How could I begin to explain to her what it means to be forty-two years old, to read the next thirty years as if they had already been written, to be choked by the twin pains of longing and regret? That such pains, no matter how clichéd, can drive weak souls into the arms of willing accomplices, and souls weaker still into the passive madness of bitter daydream? That to forgive oneself, and thereby embrace the forgiveness of God, would require—for the sake of virtue—a forfeiture of dream and desire?

In the room above our garage, the windows face east, and during the summer there is not a morning that is not clear. The sunrise above the Sierra is magnificent, the sky gradually lightening, the red glow of morning throwing the dark mountains into stark relief. These days, since my unconscious heroism and surrender of this past June, I am awake to see the daily miracle of rebirth and admonition; it washes me with its tides of honesty and grace, and I am reminded that long before my family left, I had already orphaned myself with yearning and self-indulgent woe.

At these moments of reminder, I become—for a small space in time—them all; I know their lives intimately, projections of my own failure, my own pain: Max and Lennie, Patrice and Sylvia, Doctor Klinefelter and Virginia, my departed family, the cretin on the bathroom floor whom I no longer claim. They are mine, after all, my responsibility, my children, adopted without their knowledge or consent. I pray for them to understand that in a choice between inevitable evils, the noble embrace the greater hurt.

What am I to say to such things? Where, after all, will this catechism lead?

That in this land of light and shadow and make believe, the dream may school the dreamer?

Oh, yes.

And that the character that is my own—poor, passing fact if ever there was one—may find within that dream the breath that will let him live?

Yes.

Yes.

Absolutely.

Yes.

The Iowa Short Fiction Award and John Simmons Short Fiction Award Winners

1996
Hints of His Mortality,
David Borofka
Judge: Oscar Hijuelos

1996
Western Electric, Don Zancanella
Judge: Oscar Hijuelos

1995
Listening to Mozart,
Charles Wyatt
Judge: Ethan Canin

1995
May You Live in Interesting Times, Tereze Glück
Judge: Ethan Canin

1994
The Good Doctor,
Susan Onthank Mates
Judge: Joy Williams

1994
Igloo among Palms,
Rod Val Moore
Judge: Joy Williams

1993
Happiness, Ann Harleman
Judge: Francine Prose

1993
Macauley's Thumb,
Lex Williford
Judge: Francine Prose

1993
Where Love Leaves Us,
Renée Manfredi
Judge: Francine Prose

1992
My Body to You, Elizabeth Searle
Judge: James Salter

1992
Imaginary Men, Enid Shomer
Judge: James Salter

1991
The Ant Generator,
Elizabeth Harris
Judge: Marilynne Robinson

1991
Traps, Sondra Spatt Olsen
Judge: Marilynne Robinson

1990
A Hole in the Language,
Marly Swick
Judge: Jayne Anne Phillips

1989
Lent: The Slow Fast,
Starkey Flythe, Jr.
Judge: Gail Godwin

1989
Line of Fall, Miles Wilson
Judge: Gail Godwin

1988
The Long White,
Sharon Dilworth
Judge: Robert Stone

1988
The Venus Tree, Michael Pritchett
Judge: Robert Stone

1987
Fruit of the Month, Abby Frucht
Judge: Alison Lurie

1987
Star Game, Lucia Nevai
Judge: Alison Lurie

1986
Eminent Domain, Dan O'Brien
Judge: Iowa Writers' Workshop

1986
Resurrectionists,
Russell Working
Judge: Tobias Wolff

1985
Dancing in the Movies,
Robert Boswell
Judge: Tim O'Brien

1984
Old Wives' Tales, Susan M. Dodd
Judge: Frederick Busch

1983
Heart Failure, Ivy Goodman
Judge: Alice Adams

1982
Shiny Objects, Dianne Benedict
Judge: Raymond Carver

1981
The Phototropic Woman,
Annabel Thomas
Judge: Doris Grumbach

1980
Impossible Appetites,
James Fetler
Judge: Francine du Plessix Gray

1979
Fly Away Home, Mary Hedin
Judge: John Gardner

1978
A Nest of Hooks, Lon Otto
Judge: Stanley Elkin

1977
The Women in the Mirror,
Pat Carr
Judge: Leonard Michaels

1976
The Black Velvet Girl,
C. E. Poverman
Judge: Donald Barthelme

1975
*Harry Belten and the
Mendelssohn Violin Concerto*,
Barry Targan
Judge: George P. Garrett

1974
*After the First Death There Is No
Other*, Natalie L. M. Petesch
Judge: William H. Gass

1973
The Itinerary of Beggars,
H. E. Francis
Judge: John Hawkes

1972
The Burning and Other Stories,
Jack Cady
Judge: Joyce Carol Oates

1971
*Old Morals, Small Continents,
Darker Times*, Philip F. O'Connor
Judge: George P. Elliott

1970
The Beach Umbrella,
Cyrus Colter
Judges: Vance Bourjaily and
Kurt Vonnegut, Jr.